TARGET

CRAIG CARTER

(BOOK 2)

Ilona Hawkins

TSL Publications

First published in Great Britain in 2019
By TSL Publications, Rickmansworth

ISBN / 978-1-913294-20-5

Cover image by James Sands

Author's Note

I have used the known planets as a backdrop to my story. Please bear in mind that this is a work of fiction and therefore not really an indication of the atmosphere, etc of each planet.

CHAPTER 1

Craig Carter was once again in space for his commander. This time it was only a routine flight, as he had to pick up a group of people from Solar Star 1, a recently discovered planet. The inhabitants were very friendly to the Earthlings and had requested they be allowed to visit Earth and meet the humans. As Craig had no other mission, he had been instructed to pilot the space shuttle.

The handsome young man had the ability to make friends wherever he went, and had achieved this on many alien planets, but of course he had also made some enemies. Craig steered the huge craft towards Solar Star 1, where another craft flew out to meet him. Their computers interfaced, bringing the two vehicles alongside one another, and then both airlocks opened simultaneously, allowing the passengers to simply step from one craft directly into the other. Once everyone had been transferred, Craig had a few words with the pilot of the other shuttle, before they disengaged and went their separate ways.

Back on Earth, a huge banquet had been prepared for the inhabitants of Solar Star 1, during which they were welcomed enthusiastically by the President of the United States of America. Craig was given the afternoon off and he took Constance to their favourite restaurant where they sat hand in hand, looking into one another's eyes, for they were very much in love.

"Craig, when you go on your next assignment, I'm going to ask Commander Simms if I can come with you, because I'm tired of waiting and worrying when you go off on your own."

Carter smiled lovingly at his girlfriend. "If you can persuade the good Commander to let you come with me, I'd welcome it very much indeed! I miss you when we're separated for long periods of time!"

Craig had the following day off as well. The visitors completed their tour and were returned to their planet by another space explorer, and for the next few days, things were quiet.

Suddenly it was as though all hell had broken loose when a dangerous criminal caused havoc in space. He was an American technician who had worked in the Space Control Centre for a long time, and Craig thought of him as a friend. The Space Control department listened in shock as Jorrick Baker talked to them from outer space, after having stolen one of the fighter crafts.

"I've stolen the deadly bacteria that Ray has been working on and if you don't do as I say, I'll unleash them onto Earth and all the other planets!"

"Don't be a fool Baker!" exclaimed Commander Simms angrily. "Return to Earth and we'll forget this incident ever happened. I know you've been under a lot of strain lately, but we have excellent doctors who can help you."

"Not likely! I know what the penalty for treason is. I won't return to Earth!"

"Look Jorrick, I told you, you won't be harmed. You just need a little psychoanalysis and then you'll be fine. At least so far, no harm has been done."

The only answer was a mocking laugh.

Commander Simms' patience was wearing very thin. "Look Baker, if you don't come back to Earth willingly, I'll just send up ships to intercept you."

Jorrick laughed again. "I believe you won't, because I'm piloting a fighter craft and you know that I can shoot down anything that comes to intercept me."

Simms began to go red in the face and Craig laid a hand on his arm. "Sir, let me talk to him. He's a friend of mine and I'll try to make him see reason."

Commander Simms stepped away from the vidscreen and Craig took his place.

"Jorrick, listen to me," pleaded Craig, "you are my friend and I don't want to see you get hurt. Please come down, even if it's only to return those germs. If you don't want to land, then let me at least come up and get them from you. You could eliminate entire populations of planets and I know you don't really want to do that."

Jorrick smiled crookedly and addressed his friend. "Craig, you're a great guy, but I'm sorry, I can't do that. Don't come after me if you know what's good for you."

Carter opened his mouth to speak, but the screen went dead. He stared helplessly at his superior.

"It looks as though he doesn't want to see you either Craig. We'll have to come up with some sort of a plan."

"Sir, I request permission to go up and talk to him anyway. He's emotionally unstable at present and I need to persuade him to give up the bacterium."

Simms shook his head emphatically. "No Craig, I can't allow you to risk your life! He said he didn't want to see you and I think you had better stay away from him."

"But Sir," protested Craig vehemently, "he's unable to think clearly and might just unleash one of those vials on some unsuspecting planet. We could have an interplanetary war on our hands. Please let me take that chance."

Simms stroked his chin thoughtfully and reluctantly gave in. "All right Craig, if you can do anything, then I suppose you must try. Just be careful, okay?"

"Thank you, Sir! I'll do my best to persuade him to give up that bacterium at least," the explorer replied gratefully.

Craig collected all the necessary supplies he would need and then made for one of the spacecraft. Constance clung to him unhappily. "Oh Craig, what you are planning to do is suicide. If Jorrick wants to, he can kill you. This craft is no match for one of the fighter ones!"

"I know, but he's a friend of mine, darling. I could also use a fighter craft, but that's going to send the wrong message to him and he definitely won't want to see me if he thinks I'll be a threat to him. He's been suffering from a bout of depression and I know that once I can persuade him to return home, he'll go for the necessary help."

Gently he extricated himself from her and waved goodbye. His craft rose vertically upwards and soon Earth was far below him.

In space, all was quiet and Craig stared out of his observation window.

"The technicians got a fix on Jorrick's position and it should take me about a day to reach him. I must make him see reason and at least get him to hand over the bacteria, if nothing else."

One day later, Craig located the fighter craft, but Jorrick also had him in his sights. Baker smiled knowingly. "I'm willing to bet Craig is piloting that ship. No one else would be stupid enough to come out here and confront me."

His screen beeped and Jorrick switched it on.

"Hello old buddy!" he exclaimed cynically. "Didn't I tell you to leave me alone?"

Ignoring the jibe, Craig smiled at his friend. "Sure, but you know me better than that. We need to talk face to face."

"Well, go ahead, I'm listening."

Carter had the entire ship in his sights now and he saw a gun barrel emerge from the fighter craft.

"Jorrick, I want to dock with you so that we can discuss this. You know that my craft is unarmed. At least hear me out. I'm asking as your friend."

There was a moment's silence and Carter waited tensely while his friend thought about it. "All right then Craig, seeing as you took the time to come up and find me, let's have a chat. Begin docking procedures now."

Craig punched the relevant details into the computer and slowly the two crafts moved together, until their hatches were aligned, and the two ships bumped gently. Carter took a deep breath and stepped into his friend's ship.

Jorrick searched his friend and Carter submitted to the prodding. Once the technician was satisfied, he indicated for Carter to follow him. The cockpit of the fighter craft wasn't very big, but it could seat two people quite comfortably.

Craig stared for some moments at his friend, filled with compassion. Jorrick had rings under his eyes, which looked sunken into their sockets. He had obviously not been sleeping very well either.

"Will you hand those vials over to me please? I suppose you

won't return to Earth, but Commander Simms has assured me you'll receive the utmost care. You look tired. It will do you good to speak to a psychiatrist."

Baker shook his head decisively. "No, I don't trust the Commander. Craig, you and I have been friends for a number of years, so I've decided to put a proposal to you. I'm prepared to cut you in on the deal. With this bacterium, we could hold the universe to ransom! Just imagine what the worlds we know of will pay for their continued existence. We could become unbelievably rich! What do you say, buddy?"

Carter shook his head. "Sorry Jorrick, I can't do that, but if you don't hand them over, you know that Simms will send every available man out to capture you! I came unarmed and in a ship without weapons, because I wanted to give you the benefit of the doubt. If you don't want to hand over the bacteria, then my job here is done."

Jorrick took his gun out of a holster and stared thoughtfully at it.

"You realize that I could just stun you and then I would have both you and the germs."

Craig sighed. "Look Jorrick, you aren't scaring me. Either you give me the vials or I'll leave without them, but I won't play your game any longer."

Unexpectedly, Jorrick laughed. "You know me too well, Craig! I'll give the bacteria to you, but I refuse to accompany you back to Earth. Just wait here while I fetch them."

Craig waited and soon Jorrick emerged with several triangular bottles in a container.

"Here they are, Craig. I'll see you around sometime, I guess. Don't you want to change your mind and work with me? It'll be worth your while, I assure you."

"No thanks pal, but thank you for letting me have these vials. I knew you'd see reason."

Carter returned to his ship and they parted once again, each going in opposite directions.

Jorrick watched as his friend's craft disappeared from sight and then he laughed.

"Oh, you're such a fool Craig, you played right into my hands! You're in for quite a shock when you return to Earth. I was tempted to kill you when you came into my ship, but this is a much better plan. The great Craig Carter won't be quite so great one of these days. I've always hated him because he's so popular with everyone while I have hardly any friends. Constance was my girl until he came along and stole her away from me. I still love her dearly and I want her back. I'm going to make him suffer by turning everyone against him and I'll enjoy every minute. My plan is fool proof!"

CHAPTER 2

Craig returned to Earth and handed the bottles to his friend Ray, who stared unhappily at them.

"Craig, this isn't the bacteria I manufactured! The bottles are the same, but the contents are very different."

A dismayed Craig stared at his friend. "He lied to me, but I really thought he was being sincere!"

Simms placed a reassuring hand on his shoulder. "Look Craig, you did your best and I'm grateful to you for trying at least. Go home now and have a rest – you've earned it. We'll have to find some other way to get those vials back from Jorrick."

Sometime later an anonymous caller was put through to Commander Simms.

"You don't know who I am, but I have some information for you. Mr Carter is not as trustworthy as you imagine. Search his craft thoroughly and you'll find something very interesting inside."

"Just a minute ..." began Simms, but the caller had hung up. Mystified, he sent for some of the security forces and they began to search the ship Craig had returned in. It took a long time, but finally one of the security guards found a package, which he held up triumphantly for Commander Simms to see. He opened it and stared horrified at four bottles of the deadly bacteria. Underneath the bottles he found a schedule, listing planets doomed for annihilation, *in Craig's own handwriting!* Simms felt his chest tightening from shock and thought he would suffocate, but controlled himself. His first task was to send the list for analysis, but the findings were conclusive and he slumped unhappily at his desk.

"No, I can't believe it; not Craig! Yet the tests can't lie in this day and age. No one, no matter how talented they are could forge anyone else's handwriting, therefore he must have written this himself."

Simms reached for his mobile device to contact Craig, but was interrupted and requested to report to the radio room.

He followed the technician and saw Jorrick's panic-stricken face on screen.

"Commander Simms, something dreadful has happened! As you may remember, I stole eight bottles of the bacteria! Well I went to check up on them and four are missing. I swear that I haven't used any of them, nor had I ever intended to hold the universe to ransom! I should never have taken them in the first place. I don't know what came over me!"

"Relax Jorrick, we found the other bottles. Craig took them from you when he boarded your ship, but I regret to say he had formed a diabolical plan to kill off the people of Neptune. He wrote a note confirming his plans."

Jorrick gasped. "No Sir, Craig wouldn't do that!"

"I have the evidence Jorrick. I'm sorry I doubted you, but you've been cleared, so you can return to Earth. I'll overlook your indiscretion, just as long as you promise you'll see a psychiatrist and get that depression sorted out."

"Thank you, Sir, but I would like to stay out here in space for a while longer. I'll go to our Moon Base and stay there for a while, just until Craig is safely out of the way."

Simms returned to his office and contacted Craig. The unsuspecting explorer thought there was another mission for him and returned to the Control Centre. Simms was decidedly cool towards him and he was puzzled, especially when the Commander took a firm grip on his arm and steered him towards the laboratory.

"What do you see, Craig?" he asked angrily.

"Is that the bacteria!" he asked incredulously, "How did you get them?"

"Perhaps I should be asking you that question, Craig," he replied crossly.

"Me? Why? I have no idea where they came from!"

"Perhaps *this* will refresh your memory!" exclaimed Simms angrily, as he threw the note contemptuously down on the table in front of his explorer.

Craig read the note and was horrified. "But Sir, I didn't write this, I swear it!"

"I had my doubts too, Craig, so I had your handwriting ana-lyzed and it was a perfect match! I didn't believe it either, so I had the paper tested for fingerprints, and guess what; only your fingerprints were found on all the pieces of paper. I'm disap-pointed in you, because I trusted you implicitly. Jorrick contact-ed me a short while ago, when he discovered that half the batch he had stolen was now missing."

"*Jorrick contacted you?* Sir, he is a liar and you know it. Someone has set me up and I need to find out why ..."

A Venusian who hissed in rage interrupted them. By using their translators, they were able to decipher his message as he transmitted it to them.

"Earthlings, we are angry with you! We have never treated you badly, yet this is how you repay us. Half our vegetation has been destroyed, but we found a piece of paper staked on a pole amongst the ruins and it was signed 'C. Carter'. I demand an explanation for this atrocity, or there will be an inter planetary war between our worlds."

The screen went blank and all eyes turned towards Craig, who backed away when he saw the security guards going for their weapons.

"*I don't know what's happening, but I'm innocent! I would never do anything to harm anyone, I swear it! Please Sir, you have to believe me!*"

Commander Simms looked unhappily at his employee. "Craig listen, we have to discuss this. I'm sure you had your reasons for what you did, but it cannot be allowed to continue. I'll schedule an appointment with Dr Brown for later today. If anyone can sort this out, he can."

Carter backed further away. "Commander, I know absolutely nothing about this. I never had any intention to harm any of our friends in the galaxy. I don't know how Jorrick did this, but I'll find out, I promise you."

Simms tone became calm and condescending. "Craig, it's okay! Dr Brown will get to the bottom of this I'm sure. You are just a little confused right now!"

"I'm not confused or sick and I never did this terrible thing," he objected. He looked up, only to see Constance staring at him with a shocked expression on her face. The security guards began to draw their weapons which he knew would be put on "stun" in order to capture him.

Carter's instinct for survival took over and he overturned a nearby table, which crashed into the legs of the closest space policemen, causing them to tumble into one another. In the ensuing chaos, he made a wild dash for the hangar and dived into his spacecraft, noting with satisfaction that it had recently been refuelled. Before the space police could reach him, he had blasted off and was gone from sight.

Out in space, he tried to collect his shattered thoughts.

"I don't believe this! One moment I'm minding my own business and the next, I'm wanted for something I didn't do! Jorrick had someone on the inside obviously, because I know that I would never have taken the bacteria unless he gave me permission to do so. I don't remember writing those notes, nor signing my name on that piece of paper, but Simms is right, no one can forge anything these days, no matter how good they are. I'll just have to track Jorrick down and make him tell me how he did it. I have enough supplies of fuel and food to last me three months, so I'd better have answers by then. Meanwhile, the space police will probably come searching for me, so I'll need to be on the lookout for them."

⁄ ⁄ ⁄

Simms in the meantime had managed to contact Jorrick.

"Jorrick, Craig has escaped, but the space police will find him, I'm sure of that. In the meantime, I think you had better return to Earth, because if he finds you, he'll kill you as he is convinced you framed him."

"Very well, Sir, I'll do as you say."

He broke transmission and smiled happily. "Ah yes, phase one went off very smoothly, I must admit, now for the second part. Craig is mystified how I managed to frame him, but it was very simple really. I simply used a portable mind probe on him and ordered him to write that incriminating note and sign his name on various pieces of paper. While he was still in the trance, I hid the real bacteria on his ship and ordered him to wake up an hour later and not remember anything that happened. I had already told a friend of mine when to phone with that message about the four bottles and it worked wonderfully. Now Craig is a fugitive who daren't show his face near Earth again. I'll go back a hero and Constance will love me once again, like before."

Two days later, Jorrick was once again on Earth. Commander Simms was talking to him when a technician interrupted them.

"Sir, we've managed to contact Craig. He says that he would like to speak with you."

The Commander hurried to the control room. "Craig, don't be a fool! The space police are closing in on you. Give yourself up and your sentence will be lighter."

"There is no way I'll do that, Sir. Somehow Jorrick has managed to turn this to his advantage and I won't rest until I get some answers from him."

"Well if it's answers you're looking for, Jorrick has returned to Earth, so you'll have to come here if you want him."

"He came back to Earth? Well he must be feeling pretty confident then! I'll think of something, don't worry, but I'm sorry, I can't give myself up, not until I can prove my innocence."

Craig broke transmission and sighed unhappily. Suddenly he saw two space police cruisers flanking him and he was ordered to surrender. Grimly, he pressed a switch on his console and vanished into time lapse, leaving them guessing, while he sped away to safety.

Back at the Space Control Centre, Jorrick was playing his

cards well. He went in search of Constance and found her sitting miserably in the canteen, a cup of cold coffee in front of her. He replaced the cold one with another that was piping hot.

"Hello Constance, it's been a while. How have you been holding up lately?"

She blinked back tears and fought for self-control. "I'm okay, I guess. I just can't believe that Craig would do such a terrible thing! I love him so much and I never expected him to do something so horrible. This isn't like him at all," she sniffed.

"There there, don't cry," said Jorrick as he gathered her tenderly into his arms. "The police will find him and save the rest of the universe, I'm sure. I know this isn't the time to bring this up, but I still love you Constance. I'll help you get through this, I promise."

She didn't pull away, but sagged against him and began to sob unhappily.

"Look, let me take you out to dinner tonight, just for old time's sake, okay?"

She nodded and dried her eyes and when she had left, Jorrick smiled triumphantly. "Well, things couldn't be better! I've framed Craig and gained his sweetheart, as well as a little more respect from Commander Simms, so what more could a man want?"

In the meantime, Craig felt the need to speak to someone whom he knew respected him, so he made for Neptune. He landed and called to Lolita, who came to the surface, but she didn't climb out of the water.

"Craig, what are you doing here?"

"I had to talk to someone Lolita. You don't believe that I was responsible for destroying some of Venus's vegetation, do you?"

"I don't know what to think, Craig! I cannot imagine you being a criminal because you've always been kind to me. Yet your own people are saying that you left a piece of paper on a stick and it contained your signature. All the evidence seems to be conclusive as I understand it, but if you are innocent, then how did the paper get there?"

"Someone put it there deliberately, so that I would be blamed," he remarked unhappily.

"I'd like to believe you, truly I would but the evidence against you is so damning! Anyway, my father was told to be extra careful because our planet was targeted. Apparently, you wrote a note and in it you said that you wanted to unleash some of the bacteria on Neptune. Why would you want to harm us? Haven't we always considered Earth and especially you, one of our allies?"

"Lolita, I assure you that nothing has changed! I would never harm anyone on Neptune, or anywhere else for that matter! I never wrote that letter! Please believe me!" he pleaded earnestly.

"I want to, but the facts speak for themselves. Everyone your planet has befriended over the last couple of years has been threatened. You told me once that the Saturnians are your best friends in the universe, yet they were also mentioned on your list. I just don't understand what's happening to you. You should go back to Earth and get the help you need before you cause more damage! Please do this for me. I only want what's best for you!"

"Yes Lolita, I believe you mean well and I appreciate your concern. You're trying to tell me you think I was responsible, but in a tactful way, so that you don't hurt my feelings. I'm not angry with you, how could I be when the evidence is so damning?!"

The Queen, who had come to look for her daughter, interrupted them and an awkward silence developed. Finally, she broke it. "What are you doing here?" the Queen asked the explorer coldly.

Craig bowed low. "Forgive the intrusion Your Majesty, but I just wanted to be among friends. I would never intentionally harm anyone I cared about, I swear."

The Queen's eyes were cold and her stare was icy. "We trusted and believed in you Craig! You have helped us on many occasions, but what you are doing now is unforgivable! How could you even think about poisoning the planets that have alliances with Earth? We were warned that you planned to unleash the bacteria on us as well! Is that why you're here; to carry out your threat?"

Carter shook his head miserably. "Of course not; how could you even think that?! I would never harm a hair on anyone's head, not here or anywhere else. I wouldn't even do such a loathsome thing to my enemies! No one deserves such a terrible fate! Someone else is doing this and I am the scapegoat."

"The signatures matched yours in every case," the Queen continued dogmatically. "How do you explain that?"

The explorer shook his head. "I don't know! I was tricked somehow and I'll get to the bottom of this, you have my word."

The Queen of Neptune took her daughter firmly by the arm and turned away from the earthling. "Get away from here and never come back!" she exclaimed angrily. "We want nothing to do with you and as far as we are concerned, until you are apprehended and made to pay for your crimes, we'll boycott Earth until this matter is satisfactorily resolved."

Carter went down on his knees. "Your Majesty, don't turn your back on Earth! It's not their fault this unfortunate situation has arisen. If you want to hate me, then do so, but my planet cannot be held responsible for these circumstances."

The Queen however was no longer listening. She took Lolita by the hand and began leading her away. "Come along my dear, you shouldn't be associating with this man. You are young and so impressionable and he has a persuasive way about him. Your father was looking for you and it is best not to keep him waiting."

Lolita smiled tentatively at her friend and he waved to her. "Well anyway, I'm glad I saw you Lolita, even though you suspect me. Goodbye Your Majesty, Lolita."

"Bye Craig," said Lolita timidly, and her mother steered her firmly away.

Lolita watched her friend as he sat mournfully on the embankment and put his head in his hands. She dived down with her mother and returned to the palace.

"Lolita, you took a chance going up there to see him," her father admonished her. "He could so easily have killed you, or caused you some harm at least."

Lolita's eyes were wet with tears. "He would never harm me!" she exclaimed miserably. "He likes me."

"He has helped us a great deal in the past," her father agreed, "but something has changed and he has become dangerous. You are never to speak to him again, especially not alone! I have already informed Commander Simms that we will be sending some of our spaceships into space to help Earth look for Craig Carter. He must be apprehended before he can place those cursed germs on any other planets!"

The King stopped a passing technician. Bron, tell the pilots to launch immediately. Carter is right here on Neptune! If we hurry, we can stop him before he lifts off again. Send our fastest crafts to apprehend him."

The man nodded and hurried to their control room.

Lolita sniffed and bowed to her father. "May I leave?" she asked timidly.

He waved her away irritably and Lolita went to her beautiful garden where she sat on a bench, put her head in her hands and wept for a friendship lost. "Why have you done this terrible thing Craig?" she asked miserably. "What made you change so?"

Carter climbed back into his ship and stared at the tranquil blue water below him. He knew things between him and the Neptunians would never be the same ever again, unless he could prove his innocence beyond any shadow of a doubt. Suddenly he saw the water churning and heard the sound of engines.

"Oh no! I wasn't expecting them to come after me so soon. I had better get going!"

He spoke to the computer. "Initiate take off immediately!"

The display lit up and the ship began lifting off Neptune, just as the first fighter craft rose out of the water. Craig barely had time to fasten his seatbelt before the Neptunian craft had spotted him. He knew it would take them a few minutes to get their guns online and he was a sitting duck. It was too soon for him to go into time lapse, as his engine needed to warm up some more, so he pointed the ship's nose upwards and hoped he had enough thrust to avoid being hit. The Neptunian ship quickly closed the distance and they hailed him.

"Give up now, or we will disable your ship!"

He didn't even bother to answer them, but spoke urgently to

the computer. "Increase power!"

The turbines groaned loudly, but he felt the thrust which slammed him into the back of his seat, and slowly, agonizingly, the distance between the two ships increased. The computer sent out a warning. *<Enemy ship has locked on us and will fire soon.>*

Craig swerved violently to the left and the laser beam passed narrowly on the right. He coaxed more power from the motors, and the distance increased marginally once again. The Neptunian ship also increased power and fired once again. This time their laser beams shot under the ship, also narrowly missing its target. Carter knew that eventually they would find their target and it would all be over. The engines began to revolve more smoothly and he ordered the computer to go into time lapse mode. He sighed with relief when he saw his ship had done exactly that. Just to be on the safe side, he kept the ship at a higher speed until he was sure the Neptunians had been left behind, then he slowed down.

"I can't blame them really, because what happened was pretty awful," he rationalized. I dare not go to Venus and try to explain either, because I don't know how that piece of paper bearing my signature got there, and anyway, they'll probably kill me on sight. Who can I turn to for help? The Saturnians are friends of mine and only use violence when it's absolutely necessary. Maybe they can help me. I'm not going to land on theirs or any other planet though, because I'll be a sitting duck if they choose to come after me. It was a close call with the Neptunians and I won't try that again."

Craig hailed Saturn and Karnd stared hostilely at him. He smiled, but the Saturnian didn't return the gesture.

"Hey, surely you don't believe all that rubbish you've been hearing about me?" he asked plaintively.

In response, Jorrel approached and he held a limp form in his arms.

"Do you want to see the results of your handiwork, Craig? This child is dead and you killed her!"

"How is that possible when I have not been anywhere near your planet since I began my journey?" he wanted to know.

"Oh, you killed her all right. I'm not interested in any excuses. That deadly bacterium you stole was sprayed on the far side of our planet and this child went to sniff a flower over there. She died as a result of that act. We have to wear protective clothing, because we don't know how much of our planet is contaminated. We are peaceful people as you know, but there are exceptions and this is definitely one of them. Even now we are tracking your location and we will be seeing you soon. When that happens, we will blast you out of the sky. I have heard Earth has made capturing you their number one priority, so maybe they will find you soon and punish you for your crimes; oh and while you are chatting to us, this is what we think of your calling card!" said Karnd viciously, as he tore up a piece of paper and allowed the pieces to drop to the ground. Craig caught a glimpse of it before it was shredded and his signature could clearly be seen. The vidscreen switched off and Craig found himself staring at the blank screen.

"Damn that Jorrick Baker! Because of him I'm not welcome even amongst those I consider my friends!" he stormed.

CHAPTER 3

Angrily, Craig chose a destination at random and decided to just stay out of the clutches of any of the known planets. He was so deep in thought that he failed to see a line of meteorites until his ship collided with them, jolting him off his feet. He slammed into a part of the console and hit his head, blacking out for a second. Carter woke up to find his ship lurching and tilting dangerously and the computer's alarm screaming, alerting him to the fact that he had sustained some kind of damage to his craft. With an effort, he managed to right it and began running a diagnostic check.

"I'm going to have to make an emergency landing somewhere to

check my ship," he thought desperately. He began scanning the surrounding area to find a safe planet, when suddenly he looked up and discovered, to his amazement, that the sky above him was no longer black, but blue.

"Oh no, where *am* I? I must have been hit harder than I thought, because it looks as though I've entered another universe. The sky is blue, as blue as the ocean on Neptune!"

His craft seemed to develop a mind of its own and made for a yellow planet in the distance. Although badly damaged, the ship made a perfect landing and Craig climbed warily out and looked around. As he watched, something moved in the distance. The stranger came closer and Carter noticed it looked like a dwarf. It had two arms and two legs, and a very round shaped body. The creature's head seemed to be very large. Craig saw two ears protruding from the top of the being's head. The being was blue all over, including its clothing.

Carter's hand hovered close to his laser gun just in case the being wasn't friendly. When it was very close, the explorer took out his mobile device and activated the built-in translator. The small being spoke very softly. "I greet you, strange one. I have never seen your kind here before."

Craig smiled nervously. "Er, well that makes two of us. You are strange to me too."

The being was quiet for a second, obviously considering this fact, and then spoke again. "You are the stranger here, so you can go first. What planet do you come from?"

"It is known as Earth."

"Earth; where is that? I have never heard of such a place. Do all the creatures look like you?"

"Um, yes," he replied warily.

"You look most peculiar! Your mode of transport is also very strange to me."

"What is the name of this planet?" he asked curiously.

"It is one of the Meltonian planets in the Golden Way."

Craig nodded. "I see, but I have never heard of you or your planet before today. Do all the beings living here look like you?"

"Yes, we are all the same, but also different. There are several more like me, but then there are others as well. Would you like to meet them?"

"I guess so," he said hesitantly.

The being noticed his discomfort and began to reassure him. "Stranger, we are a peaceful planet and only harm those who would injure us, yet I feel that you are trustworthy. I have already discovered that the object you are holding in your appendage is a translator, so you are obviously an intelligent being," he said, pointing to Craig's mobile device. "I am sure you have many questions to put to us, and I am also very curious to learn about your people and planet."

Carter couldn't deny the fact that he was extremely curious, so he began to follow the strange being, who despite its small stature, walked very fast. Craig ran after it, but began to lag behind. Then, realizing he wasn't nearby, it retraced its steps.

"Aren't you coming?" it wanted to know.

"I'm sorry, but I just can't keep up with you. Could you slow down a little perhaps?"

The creature chuckled. "Oh, forgive me, I have forgotten my manners. You are definitely not like us."

They came to the top of a hill and the explorer could see a great deal more of the planet, and it fascinated him. Everywhere he looked, appeared to be green, but it wasn't grass. He took out his mobile device and pressed an icon, but his phone remained blank and a "no service" icon flashed. In the distance, he could see several other creatures, all basically round, but they were all different colours of the rainbow, red, blue, green, purple, orange, pink, etc. His new friend went into the midst of them and introduced him to more of the inhabitants, who were just as curious about him.

"By what name should we address you?" a purple one enquired.

"I am Craig Carter, from the planet known as Earth."

"That place is unknown to us," replied an orange being.

"Until today, I didn't know about this planet's existence either, but nor did I know about this universe. Somehow I left my own universe and ended up here."

A green being spoke, "Ah yes, we have heard rumours that another universe exists. It has been said that the sky is black when you are in deep space."

"Yes, that's true, but I don't understand how I came to be in this universe all of a sudden. I am not surprised we haven't heard of you either, because we were not sure if other galaxies existed. All I can remember is that I found myself in a field of meteorites in my own universe and the next thing I knew was I was here in yours. I passed out briefly, so I never saw how I came to be here."

An orange being moved forward. "I think I know what happened. When you hit the meteorite shower, it must have pushed you through the entrance to our universe. You said you passed out, so that explains why you suddenly realized our sky was a different colour."

"I guess that makes sense," agreed the explorer.

"What I cannot understand, Craig Carter is the fact that you allowed yourself to get into trouble in the first place. Surely your craft has warning signals for just such an event?"

"It does, but I was ... er ... distracted at the time. I had a problem I was trying to solve," said he evasively. "Please call me Craig – it is simpler."

Some of the beings moved around and began to inspect his ship. "Your ship has quite a bit of damage on it. Can you repair it?"

Carter followed the beings and stared at his craft, which was pitted with several dents.

"Most of this damage is superficial anyway. The ship will hold together, it just needs some fine-tuning to check that the guidance system is operational. Actually, I need to work on it really soon, so that I can get it running again, but how will I manage to leave this universe again when I don't even know where the entrance is?"

"Relax Craig, for we have something to assist you. A machine exists which can hurl objects far out into space. If we can perhaps match the speed at which you approached, you could probably reverse the procedure again. However, you will black out again, for a time."

Craig thought about this and nodded. "I have to trust you because I can't do this on my own."

"Very well," remarked the blue being he had met first. "Come and eat with us and then you may set about repairing your vehicle."

Carter was doubtful, but they were very friendly and he didn't want to offend them, so he agreed, hoping all the while that he wouldn't get ill from their food.

He was taken to a part of the planet where the strangest vegetation grew. One creature bent down and plucked an orange sphere from a vine and handed it to the explorer. Craig took a deep breath, then bit into it and was pleasantly surprised, for it tasted deliciously sweet. He was handed other plants and each one had its own special flavour. Nothing tasted the same. When he had eaten enough, they handed him another plant, which contained some liquid, and he drank. It tasted like fruit juice and was quite refreshing. Afterwards, he returned to his ship and began the repairs. Several creatures watched as he worked and asked questions which Craig answered as best he could.

It took some time, but several hours later the work was done and Craig prepared to leave the planet once again. "Thank you for your hospitality. I'll always be grateful," he said as he climbed the stairs of his ship.

"Craig?"

"Yes?"

"I sense you are distressed about your world, but I understand if you don't want to talk about it. If things become unbearable out there in your universe, you are welcome to return here. We will give you sanctuary."

"Thank you very much; I'll remember that," he responded gratefully.

When he had strapped himself in firmly, he gave the go ahead and a powerful beam shot out, catapulting him at great speed back into space. He was conscious only of being shoved violently, before he passed out.

When he regained consciousness, he shook his head and unbuckled his harness. He looked outside his window and the sky was black once again.

"So, they did it! Well now I need to find out exactly where I am."

He asked his computer and it told him he was near Mars.

"So, what happens now? I don't know if I did the right thing by coming back here, because I am still a wanted criminal."

His train of thought was interrupted by an insistent beep from his vidscreen and he switched it on, only to be confronted by Commander Simms.

"Where the devil were you, Craig! I've been trying to contact you for ages."

"Sorry Sir, but my radio malfunctioned and I have only now finished repairing it," he lied. "Why did you contact me?"

"I want you to give yourself up and come back to Earth! Several planets have been targeted, but the damage has been slight. If you don't stop this madness soon, we'll have a full-scale war on our hands!"

"What planets have been harmed, Sir?"

"You know which ones, seeing as you are the one responsible for this."

Craig opened his mouth to protest, but thought better of it.

"Where have you been, Carter? Even if your radio was broken, we should have had a visual on you from our various satellites, but it was almost as though you vanished from sight. We tried to get a lock on your mobile device as well, but that was also unsuccessful. I feel it's my duty to inform you that the entire space police force is out looking for you, as well as many of your former friends on the various planets. It is only a matter of time before you will be apprehended. I'm giving you a direct order to surrender!"

"Sorry Sir, the evidence is just too damning. I'm innocent even though things look bad, but I can't give myself up until I find a way to prove it. I'm not prepared to tell you where I was either; not just yet anyway."

"You realize you are disobeying a direct order," stated Simms coldly.

"Yes, Sir, I do."

The screen went blank and Craig stared at it for a time.

"Oh well, he can just add that charge to all the other trumped up ones. I can only be convicted once, but getting caught now will mean the end of my career as a space explorer. I have to find a way to stop Jorrick, but I don't know how to do it without getting arrested."

A few days passed before Craig received a nasty shock. He recognized several ships from other planets, bearing down on him. The Saturnians, Neptunians and several of the ships from his Moon Base were in pursuit. Craig didn't even bother talking to them, but instantly put his spacecraft into time lapse, thus escaping the tractor beam which shot out from one of his fellow explorers' ships.

He travelled in time lapse for a while and stared disconsolately around him.

"I didn't expect the Saturnians to find me so soon. I'm in big trouble now because their ships are the fastest in the universe. Damn Jorrick Baker and all that he stands for!" spat Carter viciously.

He travelled in time lapse for a while and when he judged it to be safe, the explorer reappeared. Suddenly, from out of nowhere, Sonambro's ship appeared and latched onto him. He knew it would be useless to try and escape from the beam so he sat with his fists clenched, waiting for whatever beheld him. Sonambro appeared on his vidscreen and he was requested to descend into the underground facility. Craig stepped out of his craft and was met by Sonambro, who made him immune to radiation before indicating that he should follow him to his quarters.

"Hello Sonambro; I guess the alert for my capture has gone out to every planet in the galaxy."

"It certainly has. It seems you are very unpopular right now, Cragus. You have achieved world status and everyone who knows you admires you. Why then would you turn on your friends in such a manner?"

"Don't tell me! Your planet was also targeted I suppose."

Sonambro shook his head. "No, what would be the point, for

we are immune to all your bacteria. I just want you to give yourself up. You are a good person and I can only surmise that too much space travel has interfered with your logic. Perhaps you just need a few counselling sessions with one of your psychiatrists on Earth."

Craig sank down on one of the nearby chairs and shook his head. "Look Sonambro, I respect you and I owe you my life. I don't expect you to believe me because Jorrick made sure the evidence against me is irrefutable. I can't deny my signature was left on the various planets, but I don't remember signing those slips of paper. Are you going to hand me over to my people by force?"

"No Cragus, I can't do that, not without contaminating the other crafts and planets. At the moment, I have a protective shield about my ship, which prevents radiation from escaping. I can't judge if you are innocent or guilty, it's up to your Earth courts to decide. If you are innocent as you claim, wouldn't it be better for you to give yourself up voluntarily?"

"Too much has happened for me to do that. If I give myself up now, all the planets that have been harmed will fight over who should have the privilege of putting me on trial and then there will definitely be a war between them. Anyway, while I'm free, I can still figure out a way to bring the real culprit to justice. I'll find some way to prove my innocence, but I need time."

The sun creature stared at his friend. "Very well, Cragus, I'll let you go, but I hope you are telling the truth."

Craig returned to his ship and was allowed to leave.

⁄ ⁄ ⁄

It was then the space criminal made a terrible mistake and placed some of the germs on Tyrome where the silver human-oid-like creatures lived. The wind factor wasn't considered and a third of this planet's inhabitants were destroyed. As a result, Tyrus declared war on Earth. In a broadcast to Commander Simms, he delivered his ultimatum. Craig was to give himself up to Tyrus, who would perform the execution himself. If the explorer refused, there would be mass destruction on Earth. A frantic Simms made contact with Craig once again and told him of Tyrus' threat. Now the explorer was faced with a difficult decision. He could stay free and put his planet at risk, or surrender to the silver creatures. Carter was silent for a while, but he knew what his decision had to be.

"Commander Simms, I'll give myself up to Tyrus, but promise me just one thing please. Tell Constance that I love her and there are no hard feelings on my part. Also, you need to contact Tyrus and ask him to fetch me, because I don't know how to get to his planet."

"I'll do that, lad and I regret things turned out the way they did. I admire your courage even though you are, I mean, have become a criminal."

His boss disconnected and Craig stared sadly out of the observation window. "How beautiful my planet looks this time of day. It's clear the sun is setting on this side right now. I shall never see this spectacle again, so I'd better make the most of it."

He was still gazing at Earth when Tyrus appeared in his ship.

"We meet again eh Carter! How pleased I am that I can have the honour of executing you. I'll do it slowly and painfully, for I owe you that much. You made a fatal mistake when you attacked our planet with that deadly bacteria, now come here and I'll give you instructions on how to land your ship on my planet."

Craig obeyed and followed the creature's directions, and then moved to the observation window and watched as Earth receded in the distance. He didn't say much, but Tyrus was too absorbed to notice anything. When Tyrome came into view, Tyrus handed the explorer a strange looking suit, which reminded him of the ones astronauts used a few centuries before on Earth.

"What's this for?"

"I may be the leader of Tyrome, but my people are anxious to finish you off quickly. That honour will fall to me alone. That suit will protect you from our electrical impulses, for a short while anyway."

Craig put it on and began the procedure to land on Tyrome, while Tyrus gave him instructions on where to land. Once the craft had been put down safely, the silver being took Carter firmly by the arm and led him out of the ship. As Tyrus had promised, his people were very angry and did their best to get to the man they thought was responsible for their plight.

Craig was marched off to a cell and imprisoned. The door was sealed behind him and energy coursed through it, effectively turning it into a high voltage death trap. The bars on the window were not electrified though and he stared miserably outside.

"Well it looks as though this is the end of the line for me. I'm going to die with my reputation in tatters. All I've ever worked for at the Space Control centre was for nothing! Now I'm going to pay for someone else's crime," he thought bitterly.

He thought back to his life up to the present moment, reflecting for a long time on his childhood. He remembered his father throwing a ball for him and how he laughed proudly when Craig caught it. He knew he had always been surrounded by love, and sighed deeply. "I'm glad he isn't here to see me at this moment. I dare not return to Earth, even if it was just to reassure my parents of my innocence. How upset they must be right now! Well as much as I hate the idea of dying, it won't be in vain if Jorrick is found out and made to pay for his crimes."

Carter dwelt on memories of when he first joined the Space Control Centre and how difficult the admission tests had been. Again, he relived the excitement of being accepted.

It wasn't long before Tyrus came to collect him. "It's time, Carter."

There was a bitter taste in his mouth as Craig moved forward and he hesitated just for a second. Squaring his shoulders and head held up high, he walked in front of his executioner. Amidst jeers, Carter was marched into the centre of a clearing. His arms were tied behind his back and secured to the trunk of a tree. He prayed it would be over soon. While Tyrus got ready, Craig looked into the sky and saw a Saturnian ship watching the proceedings.

Tyrus laughed. "I think your ex-friends are here to confirm

you really are going to die. Well I won't disappoint them. Are you ready, Earthling?"

"Just get on with it!" said Craig, through clenched teeth.

"Ah but of course, you wish this moment to end quickly. Why did you destroy one third of our planet in the first place? Surely you must have known we would retaliate."

Craig's expression was stony. "I have nothing to say. As far as I'm concerned, the universe has already judged me guilty. No matter what I say, you're going to kill me anyway, but if you want the real truth, I'm innocent. The evidence is conclusive I know, but I want to state categorically that I had nothing whatsoever to do with the destruction on any of the planets that have been harmed. You are telepathic Tyrus. If you probed my mind you would know this."

Tyrus grinned maliciously. "Actually, I already have! You are genuinely confused about this situation, I can tell. You have no idea how this happened do you?"

The explorer glared at his enemy. "So, you know I didn't commit these crimes, yet you're still going to kill me. I don't like you, and I know you feel the same way about me, well tough. I did what I knew was right and saved the Saturnians from extinction. You have a grudge against me for doing this, so your motives are biased! This isn't about the bacterium landing on your planet – it's about revenge."

"You catch on quick Carter! You have been a thorn in my side since we first met, and now I have your government's permission to execute you. How does that make you feel? You work for someone you admire and respect a great deal, and this is how you are repaid. See, those you rescued from me are here to witness your execution. Talk about double standards! Well I get my wish and that is to see you die."

"You know I wasn't responsible for unleashing that bacterium! Do the right thing and tell those who are watching, that I am innocent!"

Tyrus smiled evilly at him. "I don't care. I have been given permission to execute you and I will be happy to do it. Goodbye Craig Carter!"

Craig lapsed into silence and stared at his executioner. His face betrayed no emotion as Tyrus raised a hand and aimed it at him. A soft breeze seemed to caress Craig's face and he closed his eyes.

CHAPTER 4

When he opened them again, he was surprised to find himself lying on a bed in his own spacecraft. He turned his head and saw he was back in space, but he had no recollection of how he got there. Carter stood up and moved towards the cockpit, where he stared in amazement at the pilot, for it was a shapely woman.

"Excuse me ..." he began.

The woman turned to face him and her incredible beauty stopped him in his tracks

At first glance she looked human, but Craig knew she couldn't be. She had long red hair and wore a red tank top, with a skirt that stopped just above her knees. Her clothing was the same colour as her hair. She also wore red boots that covered her ankles. However, it was her eyes that mesmerized him, for they too were a piercing red. In contrast, her skin was green. Craig thought he had never seen anyone quite so breathtakingly beautiful as this creature before him.

"Who are you and how did I get here?" he asked.

"I'm a friend. My name is Andocia."

"Well Andocia, I have never seen your kind before. Where did you come from and why have you rescued me?"

"You interest me, Craig Carter. The universes have been abuzz with news of your diabolical exploits."

"Bad news travels fast. In that case, you must know I'm a wanted criminal."

She nodded. "Yes, I know and that's why I have rescued you."

"I don't understand!" he replied.

"You will when I explain it to you. I wonder what Tyrus is thinking now? The Saturnians must have been really puzzled when you suddenly disappeared from under their noses!"

"How did I get here? The last thing I remember was closing my eyes when Tyrus was just about to kill me. It feels as though some time has passed."

"That was two days ago. I teleported you to your craft and then piloted it out of there. You must have been very tired because when I got you aboard, you fell asleep immediately. I decided to plot a course for my home while you slept."

"But Tyrus and the Saturnians must have seen you take me. How come they never stopped you?"

She smiled secretively. "Well they didn't actually see me. I brought your ship up here first and then fetched you, using the power of my mind. My powers exceed any that you could ever imagine."

"All right, then why are you taking me to your planet?"

"I would like to study you, of course. Your species are very intelligent and my people will welcome such an opportunity."

Craig backed away slightly. "Hey just a second; don't I have any say in the matter? I mean, I'm not a lab rat that will submit kindly to being poked and prodded."

She laughed and it had an edge of menace to it. Craig's stomach tensed and he wondered if he had been rescued from one fate, only to be thrust into something worse than the one he had been saved from.

"You have no choice, Craig Carter. If I wanted to, I could return you to Tyrus and let him finish the job, or I could just disable your ship and leave you here for the rest of your universe to find."

"Andocia, do you live in the Golden Way?"

Her eyes narrowed suspiciously, "Yes, I do, but how did you know?"

"I thought so! Not long ago, I landed on Melton and met the inhabitants, but I don't know how I managed to get through, because I was unconscious at the time."

"Do the rest of your people know about the Golden Way?"

"Not yet; I haven't had time to tell anyone."

"That's good," she said, pleased.

Craig felt chills run up his spine and his every instinct was telling him to put as much distance between this woman and himself as he possibly could, but curiosity won in the end.

"Andocia, if you live in the Golden Way, then you must obviously know where the entrance is."

"Yes, I do. Actually, there are several, but you needn't trouble yourself about that fact now."

Carter gasped as realization hit him. "You knew that I had landed on Melton, didn't you? In fact, I'm willing to bet that you saw where the Meltonians catapulted me and probably followed me out."

Andocia clapped approvingly. "Oh excellent; I said you were an intelligent species and I was right, but there really are several vortexes. I'm going to enjoy visiting your universe at a later time, but right now you are my first priority."

"Why did you rescue me?" he asked curiously. "Every other planet just wants to kill or capture me."

"I know and that's why I helped you. You are an intriguing man, Mr Carter and the very nature of your deeds is the reason why I'm interested in you."

"I'm sorry, but I don't understand."

"It doesn't matter right now. We have plenty of time to discuss this later."

There didn't seem to be anything more to say, so Craig moved back into the rear of his ship and sat down heavily on the bed once again. His mind was racing.

"Oh, this is just great! She is a conqueror and I have unwittingly put my universe and my world in jeopardy! Well if I didn't feel I was a criminal before, I sure feel like one now. What Jorrick did to me is nothing compared to what this woman can unleash on our unsuspecting universe. I have to think of some way to get rid of her and return to Earth. Even though I'm wanted on my planet, I'm prepared to give myself up to the first space police craft I see, just so I can warn them of this impending danger. I don't know if she'll want to conquer Earth in the near future, but we'll have to be prepared. I need to do something before we reach the Golden Way, because I won't know my way back from that universe."

Craig went to his toolbox and picked up a heavy wrench, then he crept stealthily back into the cockpit where he raised the tool high above his head. Andocia didn't even turn around, but the wrench was tugged from his grasp and he watched in amazement as it flew back to its original place.

"What ...?"

She turned around and faced him, red eyes flashing dangerously. "Is that how you repay me for my kindness, Earthling?"

"How ... how did you *do* that?" he gasped.

"I told you; with my mind. However, you need to be taught a lesson, for no one dares to go against me."

In that instant, Craig knew real fear. He realized that he was up against something so evil that he couldn't even begin to comprehend the magnitude of it. Andocia's red eyes caught his gaze and held it, and he couldn't look away. Her eyes seemed to enlarge until he could see only them, and he felt himself succumbing to her will. For a while he fought to regain control, but it soon became obvious who would win this battle. He heard a tortured scream, like an animal in pain, and then realized it was coming from him. He heard eerie laughter and then mercifully, there was only darkness.

"*I have him ... ha ha ha, I have him. He'll be in my power soon!*"

However, before she could continue, she saw something in the distance and gasped. Then she vanished from the craft, leaving the unconscious Craig to the mercy of whatever was approaching.

↙ ↙ ↙

The explorer was unaware of the hands that picked him up gently and transported him to some unknown destination.

"Will he live?" enquired one.

"I think so; we got to him just in time. We must make haste though, for the trauma of what he experienced could kill him otherwise."

↙ ↙ ↙

When Craig Carter regained consciousness, he found himself in a bed, but there was only darkness around him. He was aware of someone approaching and gentle hands propping him up. Something was pressed to his lips and he was made to drink some liquid.

"Who are you and where am I? Please switch on the light, I can't see,"

"Now, now," admonished the gentle hands, "Please just relax and try to get some sleep. You have been traumatized and need time to heal."

The young man wanted desperately to question the kindly soul who was ministering to him, but felt his eyelids growing heavy again and slept. The nurse left and went to speak to the doctor. Unbeknown to Craig, his rescuers were so grotesque that one glance would cause him to have a heart attack. However, they were friendly and compassionate and they too lived in the Golden Way.

The nurse entered the doctor's office. He looked up from his work and spoke to his assistant. "Yes nurse?"

"It is as we feared doctor. The Earthling, Craig Carter is blind! His eyes are open but he can't see anything."

"Thank you, nurse."

"Is there some way we can cure him, doctor?"

The being shook his head regretfully. "No nurse, for we know so little of the human anatomy. The only ones who can help him right now are the Saturnians in his own universe."

"But doctor, the Meltonians mentioned he is a wanted criminal in his own galaxy."

"I know, but it is not for us to judge his innocence or guilt. We are here to cure people of ailments, not condemn them for crimes which they may or may not have committed."

"I understand, but he'll have to be told the bad news, doctor."

"Yes, I realize that. I'll tell him, nurse."

The nurse went to attend to her other patients, but her thoughts were with the unfortunate space explorer. "Oh dear, the poor Earthling – and he's so young too. It seems so cruel that such a handsome man should be blind."

◢ ◢ ◢

The doctor went to Craig's ward and spoke gently. "Mr Carter, are you awake?"

"Yes doctor; please switch on the light. I would like to thank you face to face for saving me."

"I have some bad news for you, Mr Carter. It's daylight outside."

There was a moment's stunned silence before Craig spoke. "Then ... then you mean that I'm ... blind?"

"I'm afraid so. Andocia's gift to you," he said angrily.

"How is that even possible?! I know she is thoroughly evil, because I have never experienced such fear before! Am I back in the Golden Way?"

"Yes, you are. Perhaps I should explain something to you. Many years ago, there lived a race of women who worshipped Andocia, and she was their leader. Her followers terrorized all of us in the Golden Way and we lived in constant fear of them."

Craig shuddered when he recollected his brush with the terrible woman. "I can believe that," said Craig emphatically.

"Well anyway, some of the planets got together and managed to wipe out the entire planet and all its inhabitants, leaving Andocia all alone, but when our allies looked for her, she had disappeared without a trace. Now she's back and looking for trouble once again. We know you have befriended the Meltonians, as word gets around quickly in this universe. We have heard that in your own galaxy, you are a wanted man, but it's not for us to judge why this is so. For my own part, I don't believe all the rumours. Andocia wasn't aware that another universe existed and I think that was why she was so interested in you. She had hopes of making you one of her loyal subjects and as you may have guessed by now, the first stage is to blind her victims. You were lucky we got to you in time, because she never succeeded in completing the task."

"Will she return for me, do you think?" he asked nervously.

"It's a possibility, but we'll do what we can to protect you," he remarked reassuringly.

"Thank you, but I need to know if you can reverse the damage to my eyes at all."

The doctor spoke compassionately. "I have to be honest with you. The answer is no, we cannot help you. There's only one planet that may be able to do something for you and that is Saturn."

Craig shook his head. "Then I might as well resign myself to being permanently blind. They were watching when I was nearly killed by Tyrus and his pals!"

"Tyrus?" the doctor asked in a puzzled tone.

"He's one of my enemies in my own universe, but he pales in comparison to Andocia."

"I see," said the being reflectively, "But we are digressing from the main topic – that of your blindness. How will you manage without your sight?"

Craig was silent for a while, and then he spoke in a shaky voice. "Please could you leave me alone for a while? I have plenty to think about."

"Of course, I understand," replied the doctor kindly as he took his leave. He moved out of earshot and took the nurse aside. "Get someone to guard the Earthling. I am worried because Andocia could return for him at any time."

She nodded and went to organize it.

Meanwhile, Craig was trying to visualize what his new friends looked like. They had gentle voices and their touch was soft and comforting, but he had no idea how grotesque they really were. He tried to think of some way out of his predicament, but the future looked bleak for the space explorer. Finally, after tossing and turning for quite some time, he fell into a troubled sleep.

⏳ ⏳ ⏳

Meanwhile, back on Earth, Commander Simms was angry and confused, for every effort he made to contact Craig was unsuccessful. The Saturnians had informed him that Craig had been facing death one minute, and then had just disappeared from their sight. Unaware of the drama that had taken place, he continued to search for the missing man.

Jorrick and Constance came into the control room holding hands.

"Sir, have you managed to contact him yet?" asked Constance.

"No, I haven't, my dear, but I'll keep on looking."

Jorrick was pensive. "Sir, you have police patrols out everywhere and no one has managed to find any trace of him. Do you suppose he had an accident of some sort?"

"It's possible I suppose Jorrick, but Craig is very careful and also very clever. He isn't one of my top space explorers for nothing, you know. However, he can't hide forever. Sooner or later, someone will find him."

The young couple walked arm in arm out of the office and Jorrick stroked Constance's face gently. "Cheer up my angel, he'll be found. Why are you bothering with that space criminal anyway?"

Angrily Constance pushed him away. "Jorrick, Craig may have become a criminal, but you seem to forget that I was going out with him not so long ago. I'm still curious to find out what happened to him."

"I'm sorry! That was very inconsiderate of me. Craig was my friend too you know, but let's forget about him for the meantime. I'll buy you lunch in the cafeteria."

Constance smiled at Jorrick. "Thank you, but I'm not really hungry right now and I have a headache. I think I'll just go home and lie down for a while."

When Constance reached the car park, she stopped and turned around. "No, I'm feeling very uneasy about Craig. Somehow, I sense he is in more trouble than we realize. I have to persuade Commander Simms to let me go out into space and look for him by myself."

Thus, Constance returned to the Commander and put her request forward. At first, Simms was sceptical, but he realized the sense in her argument, so he gave her permission to search for her ex-boyfriend. Jorrick tried to persuade her not to go, but she was adamant and before long, she was in deep space.

CHAPTER 5

Back in the Golden Way, Craig had got used to walking about the planet. Outwardly, he greeted everyone cheerfully, but he was depressed about his condition. There had been a few close calls when Andocia tried to kidnap him once again, but the vigilant guards had always sounded the alarm in time, and this too weighed heavily upon him. His kindly benefactors got together and held a secret meeting, because they knew he was only pretending everything was fine. Together, they formulated a plan, but decided not to tell the blind explorer about it. Instead, his doctor came and spoke to him.

"Craig, we can't keep you here indefinitely. Andocia will succeed in kidnapping you again if you stay here. Perhaps if you returned to your own universe, she would leave you alone. If we took you to your ship, would you be able to pilot it?"

'Yes, of course I would. I know my ship like the back of my hand, and anyway, once the correct coordinates are punched in, the computer will control my craft. I can also communicate verbally with it."

"Very well then, if you tell me how to work your computer, I'll put all the relevant data in for you. However, before you leave, I want to give you a final examination."

Craig agreed and together they made their way to the surgery, where the doctor strapped a queer contraption over his eyes. Unbeknown to Craig, this was not part of the treatment, but the doctor had a suspicion that something else was worrying him. When the examination was complete, the doctor ordered one of his staff members to help Craig pack his things so he could leave.

While this was being attended to, he called an emergency meeting with the planet's technical staff.

"I have encountered a problem. I probed Carter's mind and he's determined to commit suicide by crash landing on one of the uninhabited planets in his universe. We can't allow this to happen, for the Saturnians may yet be able to save his sight. No matter what he is alleged to have done, he deserves to get the help he needs. You will have to sabotage his craft in such a way that he is unable to change anything on his computer, but go directly to Saturn, whether he wants to or not."

There was a collective nod of agreement and the plan was put into motion. The unsuspecting explorer climbed into his ship, thanked his friends for all that they had done and then lifted off vertically. A while later he was again cruising in the universe he knew so well, but he couldn't see the black sky. He only knew where he was because he asked the computer.

Some time passed and Craig became aware of a gentle bump as another ship docked with him, but he received no communication. There was a soft hiss as the doors opened simultaneously and Craig smelt a familiar perfume. He turned in the general direction of the door and stared at the intruder.

"Constance, what are you doing here?" her boyfriend asked crossly.

"I came to talk some sense into that stubborn head of yours. Everyone has been on the lookout for you. Jorrick thought you had crashed somewhere, but I knew you were too experienced to let that happen. I want you to return with me to Earth and face trial for your misdemeanour. You're only making things worse by staying out here. At least if you give up voluntarily, your sentence will be lighter."

Craig snorted angrily. "Huh! I loved you Constance and I thought you at least would believe me when I told you I was innocent, but you condemned me, just like the rest of the world has. Go back to Earth and forget about me!"

Craig turned his back on the woman he loved and began to walk away from her, but he didn't see the chair right in his path and with a muttered oath, fell over it and crashed to the floor. For a second, he was disorientated and never realized Constance had now moved in front of him. He struggled to his feet and was startled when he felt her arms on his shoulders. "Craig, what's happened to you?" she cried, alarmed. "You're blind!"

"So, what if I am?" he remarked sullenly. "You don't care and nor do the rest of the worlds. Go back to your precious Jorrick! He never forgave me for stealing you away from him in the first place! Well now the two of you can get on with your lives."

He shrugged himself loose and walked away from the woman he loved so dearly.

Constance went to the vidscreen and contacted Commander Simms.

"Constance, what is it, why are you crying?"

"I … it's Craig. I have found him, Sir."

"Has something happened to him, my dear?" asked Simms gently.

"Yes, Sir ... he's ..."

Craig grabbed Constance roughly and pushed her away from the screen. "All you need to know Simms is that I'm alive and well and I refuse to return to Earth. I was just about to send Constance back to you, and for the last time, *leave me alone!*"

He broke transmission and hustled Constance off to her ship. The malicious words tumbled out of his mouth before he could stop himself, and Constance left in tears as the two ships separated. Craig listened as the sound of her ship's engine grew fainter.

"Farewell Constance, I've hurt you terribly, but I want you to forget all about me, because I'm going to kill myself. I can't live, knowing that I'm blind. All I have ever wanted was to be a space explorer, but that's impossible now. Even if I wasn't blind, everyone thinks I'm a criminal so I'll never be allowed to explore space ever again."

Craig moved unhappily to his computer and gave it instructions.

"Computer, set this craft on a crash course for any uninhabited planet nearby!"

<Sorry Craig, but I am unable do so.> It replied apologetically.

He rounded on the computer and slammed his fist on the console. *"Damn it, I gave you a direct order!"*

<Yes Sir,> replied the computer patiently, *<but there is an override switch which prevents me from carrying out your orders. I am unable to reverse the process.>*

Craig sighed heavily. "Oh, very well then, computer. Cancel the previous instruction."

He was conscious of feeling very tired, so he lay down on his bed to have a nap.

♩ ♩ ♩

When he woke, he found he was once again in a bed, but had no idea where he was. A door opened somewhere nearby and Craig heard footsteps coming towards him.

"Hello Craig. It's just me."

"Lara, is that you?" he asked. "How did I get to Saturn? I don't remember anything at all."

"Just take it easy right now. You were pretty out of it when we found you floating in our orbit. You have been under quite a strain lately, haven't you?"

Craig reached up to touch his eyes, but they were swathed in bandages. Lara gently took his wrists and placed his hands by his side once again.

"Leave them alone for now, Craig. The operation was a very delicate one and your eyes need to heal."

"You operated on them already?" he asked in amazement. "How did I get to Saturn, because I didn't plan on coming here at all?"

"I know; you had other plans, but someone foiled them and they did the right thing. Killing yourself isn't the answer, no matter what the circumstances."

"You used a mind probe on me, didn't you?" he asked angrily.

"No, we were unable to do so because of the damage to your optic nerves and a section of your brain. A doctor from some planet called Bartha left us a note on your computer explaining the situation. When you are well enough, my people have many questions that need to be answered, but that will come later. I feel it's my duty to tell you that this operation was a very complex one and it's possible that even with our advanced technology, you could still be blind."

"I understand, but when will I know the answer?"

"It will be confirmed in a few days only. You've been blind for a fairly long time now, so a few more days won't hurt you. Why, did you have other plans?" she remarked snidely.

Carter decided to ignore the jibe, as it was obvious he was still a wanted criminal, however something worried him. "Lara, why did your people operate on my eyes when I'm obviously going to prison for my so-called crimes anyway?"

"Your life isn't over, even though you may think so Craig. Because you are a first-time offender and obviously because of the good work you've done up until this crime spree, maybe your term won't be long and you can return to civilian life after a few years. Besides, we would help even the most hardened criminal if Earth asked us to. Your planet has been good to us in the past. We can't break off the good relations just because of one criminal. However, we have taken the necessary precautions and some of your space police have been ordered to guard you. If you need something, ask the guard on duty to call one of the nurses."

Craig replied angrily. "You're right of course! You mentioned civilian life! No way will Commander Simms allow me to explore space again. As far as he is concerned, I'm guilty as charged, but I would never do such a terrible thing. Why won't anyone believe me? I'm not a criminal!"

An awkward silence developed and Lara tentatively touched his arm. "Just try to relax for now." She turned away and her voice broke. Lara spoke quietly, but it was loud enough for Craig to hear. "I'm truly sorry!" she sniffed, and then she was gone.

The days passed slowly for Craig, but finally the moment of truth arrived and the doctors clustered around Craig's bedside. Slowly, they began to unravel the bandages and he tensed, not sure what would happen. The last piece of cotton wool was removed from his eyes and he opened them slowly and blinked carefully. At first the images swam in front of his eyes and blurred into several faces. Gradually they cleared and he stared at Jorrel and Lara.

"I can see!" he exclaimed, relieved. "You did it!"

They smiled, but it was tinged with sadness and he knew that it was a hollow victory for them. Carter looked around the room and saw he was in a prison cell. A policeman inclined his head and greeted the explorer. They stayed only a short while and then left the cell.

Jorrel went to the vidscreen and contacted Commander Simms.

"Commander, the operation was a success. Craig Carter can see again."

"I'm glad for his sake. Did you find out what caused it?"

"Yes Sir, we did, but it was completely unknown to us. I am requesting permission to question Craig about it, but he's been through a traumatic time. We were unable to use a mind probe on him, as the extent of his injuries were quite severe and we were afraid to inflict even more damage. I suppose you would like him returned to Earth for trial as soon as possible, but we need to keep him under observation here for a few days at least."

"Then you must do so. When you have completed your investigation and he's fit to travel, the space police on your planet are to return him here. Will you give me a copy of your investigation for our files?"

"We'll do that, Sir. When he's ready to travel, I'll inform you, so that you'll know when to expect him."

Jorrel allowed some time to pass and then went to visit Craig in his cell. "Craig, I need to ask you some questions, but they aren't related to your crimes. Will you give me your fullest co-operation?"

"Do I have a choice?" he replied sourly.

"I'm trying to help you, not make things worse!"

Craig sighed. "Oh, very well, what do you want to know?"

"How did you become blind?" asked Jorrel curiously.

Craig once again had a vision of the devilish woman and he shuddered involuntarily.

"Craig, are you okay?" asked Jorrel curiously.

"No, I'm not! I've come up against some pretty tough foes during my stint as a space explorer for Earth, but I have always kept my head and got the job done. However, this time was different. There was this evil woman who plucked me out of Tyrus's grasp, just by using her mind. She was so powerful that I felt helpless in her clutches. She tried to make me her willing subject by mental brainwashing, and that's when she blinded me. It's so hard to explain, but I have never in all my life known of any power as awesome as hers."

"I believe you, because you disappeared right under our noses and we never saw a thing. Craig, where did you go to afterwards? Every planet in the universe was on the lookout for you, but no one saw you at all. It was almost like you disappeared without a trace for a time."

"That's because I did, literally. This woman lives in another universe known as the Golden Way."

"Then there *is* another universe beyond ours!" exclaimed Jorrel excitedly.

"Yes, there is," he assented.

"We suspected as much, but were never able to prove it, until now. What do the beings look like?"

"Well apart from Andocia, they were very friendly, but I only know of two planets and I never got to see the second one, because I had already been blinded. They rescued me from that she-devil and they are the ones who sent me to Saturn. The doctor who left you that message on my computer lives on that planet."

"Fascinating!" exclaimed Jorrel excitedly. "I would love to meet them some day so we can swap ideas."

"Jorrel, I hate to disappoint you, but I don't know how to get to the Golden Way. Each time I passed through the portal, I was unconscious."

Jorrel gasped as a disturbing thought came to mind. "Craig, this Andocia woman captured you in our universe! Do you think that she might decide to conquer our galaxy?"

Craig shrugged. "How would I know? I'm not the scientist, you are!"

After a while, Jorrel left Craig alone. The explorer had plenty to think about, but he was determined to escape. He knew he couldn't rest easy until Jorrick had paid for his crimes.

CHAPTER 6

Much later that night, Craig was asleep in his prison cell when he heard a muffled sound. He was instantly awake, all his senses alert to danger. The key turned quietly in the lock and a figure dressed all in black and wearing a hood over its face crept stealthily inside. Carter tensed as he heard his name being whispered. "Mr Carter?"

"Who are you and what do you want?" he demanded.

"I'm a friend. I believe you've been framed for something you didn't do and I'm here to rescue you. Quickly, we haven't got much time. I have knocked out the guard at your door. We need to get out of here before his colleague finds him. I have a ship standing by to take you anywhere you want to go."

Craig hesitated for a second and a hand gripped him tightly. "I heard you are to be returned to Earth tomorrow morning where you'll be sentenced for your crimes. If we don't go now, it'll be too late."

Carter followed the person out of the cell and down the passage. The figure didn't hesitate as it led him in total darkness down passageway after passageway until they reached the outside of the building. In the distance, Craig could see the outline of a craft and he headed for it. The design was unfamiliar to him and as he and his rescuer approached, a portable stairway came down. The door closed behind the twosome and Craig blinked in the light. Even before he had time to focus, the craft had lifted soundlessly off Saturn.

Carter blinked once again and gasped as a familiar face greeted him.

"Well, look who came in from the cold! Colonel Ivan Petrovsky! You were the last person I was expecting to see!"

The Russian smiled pleasantly and Craig stared at the gun in his hand. He had never seen anything like it before either.

"Well it looks like you Russians have been busy lately. Your ship's design was unknown to me, and that weapon looks pretty lethal."

"Ah comrade, you are quite correct. This ship is a new prototype I have been given permission to test, and so is the weapon. I'll be glad to give you a demonstration, if you like."

Craig grinned as the irony of the situation hit him. "No thank you, Comrade, that won't be necessary. The odds aren't in my favour anyway."

Petrovsky nodded to his friend and the man removed his hood and patted Craig down expertly, but of course there was no weapon. Carter ignored the guns trained on him, and sat down on a chair.

"I suppose I owe you my thanks, but why would you rescue me? – No wait, let me guess! You want me to return the favour somehow, am I right?"

"Ah Carter, you catch on very quickly. I must say that even though we are enemies, I have always admired you, for you are a worthy adversary. Imagine my surprise when I learnt that the esteemed Craig Carter had become a criminal."

Craig grinned but didn't deny it. "Ah well, stranger things have happened before. Tell me Petrovsky, what did you have in mind?"

"Well I thought, seeing as your country hates you so much, perhaps you would like to get back at them. We'd like you to be our guest on the Russian Space Station, where we hope to convince you to part with the secret information regarding your new weapons and fighter craft blueprints. You can disappear from sight if you want, or Russia will give you sanctuary. If you would like to continue exploring space, then you'll be welcomed with open arms by Russia. You'll be given a new face and identity. We can get what we want by force, as you know, but it would be better if you'd co-operate fully with us."

Carter nodded. "I'm tempted this time, I must admit. All my life I've worked my butt off for Commander Simms, and this is how he repays me, by hunting me down like a wild animal, but I'm curious, Petrovsky. Why would Russia want someone who goes around poisoning other planets and taking credit for it?"

"I'm sure you had your reasons, comrade, but you're not a fool so you know there will be some … er … mind altering involved."

Craig laughed. "Oh, come on Petrovsky – you mean brainwashing, don't you?"

Now it was Petrovsky's turn to laugh. "Ah comrade Carter, your forthrightness has always amused me. Does the prospect upset you?"

"I hate to disappoint you Petrovsky but I wasn't the one responsible for poisoning the planets. I don't expect you to believe me, as the evidence against me is pretty damning. I know who was responsible for this, but he's covered his tracks very well, so my reputation is in ruins. Whichever way you look at it, I'll never explore space under the American flag again, so Petrovsky, if Russia will have me, then I'm yours. However, I have no wish to be brainwashed. I'll come over to Russia willingly. Do we have a deal?" asked Craig as he extended his hand in friendship.

Petrovsky shook the extended hand vigorously. "Yes, indeed Mr Carter, now let's have a drink to celebrate!"

Both he and his companion replaced their guns in their holsters and Petrovsky poured some Vodka into glasses standing on a cabinet nearby.

"Here's to a wonderful new partnership, Carter."

They clinked glasses and sealed the deal. After quite a few more drinks, both of them staggered to the sleeping quarters and Craig was shown to an empty bunk. He fell asleep fully clothed and Petrovsky did the same.

When morning came, both were considerably the worse for wear, and Craig held his head tightly. "Owww Petrovsky, just how many Vodkas did we drink?"

The Russian moaned. "I'm not sure, but it was plenty. It's breakfast time so we had better go to the dining area."

"You want to have breakfast?" Carter asked incredulously. "No way will I keep it down!"

"I know how you feel, but you have to keep your strength up. You'll feel much better when you've eaten. Somehow, having a hangover in space is worse on an empty stomach."

Petrovsky put his arm around Craig's shoulders and they weaved their way to the dining area. Both sat down heavily on some vacant chairs and looked around blearily.

Without being asked, Petrovsky's assistant from the previous night, came to the table and placed two cups in front of Ivan and Craig. The American explorer stared dubiously at the container of blue liquid, which bubbled ominously.

"What is this stuff?" he asked suspiciously.

"Relax Carter, we won't poison you! Uri is my most trusted aide and this is a hangover cure, known as Rat Poison."

Craig sniffed it tentatively. "Well it's aptly named. Oh well, I guess I can't feel worse than I already do so here goes!"

Both men tilted their heads back and swallowed the liquid simultaneously, in one single gulp. They choked and tears came to their eyes, but the effect was almost instantaneous, for the floor had stopped spinning. Craig's appetite returned and he found that he was in fact very hungry. After a hearty breakfast the twosome returned to the flight deck.

"Well comrade Petrovsky, what happens next?"

"Our Space Station isn't far away now. Commander Trotsky is waiting eagerly to greet you. I'm glad you chose to come over to our side willingly; it's so much more convenient. Russian torture is very effective, but so unnecessary!"

Craig didn't answer. He knew that no matter what Petrovsky said, they didn't trust him at all. There were always guards nearby, alert for any trouble that may occur. He decided he couldn't really blame them, for if the situation had been reversed, Colonel Petrovsky would have been treated in exactly the same way. Petrovsky pointed out the window at something in the distance.

"There's our Space Station, Comrade. We should be landing in about ten minutes."

Craig watched as the dome shaped construction moved closer and the landing doors opened. They flew inside and the doors closed behind them once again.

Craig hung back, but Petrovsky pushed him gently from behind. "You go first, Comrade Carter."

Craig climbed down the steps and stared at the group of people who had come to meet the Russian ship. Petrovsky moved ahead of Craig and Uri came to stand unobtrusively beside the American explorer. He watched as the Colonel approached a man and saluted smartly. "Greetings, Commander Trotsky!"

The man returned his salute and then stared at the American piercingly. "So, this is the infamous Craig Carter!"

Uri nodded and Carter went to stand next to Colonel Petrovsky and extended his hand. "Sir, I'm honoured to meet you."

"I'm pleased to meet you too, Comrade Carter. Ivan here tells me that you wish to join our ranks. America's loss is certainly our gain and I bid you welcome."

Commander Trotsky indicated to Uri and the three of them

fell into step behind him, while he led the way to his quarters. Once they were all seated, he moved to a bar and offered drinks, but Craig declined, the memory of his hangover still fresh in his mind.

Trotsky was courteous and respectful of the American space explorer and for a while the discussion centred on the various achievements by both the Russians and Americans in the quest to conquer space. After some pleasant small talk, Craig was asked to follow the Commander, and again the threesome moved off. Uri had gone to attend to other duties.

Trotsky led the way into what looked like an interview room. At the doorway, Carter hesitated.

"Is something wrong, Mr Carter?" asked Trotsky pleasantly.

"Well no, but I had hoped to shower and change into some clean clothes first," replied the American space explorer.

The Russian commander smiled disarmingly. "I understand of course, but business before pleasure. Later on, you'll have all the time in the world to attend to such matters. Why do you hesitate, Comrade? It was my understanding that you came here of your own free will."

Craig nodded. "I did and I intend to co-operate; I just thought you would conduct this interview tomorrow."

Trotsky smiled again. "Ah Mr Carter, why put off for tomorrow what can be achieved today. Please take a seat in that comfortable chair over there."

Craig did as he was told and rested his arms on the armrests. To his amazement, two steel bands emerged from the chair and encircled his wrists.

"Hey, what's the meaning of this? I said I would co-operate fully!"

Trotsky smiled again, but his eyes were cold. "Oh, come on Mr Carter, this is just a precaution. You didn't really think we would accept you at face value, did you? However, if you have been telling us the truth, then there is nothing to fear."

Petrovsky moved forward holding a strange device and Carter squirmed uncomfortably. Perspiration began to break out on his forehead. "Hey, what are you doing?" he exclaimed nervously.

"Take it easy, Comrade Carter," remarked Petrovsky, "You

won't die, but this is our insurance. It's truth serum, which I'm going to inject into your body. I assure you, you will remain awake and alert the whole time."

He held the device against a vein in Craig's neck and Carter gasped as he felt the prick of a needle. He could feel the liquid surging through his body, but he tried to fight it anyway. The explorer began to perspire and Petrovsky's face swam out of focus for a second. The Russian took a nearby towel and mopped the American's sweaty forehead.

"Fighting the drug is useless, Comrade. It's one hundred percent effective," said Trotsky softly.

Craig realized he was in a bad situation. He knew beyond a shadow of a doubt, he would answer anything truthfully, even against his will. Petrovsky examined his eyes. "Can you hear me Carter?"

His head felt clear, but his tongue seemed to go lame, and he spoke with an effort. "I hear you, Comrade."

Ivan turned to his superior. "Comrade, the drug has taken effect now. You may proceed."

Nodding, Trotsky pulled up a chair until he was facing Craig.

"Mr Carter, do you really want to defect to Russia and join our space program?"

The words formed in Craig's head, but something entirely different came out.

"No, I don't! I could never turn against my colleagues in America."

"Why did you go along with Colonel Petrovsky then, if you had no intention of joining us?" Trotsky queried.

"I was waiting for the right opportunity to escape."

"Why did you unleash dangerous bacteria on your friends? Have you decided to go into business for yourself?" the Russian asked.

"I wasn't responsible for that. Jorrick Baker framed me."

"But your signature was found on every planet that was affected! How could he forge that?"

"I don't know!" Craig replied.

"How do you feel about America now? They think you are a

criminal."

"I'm upset about it, but my loyalties still lie with my country."

"How do you feel about giving us some top-secret information?" asked Trotsky slyly.

"I don't want to!" Craig replied truthfully.

"But you will, won't you?"

"Yes," confessed the explorer

"What is your opinion of Comrade Petrovsky?"

"He's good at his job and a worthy adversary."

The questioning went on for quite some time and Craig answered every question, but Trotsky grew impatient.

"Before the effects of the drug wear off, we need to question him about the new spaceships that America will be building."

Petrovsky consulted his watch. "Very good, comrade, we have still another half an hour to go."

He moved over to Craig and confirmed that the explorer was still under the influence of the drug, but Craig turned his face away, knowing he was going to betray his country, and there wasn't a thing he could do about it. Trotsky cupped Carter's chin in his hand and turned his head so that he could look directly into the explorer's eyes.

"This is your big moment, Carter. Is America busy building a new spacecraft?"

"Yes."

Trotsky and Petrovsky exchanged satisfied looks and the Commander peered intently into Craig's eyes. "Come on then, tell us everything about it."

Craig opened his mouth to obey, but suddenly Trotsky's face seemed to disappear and he found himself looking at Andocia. He screamed in mortal terror and in that instant, he went blind once again. His face was slapped repeatedly, but he wasn't even aware of it. Finally, he slumped down in the chair. Trotsky looked enquiringly at his officer.

"What happened, Comrade? Everything was going fine, but he seemed to go mad suddenly."

"I don't know, Comrade Commander. Perhaps we taxed his brain too much. We must continue tomorrow and allow him to rest."

"Very well then, have him taken to a maximum-security cell in the meantime."

"I'll do so at once, Comrade." Petrovsky saluted and his superior left. The Colonel called two men stationed outside and the senseless man was carried to a cell.

Craig came awake suddenly and his heart was pounding. He discovered, to his relief, that his sight had returned, but the fear remained.

"I have never felt this way about anyone before. Andocia's attack on me must have left me with some side effects, because I keep having flashbacks of the time when she blinded me. I guess the stress of having to sell my country out to the enemy must have set it off. I didn't reveal any secret knowledge, but it won't stop Trotsky. They know I lied about my defection now and won't rest until they know everything. That truth serum worked and once the Russians have what they want from me, I'll be expendable."

That same night, Craig had nightmares every time he fell asleep, and he woke up in a cold sweat. "I can't carry on like this! What good am I to anyone if I keep having these nightmarish flashbacks?"

Morning came and when the Russians marched him out and sat him down in the chair again, he was very distressed and pale. He imagined he could hear Andocia taunting him and his breathing was very shallow. Petrovsky advanced with the needle once again and Craig stared at him beseechingly.

"Please don't inject me again. I ... I don't know what's happening to me, but I can't remember anything! I know you wanted to question me about the new spacecraft that America is building, but I cannot help you."

Despite his pleas, they injected him anyway, but his memory remained blank.

After a few hours involving torture as well, they gave up in despair. "Bah he was telling the truth. I don't know what happened, but he is of no further use to me. Take him away and dispose of him!" complained Trotsky angrily.

"I will do so at once, Comrade."

Petrovsky called to some guards and issued them with the

relevant orders.

They cruised to an uninhabited planet nearby and set down on the barren wasteland. While one remained in his vehicle, the other motioned Craig to walk, but in his eagerness to finish the job, he got too close and Carter punched him in the stomach, winding him. Before he could recover, a crashing blow sent him into dreamland, and with one fluid movement, Craig grabbed his sidearm. Seeing his friend in trouble, the other guard jumped out of the vehicle and aimed his gun, but Craig jumped to one side, firing as he did so, and with a soft groan, the man fell to the ground and lay still. The American wasted no time and jumped into the Russian craft. Free once again, he continued on his journey.

CHAPTER 7

Carter had no idea where he should go next and cruised around to find somewhere to hide while he thought about the situation. He was determined to somehow capture Jorrick Baker and make him confess to the crimes, but in order to accomplish that he had to return to Earth. He knew his arrival would cause a stir, especially if he arrived in a Russian spacecraft. If only he could arrive secretly, he thought longingly. He was tired of running!

The computer interrupted his reverie, but it spoke to him in Russian. He stared at the screen and snapped angrily. "Speak English!" he demanded.

A heavily accented Russian female voice spoke up. *<Apologies comrade! I just wanted to draw your attention to the fact that some of my power cells are becoming depleted. If they are not replaced soon, we will be marooned in space for all time.>*

Craig rubbed his aching temple where a headache had begun to form.

"Please tell me you have spare cells on board!" he asked tiredly.

<Affirmative,> the computer-generated voice replied. *<They*

are stored in one of the holds, but it requires human intervention in order to replace them. May I suggest you put down on one of the uninhabited planets nearby in order to make the necessary repairs.>

Carter sighed heavily. "Very well, show me a diagram of the solar system."

Obligingly the computer did so and a small light flashed.

<This is an uninhabited planet named Cyberion.> The computer replied helpfully.

<It has a breathable atmosphere for humans and some primitive life forms on it. They are of the insect variety and are harmless to humans. May I set down there?>

"You may," Craig replied.

<We will land in ten minutes,> the computer confirmed.

Carter went to the pilot's seat and strapped himself in. The Russian spacecraft hovered above the planet and set down slowly. Its engines stopped turning and it became eerily quiet.

<Landing successfully completed,> the computer replied.

"All right, now where do you store your spare power cells?" he asked the machine.

Once again it brought a diagram up on screen. A portion of the ship was highlighted in red.

<The power cells are stored in that hatch,> it explained. *<Directions on how to replace these follow now.>*

A diagram appeared on the computer screen and then the instructions appeared. They were in Russian, but Craig's expertise as a spaceship mechanic had never left him and he understood what the diagrams meant.

An hour later he had replaced the depleted power cells with new ones. His hands were dirty and he went to the bathroom to wash them. Afterwards he returned to the cockpit area and prepared to start the ship up once again, but the computer stopped him.

<Regrettably I must charge the new cells for thirty minutes before we can leave this planet. I am one of the older models,> it explained. *<The newer spacecraft do not require this. I apologize for the inconvenience.>*

"It's not your fault!" he sighed. "I'll explore the planet for a while and return later."

Craig Carter exited the ship and examined the ground before he put his foot down, but nothing moved and he began to walk cautiously around the ship. The ground was hard and stony and a grass-like substance grew everywhere. He walked a little further but kept the ship in sight all the time. After a while, strange insects began to emerge from the sand. They scurried around and circled the new arrival, but they didn't come close enough to harm him. When he stepped in their path, they scuttled away, only to return and stare curiously at the strange apparition that shared their space.

The explorer walked around for a while when suddenly the insects all screeched and ran away. Puzzled, he wondered what had scared them but then a shadow fell over him and he turned around hastily. He took a step backwards and dived to the ground when a bolt of electricity shot past him.

"Tyrus, what are you doing here?" he gasped.

The alien lunged for him and he rolled away, coming hastily to his feet. Tyrus didn't advance, but smiled in anticipation.

"I couldn't believe my luck when I passed by the planet and found you walking around!" he began conversationally. "I missed my opportunity before but the stars have been good to me and delivered you into my grasp once again."

Craig took a few steps backwards and wished fervently that he had a weapon of some sort with which to defend himself.

Tyrus read his thoughts and chuckled merrily. "You are at a disadvantage right now Earthling. What can you do against me when you have nothing to defend yourself with?"

The silver being circled him and the explorer kept his eyes on his adversary. "Why don't you just leave me alone? I don't need this right now."

Tyrus continued circling the explorer. "Do you know you are very popular out there in the universe? Your name is spoken often as the killer of planets. It seems those you considered your friends no longer want to have anything to do with you. I think every known planet in the solar system is gunning for you right now. I also believe there is a price on your head."

"So, what else is new?" Craig grumbled. "I know that!"

"Isn't it strange how fickle the planets can be," remarked Tyrus." Here I am, one of your greatest adversaries, yet I alone know you are innocent. It seems I'm the only one who believes you."

"What's your point Tyrus?"

"Well I just find the situation quite entertaining! You have spent your life doing the best you can for your planet and now the universe hates you."

"I'll get to the bottom of the situation. One way or another I'm going to confront Jorrick Baker and make him confess to his crimes and then my name will be cleared."

"I can offer you an alternative," Tyrus remarked slyly.

"What can you offer me?" Craig replied suspiciously. "Sanctuary on your planet, I suppose? Well, I don't trust you!"

The being continued circling the explorer. "Let's face it no one will think to look for you there!"

"True, but I don't want your hospitality and anyway I can't live there forever. I'll clear my name – I have to! I cannot spend the rest of my life running away."

Tyrus looked at his enemy and smirked. "Well there is another route we can follow, I suppose."

"Oh really! And what would that be?" Carter enquired.

"I could capture you and claim the reward! I'll be a hero!"

Craig shook his head and retreated further away. "Over my dead body!" he exclaimed fervently.

Tyrus's three eyes glittered in anticipation. "Well, your planet hasn't specified whether they wanted you dead or alive, so I'm fine with either choice. If it were up to me though, I would choose the first alternative. Imagine killing you and then still getting a reward for doing so! The idea certainly has possibilities," he chuckled.

The explorer took several quick steps back and then spun around as the humanoid-like being appeared behind him.

"You're wasting your time trying to elude me, human. Why not save both of us the trouble and just surrender to me? I promise not to kill you immediately. We can have some quality time together on my planet, and then I'll kill you later when I have learnt all I can about you and the rest of your species."

The explorer looked longingly at his ship in the distance and tried to imagine how long it would take him to sprint to the ship and blast off, but even as he thought about it, he knew half an hour had not yet passed and the ship would not have recharged its power cells just yet.

"We have reached what you humans would call a stalemate, Carter! You know your ship isn't nearly close enough to attempt a dash at freedom. Give up now and I won't have to hurt you. Or else you can try to get away from me. I'll enjoy the game, whatever you plan to do. What is it to be Carter? Choose!"

The space explorer looked around and began to run. He was determined not to go down without a fight! Tyrus teleported ahead of him and he swerved away. For a while Tyrus watched him run and chuckled merrily, knowing that soon his quarry would tire and he would be victorious. He couldn't lose!

Craig disappeared around a bush and Tyrus landed just behind him. For a moment, he stared curiously as Carter simply stood still and made no attempt to flee.

"Oh dear, are you tired already?" he simpered. "I was just beginning to enjoy this little game of ours."

The young man made no reply and Tyrus followed his gaze. His three eyes came to rest on a figure in the distance.

Something emerged from the bushes and walked towards them. Tyrus shielded his eyes as a beam from the sun blinded him temporarily. When his vision returned, he was face to face with a woman who looked human but had green skin. Craig groaned and spoke urgently to his enemy. "I think I will take you up on that offer of sanctuary. We should leave now!"

The silver creature however was fascinated by the new arrival and Craig was temporarily forgotten.

"Hello and who are you?" Tyrus asked the being.

She pointed to Craig who was now hiding behind the creature.

"I think I'll let Mr Carter do the introductions," she replied magnanimously. "Introduce us!"

Craig peered out from behind Tyrus's back and his enemy looked enquiringly at him.

"That woman is known as Andocia," he replied sourly.

Andocia grinned. "I know that your name is Tyrus," she replied. "We've met before but you won't remember that."

The electrical creature looked searchingly at Craig. "You know this being?"

"I have had the misfortune to meet her, yes," he replied guardedly. "She took me away when you were just about to kill me a few months ago."

"Impossible!" Tyrus stormed. "I would've seen something, but you just disappeared. I was going to ask you how you did that when I took you to my planet later."

Tyrus looked curiously at the woman. "So, this is your benefactor! How very interesting! She rescued you but I can sense animosity radiating from both of you. Why do you hate her so much?"

Carter gripped one of Tyrus's arms very hard. "Look I'll be glad to explain later," he whispered. "Right now, let's just get out of here! She isn't someone you want to associate with, I guarantee it."

Tyrus however wasn't about to be put off. He turned back to the new arrival. "Well Andocia, I'm pleased to meet you! Any enemy of Mr Carter's is very definitely a friend of mine. So how did you spirit him away before if I may ask?"

"Teleportation," she replied.

"Ah, so you can also teleport?" he asked. "That happens to be my talent as well!"

Andocia examined her fingernails and flexed her hands. "I can do that and so much more," she replied secretively.

"It sounds fascinating. Perhaps one day you can enlighten me. At the moment though, Mr Carter and I have some unfinished business. I'm taking him to my planet where I intend to question him at length about a great many things. It was a pleasure to meet you," he replied dismissively.

The silver being reached out its hand to the man standing near him when Andocia spoke commandingly. "Not so fast Tyrus! I want a word with Mr Carter first. We too have unfinished business and mine takes precedence."

"Here we go again!" Craig mumbled softly. He turned around and made a mad dash for his ship. Both Tyrus and Andocia hurled bolts of pure power at him. The electrical impulse from one of Tyrus's fingers went wide, but Andocia's singed his ear and he put his hand over it. Blood began to seep from the wound and trickled through his fingers and down the back of his hand.

"Stop right there, otherwise the next one will smash your kneecap," she ordered.

Carter muttered an oath, but obeyed and turned to face her.

"This is fascinating!" Tyrus replied. He was agog with curiosity. "We really should sit down and discuss your talents," he remarked.

Andocia ignored him and crooked her finger at Craig. Reluctantly he went back to her.

"You and I have some unfinished business I believe. Last time we were rudely interrupted."

The explorer sighed heavily. "What could you possibly want with me? I'm not even a threat to you; in fact I hardly know you. Why are you so interested in me anyway?"

"Mr Carter, you do yourself an injustice! I sense great wisdom and determination emanating from you. If you must know, the reason I took you away from Tyrus in the first place was because you fascinated me. News of your crimes against the planets was circulating around this universe and I knew I had to meet you. Never before had I ever heard of a human causing such mayhem on the targeted planets. When I saw Tyrus here was determined to do away with you, I rescued you with the sole intention of finding out whether we could perhaps be friends."

"Andocia you have since learnt that I am not as evil as you supposed. You read my mind and you know I wasn't responsible for these so-called crimes. One of my colleagues framed me."

"Yes, I did learn that, but I had plans for you and these were spoilt by the Barthenians in the Golden Way. No one interferes with my plans!" she exclaimed angrily. "They should not have rescued you. I must admit though you were much more appealing to me when I thought you were a master criminal."

"I realized that long ago, yet you still tried to invade my mind. You nearly ruined my life!"

"Maybe, but you are well once again. How did you recover?"

Craig refused to answer and Andocia smiled wickedly.

"It doesn't matter; I know who helped you. The Saturnians are very clever, aren't they?"

"Leave them alone Andocia!" he pleaded. "They are no match for you. Tyrus killed some of them a few years ago when he tried to rule their planet."

"Yes, and I have never forgotten how you interfered with my plans Carter," the silver creature interjected. "Everything was going so well until you arrived on the scene."

Carter placed his hands defiantly on his hips and glared at his enemy. "Tyrus you and your kind are bullies who prey on those weaker than yourselves. The Saturnians are a delicate race and will become extinct if they continue to be targeted. They have never harmed anyone in their lives and they only use weapons to protect themselves. You were wrong and I made it right. Now if you don't mind, I'm sick and tired of you trying to justify what you did. Killing me won't change anything! I'm tired of being a fugitive and I want this nightmare to end! Right now, I just want to go home and fix this! Jorrick will pay for what he put me through. I suggest we all go our separate ways and I hope that we never meet again!"

Angrily Craig turned his back on the two beings who had caused him the most trouble and headed for his ship. He ignored Andocia's order to stop walking. Tyrus pointed a finger at his departing back. "Oh please, allow me!" he begged.

The explorer was startled to hear a bellow of pain and he spun around and stared incredulously at Tyrus, who was holding a smoking appendage and blowing furiously on it. "Why did you do that?" he whined.

"Tyrus you have a one-track mind. All you can think about is killing the Earthling and I need him alive! Now get out of my sight and go back where you came from. If you don't, I'll give you a taste of what I can really do and believe me, you won't like it, now get lost!"

Tyrus glared at her sullenly. "He's mine; I found him first. I have so many questions and not enough answers."

Andocia raised her hand and pointed a finger at the creature. "Why are you still here? Would you like another demonstration of my power? I'll start with you and then take him anyway. The only reason you are still alive Tyrus is the fact that we do have something in common; we both dislike this Earthling. If you go now, I might be in a good enough mood to leave something for you to play with later. I know where your kind live. If, however you insist on defying me, you'll die first!"

Craig saw his opportunity and decided he wanted to be with neither of his enemies. He began walking silently towards his ship while Tyrus and Andocia continued arguing. They didn't seem to notice he had moved away. Carter broke into a run and both of his enemies forgot their dispute and aimed for their fleeing quarry.

He dodged their energy bolts by not running in a straight line. Some kicked up the dirt at his feet but he ran faster. Carter vaulted onto the top step and shouted at the computer.

"*Get us off this planet now!*" he replied, slamming the hatch door shut.

<*I cannot! My fuel cells...* > the computer complained.

"*Lift off!*" he commanded. "*You have had sufficient time – hurry!*"

The engine whirred into life and Carter looked desperately at the controls.

"Engage time lapse sequence now! You do have such a facility I assume."

The computer made some strange noises and the explorer felt certain that the ship was indignant. However, it complied and they disappeared from sight. Craig just had time to see Andocia's startled face as he disappeared from view.

"Phew, that was close!" Craig gasped as he fell back into the chair. "Set course for anywhere far away from here. I have a lot to think about."

Carter went to the observation window and clasped his hands behind his back. "I have to think of some kind of strategy to prove my innocence!" he thought desperately. "Jorrick Baker must be exposed for the fraud he is so I can get my life back! I'm tired of running away! I miss Earth and my friends!"

CHAPTER 8

Back on Earth, Constance was feeling very depressed as no one could find any trace of Craig. A tear fell and she brushed it away.

"I mustn't cry for Craig. If someone has killed him, he deserved it, because I don't love him anymore. Jorrick is a much better man, or is he?"

She sat down moodily on a bench and stared up at the sky.

"Oh, who do I think I'm fooling! I'm in love with Craig! He kept on telling me he was innocent, but I doubted him. What if he really was telling the truth?"

She shook her head and stood up decisively. "No, I'm just being stupid. Jorrick will laugh when I tell him what I've been thinking about. The evidence couldn't have been forged. That really was Craig's signature on those pieces of paper."

Annoyed at herself, she went in search of Jorrick to persuade him to take her out to lunch.

At his office door, she paused when she heard him talking to someone on his mobile device. The door was slightly ajar and every word came clearly to her. "Things are going just as we planned! Craig Carter is a marked man now and if he's not dead yet, he soon will be. Thanks to you, that next container of bacteria is on its way to Jupiter. This time I've sent the whole bottle, so the inhabitants will be wiped out. Carter's signature will be there, as usual. After Jupiter's demise, the orders will be not to capture, but to kill Craig Carter on sight."

Constance moved closer, scarcely daring to breathe and she stared at the face of one of the technicians on the screen.

"*So that's how he's been doing it! Martin is in cahoots with him,*" thought Constance angrily.

Martin laughed spitefully. "That's great Jorrick! I've always hated that jerk Carter and I can't think of a better end for him than that."

"Same here, pal. I know Constance still loves him, but once he's out of the way, she'll marry me."

Stunned, Constance could only gape at the man she thought she knew, but she had heard enough and hurried to Commander Simms' office. He was speaking on his mobile device and waved her to a seat, but she interrupted him.

"Sir, please, this is an emergency!"

He stared at her and then spoke to the caller. "I'll call you back later, Mr Ambassador."

His caller disconnected and Simms turned his attention to his employee. "All right, young lady, what was so important that I had to interrupt that call from the Ambassador?"

Constance went to the door and shut it, then came and stood in front of his desk. He waved her to a seat but she declined and wrung her hands nervously.

"Commander, we have done something terrible!" she blurted out. "Craig is innocent of the crimes against the planets. He told us so, but we refused to listen!"

"Explain what you mean, Constance."

"Sir, I was on my way to see Jorrick, but he was talking to Martin in the Control Centre. Jorrick has sent off a full bottle of that virus to Jupiter, because he wants to wipe out the entire population. He plans to leave Craig's signature there, and that'll mean certain death for Craig when he's caught. Please Sir, you have to arrest them and recover that vial."

Simms went pale and pressed an icon on his vidscreen. "Chris, get some police to my office pronto!"

"Yes Sir, right away," said the Chief of Police.

Jorrick was arrested and when he heard he had been found out, broke down and confessed. Martin too was taken into custody and confessed to his part in the drama as well. The stolen bottle was recovered by a passing spaceship and returned unopened to the Control Centre.

However, out in space, Craig was still unaware his name had been cleared. Eventually he was located and surrounded by the space police, who ordered him to surrender, thinking he was a

Russian cosmonaut. He identified himself, but by now had grown tired of running away so he contacted the nearest ship. "All right, I surrender! I'm tired of running away. You may lock a tractor beam onto my craft and tow me along if you wish. I just want this to end."

"You don't understand, Mr Carter; we aren't here to capture you, but to provide you with safe passage back to Earth," replied the space policeman. "Jorrick Baker confessed to everything and Commander Simms wishes to apologize for any inconvenience you may have suffered. He'll explain everything to you when you return, but we have a passenger who requests permission to come aboard your craft and accompany you down."

"Who is it?" he asked curiously.

His heart seemed to miss a beat when he saw Constance's face on the screen.

"Can I come aboard?" she asked timidly. "We have a lot to discuss. I owe you an apology and I would like to deliver it personally if you don't mind."

The two ships docked and Constance ran into her beloved's arms. "Craig, oh darling, I never stopped loving you! Can you ever forgive me for treating you so shabbily and listening to Jorrick's lies?"

"I've already forgiven you, my dearest," said Craig as his arms encircled her waist and their mouths locked in a tender kiss. They were interrupted by one of the policemen.

"Ahem, er … Mr Carter, we would like to separate from your ship please."

"Oh, of course; right away! Would you mind if I didn't have an escort down to Earth? I promise to return shortly."

"Very well, Sir," replied the policeman obediently.

The ships separated and Constance held Craig close.

"Why do you want to return later, Craig?" asked his girlfriend teasingly.

He smiled and kissed her tenderly once again. "Constance, I have missed you so much and I just wanted to have you to myself for a while at least."

"A splendid idea, my love, so what are we waiting for?" said Constance happily.

Much later, they were nearing Earth and Craig questioned his girlfriend. "Constance, I owe you a debt of gratitude. If you hadn't overheard Jorrick and Martin talking, I would still be on the run and Jupiter would no longer exist. Did you find out how my name came to be on those slips of paper though?"

"Yes, Jorrick confessed that he had used a portable mind probe on you and when you were under his control, he made you sign those pieces of paper. Afterwards he ordered you to forget what had happened. He's gone quite insane you know."

"I know I should hate him, Constance, but he was a friend of mine. I didn't realize just how jealous he was of me and you."

"He fooled all of us, Craig, but let's forget about him now. The landing bay has been cleared."

They landed and were greeted by a very subdued Commander Simms. "Craig, I don't know what to say to you. I should've trusted you when you told me you were innocent, but the evidence against you was so damning!"

"It doesn't matter anymore, Sir. I think I would have behaved in exactly the same way if the roles had been reversed. Would it be possible to speak to Jorrick, Sir?"

"If you want to, but I don't think it's a good idea. He has done nothing but swear he'll get even with you someday. I can't allow you to enter his cell, but you may speak to him from outside if you really want to."

"I just want a few minutes with him."

Simms shrugged and a policeman led him to the cell, then stood nearby.

"So, the legendary explorer has returned from his adventure I see," he said maliciously. "My plan was foolproof, but I didn't count on being overheard and that was unfortunate! What a pity Tyrus didn't succeed in killing you, but one of your friends rescued you! I will even the score, I swear it. Do you know how much I hate you?" he asked malevolently.

A shiver ran up Craig's spine as he recalled the "friend". He could see there was nothing more to be said, so he left the cell.

Carter returned to his commander. "You were right, I was just wasting my time. Sir, could I have the next few days off? It's been pretty hectic lately."

"Yes, of course you may. You need to recover, but you know we have to debrief you first."

"I understand Sir, and I have quite a story to tell. Can Constance also be given time off?"

"I don't see why not. Is going out to celebrate, your idea of relaxation?"

"When Constance is with me, then yes, Sir."

Craig and Constance went to their favourite restaurant to talk about this latest adventure. While they were having a good time, they had no way of knowing there was more trouble ahead in the not too distant future.

CHAPTER 9

Out in space, some alien beings were discussing tactics and the subject was planet Earth. They watched Commander Simms as he bent over his data tablets.

"That man is important to us. He is in charge of the Space Control Centre and we need to target him first."

"Agreed," concurred his friend. "By controlling that place, we can stop them launching a full-scale attack against us, but what of the one our mistress met; the one called Craig Carter?"

"Bah, he is but one human against us and our sophisticated weaponry; what can he do?"

"Probably nothing, but Arvak, you shouldn't underestimate that young man. I have downloaded his file and he has quite an impressive record. He is only twenty-five human years old, but it seems his friends and colleagues hold him in high esteem."

"It doesn't matter! If he gets in our way then we will deal with him, but right now we have no instructions regarding the Earthling. Come Arno, call the men to me, because I need to make plans for our takeover of Earth."

Arno went about his duties as instructed. These men were also humanlike in appearance, with the same green skin as their mistress Andocia. They did not have her distinctive red hair or eyes, but their garments/uniforms were red. They all wore badges on which Andocia's face was engraved.

A few days later, Craig reported for duty and Simms wanted him to deliver some documents to the people on their Moon Base. They were discussing the trip, when a technician interrupted.

"Sir, I'm sorry to bother you, but we seem to have a slight hitch. The man you sent to pick up some Uranium on planet Uranus wishes to speak with you. He says it's very urgent."

"Very well then, patch him through."

The explorer's face appeared on the screen.

"What's wrong, son?" asked Simms curiously.

"Sir, I can't land on Uranus. It seems to be inhabited by some strange beings. Since when has there been life on Uranus? I wanted to get some Uranium, but they shot at me."

"That's very strange! What do these beings look like?"

Before he could describe the strangers, the man began to perspire and Craig was alarmed.

"What's happening? Tell us please!" he demanded.

"Ohh no, Craig, one of them just materialized in my ship. He – he's pointing something at me … *No please don't!*"

Commander Simms and Craig could only watch helplessly as a look of pure horror crossed their acquaintance's face and he crumpled to the deck of his craft.

Suddenly there was a huge explosion and the ship was blasted apart, ending transmission.

Simms was horrified. "Oh heavens, did you see the look on his face, Craig? It was awful!"

"Yes, Sir, but whatever's out there on Uranus isn't very friendly then. Do you want me to investigate?"

"No Craig, I don't think so. I'll send an unmanned probe to check it out, but until I know what we are dealing with, we'll have to avoid Uranus. However, I also have some news for you. Our friends on the various planets actually made a request that you visit them. One planet every few days. It seems they all feel guilty about hunting you down and wish to apologize personally."

Craig smiled, embarrassed. "Oh Sir, it's not necessary! Like I said before, Jorrick did a convincing job and I don't hold it against them. Besides, I can't afford to take so much time off when there's work to be done."

Simms grinned cheerfully. "Yes, well I've already accepted on your behalf and you may leave any time in the near future."

"In that case then, thank you, Sir. I'll just organize some toiletries, etc for me. Could Constance come with me perhaps?"

"Sorry Craig, not this time. I think you should visit your friends on the other planets and I'll ask Constance to deliver those documents to the Moon Base instead."

"But Sir, couldn't you just e-mail the documents? It would save a great deal of time," Craig asked plaintively.

"I could but these are highly confidential Craig. I cannot risk them falling into the wrong hands, therefore it will be better if they are delivered personally by someone I trust. Perhaps she can accompany you another time."

"As you wish commander. I'll just get my things together then."

⁄ ⁄ ⁄

While Craig was getting ready, Andocia's followers were discussing what they had recently done.

"It was a pity we had to kill that Earthling, but he saw us and I don't want the Earthlings to know that our weapons are made of Uranium. It was unfortunate he managed to get a message through to his Commander."

"I am impatient, my friend! When can we land on Earth?"

"Patience, Arno! We need to manufacture some more weapons before we try to take over. They seem like a civilized race, simpler than us, but worthy opponents nevertheless. They also have many friends in this galaxy who will rush to their aid when they hear Earth is under attack, so we must be patient and investigate further. Once we know what sort of fire power we are looking at, we'll be more able to counteract their efforts."

Unaware of the danger threatening Earth, Craig blasted off

from Mission Control and was soon once again in space. Constance's craft left soon afterwards, heading for their Moon Base. She was carrying the top-secret documents and had instructions to place them only in the hands of the Head of Security on the Moon.

On arrival, she was shown into the Deputy Head's office.

"Constance, I'm sorry, but Doug had to go away urgently. There was some problem with one of our satellites and he had to go and investigate. Could I have the documents?"

"Sorry Jeff, but Commander Simms was most insistent that I hand them over to Doug and him alone. How long will he be gone?"

"I have no idea, but probably no more than two days. Can you wait that long?"

Constance stared thoughtfully up at the ceiling. "I'd better speak to Commander Simms, but it should be okay."

"Sure, no problem!" assented Jeff.

Constance contacted Simms on her mobile device and told him what the situation was. He informed her that she should wait until the documents could be given directly into the head of security's hands. She was booked into one of the hotels nearby, where all visitors were generally housed. The documents were now wrapped in plain paper and she asked the front desk to put them into their safe.

Two days passed and Doug returned. Her mission completed, Constance contacted the Commander on his personal number, using the cellphone app on her mobile device, but she struggled to get through to him. She then went to the control room and asked the technicians at the Control Centre to contact him for her, but the technicians had trouble getting through to Earth.

"What's wrong with the vidscreen?" she asked one of the technicians.

"I'm not sure, but it's probably nothing. We seem to get interference from time to time, but it always clears up, so we'll just try a little later."

Constance went to make herself something to drink and was busy sipping it, when a member of their staff came to call her.

"Miss Gregg, there's a call for you. Please follow me."

She fell in step next to him, thinking that Simms was looking for her, but she found, to her delight, it was Craig.

"Hi sweetheart, it's so good to hear your voice. Where are you now?"

"I'm on Jupiter at the moment, but I should be ready to leave soon. It's great seeing all my friends again, but I really miss you," complained Craig mournfully. "I tried calling you on your mobile device, but I couldn't get through."

"I know, there seems to be some problem with the communications network, but we'll soon be together again. I miss you as well," she sighed. "Give my best to all our friends, won't you."

"I will do that! Are you returning to Earth soon?"

"I suppose so, unless Commander Simms has something else for me to do. At the moment, there seems to be a problem with the communication system on Earth as well, but it's minor I believe."

They spoke for a while longer and then disconnected. Not long afterwards, the Moon Base managed to contact Commander Simms, who asked Constance to return to Earth once more.

The woman arrived and went to see her boss, but his door was locked. She was puzzled and went in search of his secretary, but her colleagues explained she had been given the afternoon off. Constance returned to her superior's office out of curiosity, knowing he had expressly asked her to report back to him the moment she returned to Earth. The woman knew he would have rescheduled had there been a problem. As she sat down at his secretary's desk, a red button began to flash on the office phone, indicating someone inside Simms' office was making a call. Constance pressed the "speak" button and Simms' voice came clearly to her, but he sounded strange. He was talking to the Head of Security in an adjoining building.

"Listen Keith, I need a favour."

"Sure Commander, what can I do for you?"

"We need to improve the security here. Could you perhaps come over and bring me the blueprint that shows where all our triggering devices are?"

"That's an odd request, Sir. Security is tight here and I can assure you that nothing and no one will penetrate our defences, unless we want them to."

"I know that and I trust your judgment," snapped Simms irritably, "but I'd still like them on my desk as soon as possible."

"Do you need to have a meeting with me then, Sir?"

"No, just leave them on my secretary's desk. I'm not in my office at the moment. Whatever changes I'd like implemented will be given to you speedily."

"Very good, Sir; I'll bring them over just as soon as I can."

Simms disconnected, but Constance left the switch on, knowing that it would work like an intercom. Her superior's words came clearly to her. "All right, I've done what you asked, but you'll never get away with this!"

Another voice she didn't recognize, answered. "Oh, but I assure you I will! As long as you do exactly as I say, no one will get hurt. When your blueprints arrive, we are going for a little ride somewhere private."

"What will you do with me?" he asked tremulously.

"Relax Commander, the one I work for needs you alive. It will be in your own interest to come quietly and I give you my word you won't be harmed."

"But you don't understand! If I just get up and walk out of here without an explanation, my staff will become suspicious."

There was silence for a few moments and then the intruder spoke. "Commander, we'll walk out of here normally, but I want you to tell the second in command that you're feeling ill. That way, if you're missing for more than a few days, they'll naturally assume your ill health is keeping you away."

Simms sighed heavily. "All right I'll do as you say, but leave my staff out of this."

"My employer has no use for any of your employees, Commander Simms. You are the only one she's interested in."

Constance stiffened as she heard footsteps coming down the passageway. She switched off the intercom button and hid in an adjoining office, just as the Head of Security came into the secretary's office. She peeped through a crack in the door and watched as he put a data device down on the desk she had vacated only seconds before.

A few minutes later, Constance watched as Simms came out of his office, followed by a man she didn't know. Her sharp eyes caught a glimpse of the weapon he held and she noticed it was unlike anything she had ever seen before. Commander Simm's complexion was grey and he was perspiring. The woman waited until they had exited the office and then followed at a discreet distance. She watched from another office as Simms spoke to his second in command and the man nodded sympathetically. From the direction that her commander was taking, Constance knew they were headed for the car park, so she turned down another passageway, which was a short cut to the same place. By the time Simms and his captor appeared, she was in her helicar, watching the exit. She watched as the man handcuffed Simms with handcuffs that had a fiery red glow. The man ripped something off his head, and Constance gasped as she saw the green face and hands. His hair was light brown.

Simms' helicar lifted off and she followed some distance behind, always keeping a few cars between herself and the one she was following. In this manner, she kept them in sight. They came to rest on a landing pad outside a large, dingy looking building, and Constance made a note of the address. She flew a little further on and parked in an adjacent building's parking lot, unsure what to do.

"I can't go and rescue him, because I don't know what I'm up against. There could be more of them in that building and I'm the only one who knows he was taken against his will, so I'm his only hope. Craig mentioned to us that the woman who blinded him was green with red hair. The audacity of that woman! Well whatever she's planning has to be nipped in the bud soon."

Constance flew out of the building and returned to the Space Control Centre, a plan forming in her mind. On arrival, she made her way back to Commander Simms' office and contacted Craig on the emergency frequency. Her boyfriend was surprised to see she was contacting him in this way and was immediately suspicious. "Constance, what's going on? You obviously have a good reason for using this frequency."

"Listen to me Craig," she said urgently, "Commander Simms has just been kidnapped! No one knows about this, except me. As far as everyone here is concerned, he went home because he wasn't feeling well. I don't know what to do, because his kidnapper was a man with green skin."

Craig was shocked. "No! Why would Andocia want to kidnap Simms?"

"I don't know, but you met her. Did she give any indication that she was interested in Earth at all?"

"She did express an interest, but it was aimed at me personally, or so I thought. I didn't volunteer any information about the Control Centre, or Earth."

"Craig, what should I do? How can I help Commander Simms when I don't know what I'm up against?"

"There is nothing you can accomplish at the moment, so just be careful! I'm going to cancel my trip and head for home, but it's going to take a while for me to get there. If I don't make any stops, other than to collect fuel and some supplies, I should get back in a week or so. Constance, pretend you know nothing about this and don't tell anyone you called me, except perhaps for Keith. Maybe he'll come up with a plan, but we can't take any risks right now. The Golden Way seems more advanced than us as far as technology goes."

"All right, I'll do that. Please hurry home my darling!"

"I will."

Constance wasted no time and made her way to Keith's office. He waved his hand in a friendly greeting.

"Constance, when did you return from the Moon Base?"

"Earlier today already, but never mind about that; we have to talk," said the woman as she closed the door and sat down opposite him.

"Is something wrong Constance? You look upset."

"Commander Simms has been kidnapped, but only I know about it! Someone was holding a gun on him when he contacted you for the blueprints. I was eavesdropping. Look, never mind the details, but I need your help. I followed him and his captor to a building downtown and I have the address, but I don't know how many more of these beings are around."

Constance explained what transpired earlier and Keith was visibly shaken.

"Oh blast! Well the first thing I need to do is change the security codes, etc. It's obvious those goons want to gain control of this place and we can't let that happen! Constance, Craig was right; go home and pretend you know nothing about what happened and I'll take care of things at the office. When I've secured this place, I'll come to your home and we'll make plans on how to free Commander Simms, agreed?"

She nodded miserably. "All right Keith, I'll leave it in your capable hands, then."

Constance went straight home, but she couldn't settle down. She wished fervently that Craig was with her and hoped the week would pass quickly.

The following day, Keith knocked on her door and she was weak-kneed with relief. "Thank heavens! Did you manage to change the security codes?"

He nodded, but looked tired. "Constance, there's big trouble at the Space Centre. Apparently some more of those beings arrived and demanded to know who changed all the codes, so some of my friends told them it was me. They said something about national security and no one doubted their integrity. Those beings wore flesh coloured masks, just like you said you saw on one of them. I'd been out on an errand, so they never found me, but they've managed to issue a warrant for my arrest! Pictures of me are being displayed everywhere. Constance, I promised I would help you, but being with me will only endanger you. No one knows you are wise to those aliens, so you can just carry on normally. I'll contact some of my friends and see if they can help. Go back to the Control Centre and try to get hold of Craig again. Tell him to enlist the help of some of your friends out in space. I'll phone you on your mobile device later."

"Oh Keith, I'm so sorry to hear the bad news! Are you sure no one followed you here?"

"No one followed me, I'm certain of that, but I won't come back here again. Take care, Constance," he said as he held her hand tightly for a few moments, and then melted into the shadows.

Constance decided to waste no more time and went to the Control Centre. Everything seemed normal as she hurried to Simms' office, where her way was barred by one of the security guards.

"Where are you going, Miss Gregg?"

She flashed her most disarming smile at him. "I'm going to Commander Simms' office. He apparently went home ill, but he asked for some documentation that needed signing and he forgot to tell his secretary about them, so he telephoned me and asked me to take them to him and return them later. I was just on my way to collect them. You can come with me if you like," she offered.

He shook his head. "No that's okay, I believe you. Have you heard the news about Keith though?"

"Yes, I believe a warrant has been issued for his arrest. You think you know someone ..."

The man nodded. "Sure, well life's full of little surprises. I'll see you around."

Constance hurried to Simms' office and tried the emergency line, but to her dismay, it was dead. She took a deep, calming breath, and then picked up some data tablets that were in the secretary's "in" tray.

"Whew luckily I remembered she had left some papers for Simms to sign, so I have a legitimate reason for being here."

CHAPTER 10

Constance headed to the communications room and found the technicians scratching their heads in bewilderment.

"What's up guys?" she enquired.

"I don't know Constance, but all our communications are dead.

We're looking into the problem, but so far we haven't found any reason for it."

The woman felt uneasy with every passing moment, and walked to the hangars. She approached one of the mechanics.

"I need to go out into space right now. Have you just finished refuelling this ship?"

"Sure, she's fully gassed, but you'll be taking a big risk out there, because all our communications are on the blink."

"I heard so, but it's important! I'll have to take that chance."

He nodded and stepped aside. Obligingly he operated the controls that opened the doors and soon Constance was hovering above Mission Control.

However, when she tried to leave Earth's atmosphere, the computer flashed a warning on its console. *<Unidentifiable object ahead!>*

Constance scanned the skies, but saw nothing. "Negative, computer, I don't see anything. Enhance image please!"

The sky seemed to move closer and Constance stared, but she was puzzled.

"Computer, I don't see anything! What's causing the interference?"

Suddenly, without warning, a ship loomed up close to hers and she swerved violently to avoid it. The magnification disappeared and Constance found herself staring at a ship shaped like a trident. Before she could open her mouth however, a commanding voice boomed at her. *"Identify yourself!"* the being demanded.

"Constance Gregg of Earth," she responded, "Who are you?"

She found herself staring into the cold eyes of one of the green beings.

"We are the loyal followers of Andocia. Our mistress is aboard and wishes to speak with your leaders. Why are you out here, when all transport from Earth has been banned?"

"I know of no such order, but I have an important mission to fulfil."

"No one is allowed to leave your planet. A force field has been placed about Earth. You are requested to return there immediately."

The tone was firm, but polite, and Constance decided not to risk their anger. They hung back and indicated for her to lead the way. Constance scanned the ship and located several gun turrets. Nothing was aimed in her direction though and she breathed a sigh of relief. However, she realized it would be foolhardy to try and escape from them. After all she wasn't sure what the giant ship was capable of. Reluctantly she went ahead of the massive ship which followed her back to Mission Control.

Back on Earth, the trident ship cruised to a halt in the hangar, not far from Constance's ship. Her first instinct was to run, but she knew it was a foolish idea, so she forced herself to wait for the other occupants to disembark. A door slid open and several figures walked towards her. In the midst of them stood a woman with long red hair, and she got her first glimpse of Andocia. Constance admitted, grudgingly, that this woman was incredibly beautiful, but she could sense the evil radiating from her. The woman came and stood nearby, staring curiously at Constance, who stood her ground and met her gaze steadily.

Andocia smiled coldly. "Seeing as you have already met my followers, you may as well give us a guided tour of this place, starting with the communications centre."

Constance was furious, but suppressed it, for she knew this woman was dangerous, so she led the way as ordered.

Some time later, Andocia went into Commander Simms' office and demanded to see the confidential records stored on the computers, but Constance shook her head.

"Sorry, but no one has the access codes, except for Keith. He's the head of Security but he isn't here at the moment."

Andocia stared at the computer. "Bah, it doesn't matter. My followers can crack this antiquated system in no time, but I'm curious about many things and I'll need some helpers to furnish that information. What position do you occupy here, Miss Gregg?"

"I'm a space explorer. I know very little about anything else that goes on here. Any of the technicians or the secretaries can help you out."

Andocia smiled disarmingly, but Constance's stomach clenched. Without really knowing why, she knew that Andocia was aware that she was lying.

"Well my dear, you need to answer some questions for me and then I'll let you return home, but I want to know where you live."

Constance sat down facing the woman and wished she could be elsewhere and not looking into the green woman's penetrating red eyes.

"Well my dear, firstly, what were you doing out in space?"

"Our communication system failed and I decided to investigate. I was surprised to find there was a barrier, but that's responsible for the breakdown, isn't it?"

"Yes it is, because I don't want your planet looking for help from your neighbours, but there's more to the story than you're letting on, isn't there!"

Constance's mouth dropped open in surprise, but she recovered her composure quickly. "I don't know what you mean," she replied levelly.

Andocia stared at her in a disconcerting way once again, but said nothing.

Finally, Constance snapped angrily. "Look, how about you answering some of my questions. You obviously have some diabolical plan in mind and I'd like to know what you want here."

"Why not?" shrugged Andocia. "I'm looking for new worlds to conquer. The Golden Way more or less does what I tell them to, but I love challenges. I suppose you could say that Earth is another challenge. I'm going to contact all the leaders of the various countries and put my demands to them. Failure to do as I say could result in many of your people dying, but I'm gracious, so I'll give everyone the opportunity to bow down to me and acclaim me as supreme ruler of Earth. If everyone agrees, no blood will be shed and this planet will continue as before, only those in authority will be my mindless puppets."

A chill ran up Constance's spine as she remembered what happened to Craig, and she knew, without a doubt, that this wicked woman would succeed. Abruptly, Constance stood up.

"Like I said, I'm not really going to be of any help to you. I'm going home to lie down. I have a headache."

No one made a move to stop her as she headed for the door, but just before she reached it, Andocia spoke.

"Miss Gregg, I thought your name sounded familiar and now I remember why. I believe your young man and I are acquainted. Where is Craig Carter, by the way?"

Stunned, Constance whirled around. "How ... how did you know that?"

Andocia examined her fingernails thoughtfully before speaking. "You see, I learnt a great deal from your young man. Your image was imprinted in his mind; in fact, I'll go as far as to say that he's obsessed with you. Actually, I have him to thank for being here. He told me a great deal about this place and everyone in it."

"Craig would never give out sensitive information!" she exclaimed disbelievingly.

"Not willingly, no, but the mind is a complex organ and I know how to exploit it. He wasn't even aware I had obtained the information. Where is your friend?" Andocia asked again.

"Somewhere in space, far away from you!"

"Miss Gregg, let's get straight to the point. I know you went out into space to warn your boyfriend about this invasion, just as I know you hate me, well the feeling is mutual. I admire your tenacity, but my powers far exceed anything you could imagine. Go home if you want to, but I will still rule Earth and you are powerless to stop me from achieving my aim. There are several others here I can obtain information from," she said, indicating several terrified technicians who were huddled in a corner.

Constance remembered again how Andocia blinded Craig and immediately she felt sorry for the men crouched in the corner, and she made up her mind. "All right, we'll play by your rules – for now. I'll stay here, just as long as you leave my colleagues alone."

Andocia smiled victoriously and Constance's hatred of her deepened. The woman ordered Constance to get her something to drink and while she was sipping it, she questioned the explorer.

"Miss Gregg, I find your race very interesting. I sense you fear me, but your hatred is stronger. Why do the males of your species turn to quivering lumps of jelly, but the females seem unaffected?"

"I don't know," she replied. "Who are you anyway and why does the Golden Way fear you so?"

"I regret, but you'll have to remain curious for now. There'll be plenty of time to discuss this later. I need to start setting up meetings with your Heads of State in the various countries. How do I get hold of them?"

Constance led the way to Commander Simms' office and took a key out of one of the drawers, and inserted it into another locked drawer before pulling out an electronic telephone index.

"In here is every number you'll need. I suppose you'd like me to show you how our telescreens work."

"That would be most helpful, Miss Gregg," said Andocia as she sat down in Simms' chair.

For a while, Andocia sat at the desk, studying all the telephone numbers and seemed to lose interest in Constance, who walked cautiously backwards and picked up a fire extinguisher that was standing nearby. She moved forward once again and raised it high over her head, intending to strike this woman down and somehow get help. She held it aloft, using both hands and swung it with all her might, but it rebounded off something invisible and smashed into a nearby wall.

"*Oh!*" exclaimed Constance, taken completely by surprise.

The evil woman turned and pointed her finger at Constance's arm. Immediately the skin began to discolour and a small blister formed, making her gasp in surprise.

"Let that be a lesson to you Miss Gregg! I was lenient on you this time, but next time I'll cause you serious bodily harm."

"How ... how did you ...?"

"Do that? I told you, I have skills which you know nothing about. I willed this barrier to form around me and it did. I knew I couldn't trust you. This takeover is going to be quite a challenge, I can tell. I know every move you are going to make, even before you make it, so don't try that again. If you anger me once more, I'll imprison you with your precious Commander Simms – in fact, maybe I'll do that anyway. Consider yourself lucky, because I usually eliminate anyone I don't like."

Constance glared at her, but stood her ground. "Actually, you are going to need me, because the Commander's secretary and I are the only ones who can help you contact all the Heads of State you need to. I haven't given you the access codes yet, but if you're so clever, then you know that already."

"Touché my dear and, yes, I knew that. In fact, it was going to be my next question."

"I've just realized how you know my thoughts. It's because you're telepathic, isn't it! Yes, that explains a lot. You read Craig's mind and because it was a new experience for him, he didn't know how to counteract it. I'm right, aren't I?"

Absolutely!" exclaimed the delighted woman. "I must admit, I found your boyfriend very intelligent and I can see why he likes you. I wonder how he'll react when he finds out about my takeover."

"It's obvious; he'll do everything in his power to stop you."

Andocia laughed. "He can't stop me, no one can! Oh, this *will* be fun."

"Andocia, why did you choose to come to Earth? Why not any of the other planets in our galaxy? For instance, Saturn is far more intelligent than us. Surely their planet is more of a prize?"

"Probably, but human beings interest me more at the moment, so here I am!"

Constance had no choice but to furnish Andocia with all the relevant information that she required and the time passed. A few hours later, she was told to take a break. She went into the gardens of the Space Control Centre, accompanied by some of the wicked woman's followers. They stood quite a distance away from her, but she didn't want to cause any trouble until she knew more about Andocia. She plucked a flower and smelt it.

"All I can do right now is co-operate with this woman. Craig should be nearly home by now, so he'll realize something is wrong. I'm sure that he'll go for help."

Out in space, Craig was indeed close by. He tried to contact Earth, but received no answer. He checked with his computer and it relayed the information that the signal hadn't been received. He then tried Constance's mobile device, but again no one answered. Craig then contacted the Moon Base.

"I've been trying to get hold of Earth, but there's no signal! Has something happened to the transmitters perhaps?"

"We aren't really sure Craig, but we're experiencing problems as well. A crew is going out to check on the orbiting satellites, so maybe you should come here and wait for the answers."

"Thanks pal, I'll do that. I'll see you all in an hour."

An hour later, he touched down in the landing bay and went to join his friends in the control room.

"Have you heard anything yet?"

"No, we haven't. Let's go and have something to eat and then we can try again. The crew should be reporting back within the next half an hour or so."

While they were eating, one of the scientists came to their table. "You guys need to see this. It's very hard to explain!"

They all made their way back to the communications room and Ron pointed to a screen. Earth was reflected in all her glory and for a moment, Craig saw nothing, then he gasped as his friend enlarged the image.

"Ron, what's that around Earth? It looks like a huge bubble!"

"That's exactly what it is, but it's impenetrable. The crew fired laser beams at it and they just rebounded back into space. Also, several of our satellites were disabled," said Ron as he pointed to another screen.

Craig stared at the large hole in one of the satellites. "But Ron, what manner of weapon took those out? I've never seen the likes of it anywhere!"

"Me neither, but the situation isn't good at all! We must get our satellites up and running pretty soon, but we don't know if whoever did this will come back and put them out of action again, so we've placed some troops around them for now while repairs are being done. Perhaps then we'll be able to communicate with Earth, but I doubt if anything solid will get through that barrier."

Craig paced backwards and forwards. "I don't know about you,

Ron, but something's definitely wrong and I have a bad feeling about it. We still know so little about our universe and even less about the Golden Way. I wonder if the Meltonians can tell us anything about this dome."

"It can't hurt to ask, Craig," said Ron encouragingly.

Carter nodded and tried the planet. It took a while, but a Meltonian appeared on screen.

"Mr Carter, it's good to see your face once again! This connection is weak, but I can see you. What can we do for you?"

"I was wondering if you could shed some light on a problem we seem to be having on Earth. We have deliberately been sabotaged and no one can find out what's happening. There seems to be a transparent dome around Earth at the moment and we don't know what's causing it. All we know is that nothing can penetrate it. I'm sending you the image now."

There was another short delay and then the Meltonian came back on air.

"I'm sorry Craig, but that's bad news I'm afraid. As soon as you relayed that image, we knew what the problem was. Remember the woman whom you met; the one known as Andocia? Well her signature is all over this. I'm sorry my friend, but it looks as though she has taken an interest in your people."

The colour drained from Craig's face as he remembered his experience with her.

"Oh no, are you sure? But why would she be interested in us?"

"I'm sorry, but that's how she operates. She obviously realized you are intelligent beings and decided humans would be a challenge! Another trophy to add to her collection! Restoring your satellites should enable you to have contact, as the barrier only prevents matter from passing through. One thing I know for certain is that she will contact your Moon Base when she is ready to tell you of her demands. I regret, Earthling, we feel sorry for you, but we can do nothing to help you. Unfortunately, our technology isn't advanced enough to defeat her. Perhaps you should get together with those in your universe and see if they can come up with something to destroy that barrier."

"Thank you for that information anyway; at least now we

know what's causing it, so we know more than we did a while ago."

Craig disconnected and stared for some minutes at the screen, not really seeing anything.

"Constance! She's down there with that devilish woman and I'm helpless to do anything! I hate Andocia so much, yet I fear her as well and the feeling unsettles me."

Carter and several of the scientists held an emergency meeting with the Base Commander and it was decided they should contact all their friends, starting with Saturn, and see if they could find something to destroy the barrier. Once this had been done, Craig had a thought which he shared with the Base Commander. "Sir, we need to inform the Russian Space Station of this latest development. They may be our enemies, but Earth is their planet as well."

"Yes, of course we do! I'll contact Trotsky and see what he suggests."

Craig waited patiently until he was called into the commander's office once again.

"Craig, I've spoken to Trotsky and he suggested one of us team up with a Russian space explorer and perhaps with both our countries working together, we might just come up with some sort of solution to the problem. I'll have to ask for a volunteer, because no one trusts the Russians, but it is their world too, as you so rightly said."

Carter nodded. "Yes Sir, I'll volunteer. I can't sit around here all day hoping for things to improve, so I'd like to be out in space, trying to find a solution, even if I have to travel with a Russian."

The Base Commander nodded and returned to his office.

"Very well, Craig, it's settled then. Trotsky suggested you go over to their Space Station and report for duty."

⁄ ⁄ ⁄

Craig journeyed to the space station, which still held such painful memories for him. Although he didn't like Trotsky, Carter was determined to co-operate with them. He touched down in their landing bay and was greeted by Trotsky, who extended his hand in greeting. Craig stared at him for a moment, then shook his hand.

"Ah Comrade Carter, so we meet again, but this time we are allies; how strange that seems. You of all people will appreciate who your partner in this venture is to be."

Carter followed his enemy to a lounge, where he was offered something to drink and settled for a glass of fruit juice. He barely glanced at the man who had come to sit next to him, until he spoke.

"Ah Carter, so we meet again! I'm the one who volunteered for this adventure, and I look forward to sharing it with you. After all Earth is our planet and two heads are better than one, wouldn't you say?"

Craig smiled as the irony of the situation occurred to him.

"Well well, Petrovsky this is a first. Imagine being your 'friend' for a time. I'll do anything, just as long as Earth benefits from it, even if it means having to spend time with you. Well, we should leave now, because Saturn asked me to visit. It seems they may have something that can help us get through the barrier."

Once out in space, Petrovsky was glum.

"Ah, I wish we can solve this problem soon, because I long for the time when we are enemies again. It livens things up when I have a goal in mind. Trotsky was foolish when he wanted to kill you before. I don't know what happened to you that day, but I knew you would recover your senses and remember everything. You did, didn't you?"

Craig nodded. "Yes, but only a few days later."

"Carter, I wondered what happened to you that day to make you so terrified."

Craig felt his flesh crawl and shook his head adamantly. "Look, it's got nothing to do with you. Suffice it to say that this Andocia woman was largely responsible."

Petrovsky knew he had touched a nerve and decided to exploit it. "I've never known a woman to influence you so. She must be quite something!"

"Believe me, Petrovsky, you don't want to meet her – she's dangerous."

Ivan Petrovsky tried to question him further, but Carter wouldn't answer, so he lapsed into silence.

They landed on Saturn and Karnd escorted them to the laboratory, where he showed them a device shaped like a bird.

"We think this device will work, Craig. The bird is filled with a chemical compound that should explode on impact. Once it hits the force field around your planet, it will ignite and blast a hole in the bubble. If it works as planned, I'll send out more of them that have a larger storage capacity. Watch now while we have a test run."

Everyone remained glued to the vidscreens and followed the progress of the invention.

They all held their breath as they watched it approaching the force field, when suddenly a red ray shot out from Earth and the bird disintegrated, sending the particles scattering into space, where they exploded harmlessly. A collective gasp of dismay emanated from the people clustered around the screen.

"Oh no, we were so sure it would work, but the experiment failed!" Karnd exclaimed unhappily.

"No Karnd, you didn't fail," replied Craig, "If that hadn't been a threat to Andocia she wouldn't have destroyed it. If you make enough of them, I doubt she'll get them all, but we will have to be ready and move in before she has time to fix the barrier. If we're fast enough, we should manage to reach Earth before she can retaliate."

The scientist's face brightened considerably. "You could very well be right, my friend. We'll work on them, but there's no sense in you two staying here. It's going to take some time to make the quantity you will require. Go and see what the other planets suggest and maybe someone else will come up with a better idea to destroy that barrier."

They agreed and went back out into space, but before they got very far, Craig's vidscreen beeped and one of the technicians on Moon Base greeted him. Instantly, Carter knew something was wrong, for the man's complexion was a shade of grey and he was perspiring.

"Jake, what's wrong. You look as though you've seen a ghost!"

"That just about sums it up, Craig. We've managed to fix the satellites and the link to Earth has been restored, but we have a big problem. The woman known as Andocia has kidnapped Commander Simms and she's very angry right now. Craig, she contacted us here on the Moon and wanted to know who was responsible for that device. I'm sorry, but I had to tell her! Her eyes! They seemed to be boring right into my skull. She also ordered me to tell her who had met with the Saturnians on their planet, and now she wants to talk to you. She's at the Space Control Centre on Earth and she isn't very patient."

Petrovsky watched interestedly as his American counterpart's hands clenched into fists so tight that his knuckles turned white.

"All right Jake, I'll contact her now. Don't blame yourself; she would've found out later anyway."

He disconnected and pressed the relevant keys to reach Mission Control on Earth and a scared technician answered. Craig spoke to him, and suddenly he was staring at the woman he feared above everything else, but his voice was calm as he spoke. "I understand you were looking for me, Andocia."

Ah, Craig Carter, yes I was. Who's your friend hovering in the background?" she asked curiously.

"He's not my friend, but his name is Colonel Ivan Petrovsky of the Russian Space Exploration team. We teamed up out of necessity, to try and overthrow you," said Craig defiantly.

Andocia turned her gaze on Petrovsky who squirmed uncomfortably.

"Ah, so you two are also enemies! How interesting! However, seeing as I'm currently occupying the American Control Centre, my problem lies with them. Carter, your name is mentioned often, and it seems you have quite a reputation. No offence to your temporary partner though. I've decided that I'd like you under close scrutiny, therefore I'm ordering you to return to Earth."

"What have you done with Commander Simms?"

"Oh, he's fine at the moment and co-operating well."

"Andocia, I'm surprised by your request. Why is it so important?"

"I gave you an order and seeing as your boss isn't here, I am in charge. It would be better if you came willingly. Your temporary friend out there can go back to his space station, because I don't need him right now. Perhaps at another time, I may want to interview him."

Colonel Petrovsky looked nervously at Craig. "Uh, that's okay, Carter is welcome to accompany you. I'm sure the American will see me safely to my base."

Craig glared at his enemy and turned his attention back to Andocia.

"I still don't see the sense in returning to Earth, and I believe you wouldn't waste your time chasing one individual."

The devilish woman smiled wickedly. "Don't underestimate me, Carter. I've met your beautiful Constance by the way and she's been most helpful. With her help, I've contacted most of the countries and given them my demands, which they are considering at present. If you refuse me, I'll make sure she's no longer beautiful, in fact I might even kill her. The same goes for your precious Commander Simms. Do you want the consequences of your stubbornness to bring about their deaths?"

Craig looked questioningly at Petrovsky, who cleared his throat nervously. "Uh, if I were you Comrade, I'd obey the lady. I believe she would carry out her threat," he advised.

Craig turned his attention back to the woman. "If I do as you say, Andocia, how am I going to return to Earth? You still have that barrier around it."

"How long will it take you to reach the barrier if you left now?" she asked.

"Well I'll have to drop Petrovsky at the Moon Base first. I should get there in about three hours, maybe less."

"Very well, then do it. At exactly 17h30 Earth time, I'll remove the force field, but only for a few minutes, so you had better be there, otherwise your girlfriend will suffer the consequences."

Andocia's face winked off the screen and Petrovsky's eyes were wide. "Whew Comrade, I see what you mean. She scares me too and I'm glad she's interested in you and not me. This alliance was very short lived, wasn't it?"

"Not really, Petrovsky. As far as I'm concerned, we're still working together. I can only urge you to stay in touch with my friends, for Earth is your home too. I'll do what I can from Earth. You know, it's probably for the best that I return home. At least there I might be able to do something positive. Anything's better than sitting around feeling helpless."

The American explorer dropped his Russian counterpart on Moon Base and brought them up to date on the latest developments, then set course for home.

CHAPTER 11

At precisely 17h30 the barrier disappeared and as he entered, it sealed again. Craig landed in the docking area and climbed out of his spaceship. He watched warily as Andocia approached and had to fight an overwhelming urge to run away. Following closely behind her were several of her people, and in the midst of them stood Constance. For a moment, he forgot the peril he was in and hurried to his precious girlfriend, embracing her tenderly.

"Constance! Oh, thank the stars you're okay. Have you seen Commander Simms yet?"

She nodded in the affirmative. "Yes, I have, but Andocia has him imprisoned in a cell. Oh Craig, I didn't want to believe it when you decided to give yourself up to this woman. At least in space you would've stood more of a chance. Why did you come home?"

"I had no choice, my darling. *She* forced me to come here by telling me she would hurt you and Commander Simms, but anyway I prefer being here with you, because not knowing what had happened to you was driving me crazy."

Andocia sneered derisively. "Oh, how touching! Well your precious woman is unharmed, Carter, but unless you co-operate with me, I'll eliminate her. Do we understand one another?"

Craig nodded in the affirmative. Andocia waved her hand in a dismissive gesture and several of her followers approached. One took Constance firmly by the arm. "It is time to go, miss. Andocia wishes to speak with your boyfriend."

Constance stared at her loved one, but made no protest as they marched her out.

The devil woman led Craig to the conference room and ordered him to sit down. "I'm pleased you did as you were told, Carter, but then you knew the consequences of disobeying me."

Craig was puzzled. "Andocia, why did you want me here anyway? Surely it makes no difference where I am. I alone cannot change the fact that you're here, uninvited I might add."

"I have a feeling about you, Carter. Something tells me you could prove troublesome out in space, so I decided to keep you here under close scrutiny. Besides I really wanted to spend some time with you out there in space when your ship broke down. I was curious about you and the rest of humanity and I had many questions to ask, but you escaped! It was quite interesting to meet Tyrus as well, but he doesn't strike me as being very intelligent. Why were you in a Russian spacecraft though?" she asked shrewdly. "Would I be correct in assuming that somehow your Russian counterpart had captured you and you got away from him as well?"

Craig refused to answer and the woman smiled knowingly. "You are most definitely a slippery character Mr Carter. I do so love a challenge!"

"Why did you pick Earth though? There are so many planets more technologically advanced than us. Even in your universe there are planets that have more to offer than we do."

"Yes, you're probably right, but I was curious about Earth. I'm pleasantly surprised at the level of intelligence here. Your planet seems to have advanced speedily over the last few centuries as well. I'm sure you know the reason for my visit, but I'll enlighten you anyway. I get incredibly bored with the mundane and the planets in the Golden Way fear me, with good reason.

I have ruled over them for many years now, so it's time to search new horizons!"

Despite the situation, Craig was angry. "So, you just want to toy with Earth because you are bored!" he snapped. "You expect billions of people to suddenly decide that you're the best thing that has ever happened to them and they must follow you implicitly! It'll never happen! There are far too many countries on Earth. In order to reach a consensus, many governments will have to be approached. It could take ages! It won't work!"

Andocia glared at him. "I'll be the judge of that, Mr Carter. Right now, since fate has thrown the two of us together, like it or not, you are going to be my aide. I have many things to do and you're going to help me willingly. If you don't, innocent blood will be shed, starting with your girlfriend and your boss. One thing I did find out about you is that you value friends and family and will do anything to ensure their continued well-being. Most humans I have met seem to be very selfish and are only interested in self-preservation."

Craig sighed heavily. "You're quite correct Andocia. My friends and family mean a lot to me. I suppose in your case you would look upon this as a weakness, but I consider it my greatest strength. I still have no idea how I can help you achieve your impossible goal."

Andocia smiled triumphantly. "I thought you would see things from a different perspective when we had spoken and I had laid down my ground rules. You're not my prisoner, but you must make yourself available to me whenever I need you. Let's just say you can go wherever you like, just as long as you follow my orders. If I have reason to distrust you, then the situation could change dramatically."

"What about Constance? Why do you need her?" he asked curiously. "I've already said I would help you, although I'll do so with great reluctance."

"I need her because I need your expertise. She's my guarantee you'll do as I say. The same rules that apply to you, apply to her."

"Andocia, I'm still not entirely convinced you're telling the truth. You had another ulterior motive for targeting Earth, didn't you?" Craig continued doggedly.

"Ah, you're very clever, just as I always said. Well I don't see the harm in telling you now. This planet is very rich in minerals that have become depleted in the Golden Way, and we need them to manufacture our weapons."

"I knew it had to be something like that. So, you're going to exploit our minerals and build more weapons, in order to conquer even more planets."

"That's quite correct," she replied.

"Once you have what you want, then what'll become of this planet and all of us living here?"

"I haven't really given it much thought, but I need to study your kind in great detail. I know so little about humankind, so I'll be around for quite a while."

"Do I need to be here any longer? I'm tired after my journey and I'd like to go home and freshen up, as well as get some sleep."

"I suppose you might as well do that. Tomorrow will be a hectic day," replied Andocia.

He stood up and left without another word, but decided to visit Constance before he turned in for the night. As he drove away in his helicar, another set of headlights came on and followed close behind.

"Ah, so they are keeping tabs on me. Well, let them if it makes them happy!" he decided.

When he got to Constance's door, his tail moved away and settled into a doorway further down the street. For a moment, the light from inside Constance's flat illuminated the two of them as they embraced, before they went inside. Constance went to make them something to eat and drink and Craig sank gratefully into one of the comfortable chairs. Over dinner, they discussed the latest events.

"Craig, what are we going to do about this situation? We can't let her just come in and take over like this without fighting for our planet."

"I have no intention of sitting idly by, my darling, but we need to make plans secretly and it isn't easy when we're being guarded all the time. Our friends are working on the problem of smashing this barrier and I'm sure that something will happen soon. I'm surprised she let us out of her sight, but I'm grateful nevertheless. Do you know where Commander Simms is being held?"

"Yes, I was at Mission Control when he was kidnapped and I followed that woman's cohorts to the building, but it's heavily guarded by her henchmen. Keith has gone into hiding, because they are looking for him. We've been in touch a few times. Some of his security friends have gone into hiding as well and are at this moment planning how they can overthrow Andocia. I'd like to help of course, but she makes me go everywhere with her. I didn't want to help her, but she threatened to force some of the technicians to do what she wants. Craig, every man here is terrified of her, but she doesn't have the same effect on women. We all hate her, but don't fear her as much as the men do. I have to admit though that I don't like her at all."

"Everyone has a reason to fear her, I promise," said Craig, shuddering involuntarily.

Constance held his hand sympathetically. "I know what you went through and I feel so bad for you. How I wish we could get rid of her once and for all, but even if you try to go underground, Andocia will take it out on the rest of us."

"I suppose so, but I'm willing to take the risk. Did Keith leave you a telephone number where he could be contacted?"

"Yes, but we must use it only in an extreme emergency!"

Craig's face was grim. "Well I'd say that this situation qualifies, wouldn't you?"

She nodded and produced the number. Carter tried it, but was told to leave a message, which he did.

"Craig, there's something I need to tell you before we make any more plans. Andocia is telepathic, so she can read minds." Constance shifted uneasily in her chair and looked at her boyfriend, unsure how to tell him the bad news. He lifted his eyebrows enquiringly and she continued. "Darling, I don't know how to tell you this, but you're indirectly responsible for this invasion. I know you never volunteered any information willingly, but she mentioned she had read your mind and gained all the necessary information. I'm really sorry!"

Craig stared unhappily at his girlfriend. "Oh Constance, that's really bad news! I would never put my planet in jeopardy, I'd kill myself first!"

"I know you value your colleagues above everything else, but you can't be blamed for something you had no control over," she said sympathetically, "besides, I won't tell anyone about this; it'll just be our secret."

"Well then that settles it! I'll do whatever it takes to help Keith and his friends, because I owe this to my planet. The problem is how do I control my thoughts when I'm around that awful woman?"

"I don't know, but we'll have to think of something ..."

Constance's mobile device rang, interrupting them and she answered it. Keith's face stared back at her. "Constance, is Craig still with you?"

She nodded and Craig moved closer. "Keith, I don't want to talk for long, but I'm available to help you, just say the word. I'm not sure what Andocia has in mind for me, but if I can, I'll be there for you. It would be best if you contacted Constance at the same time tomorrow night if you have news, but try on her mobile device only. Can we meet one evening soon to discuss strategy?"

"Sure Craig, but what about your uninvited guests?"

"Leave those details to me, they don't strike me as very intelligent, so I'll make a plan."

Keith smiled gleefully. "Okay Craig, welcome aboard then."

They disconnected and reluctantly he got ready to leave Constance. When Craig lifted off, lights came on and he was followed back to his own apartment.

The next day, Craig fetched Constance from her apartment and they returned to the Space Control Centre, where Andocia greeted them.

"Ah, here come the two lovebirds! Miss Gregg, I need you to type some letters for me, and while you're doing that, I will require your boyfriend's assistance. It seems that some of your leaders are very stubborn."

Constance glared at Andocia. "I'm not a secretary! My job is to explore space. Commander Simms' secretary can help you.

She knows more about the running of this office than I do."

"Maybe so, but she has a viral infection of some sort. Apparently, her doctor told her it was contagious, so she's currently at home. You'll just have to do, unless you want some other typist to learn confidential things about this department."

Constance said nothing, but went to the desk and sat down. Andocia smirked and placed a recording device in front of her, and then went into Commander Simms' office, indicating that Craig should accompany her.

He obeyed and shut the door behind him, as she had ordered.

"All right, Carter, I want you to speak to the leaders of the various countries. None of them want to take me seriously and your job is to convince them that I mean everything I said, otherwise many of your people all over the world will die. Your president is especially stubborn, so start with him."

Hating every minute of it, Craig did as she ordered and soon the man himself was on the vidscreen.

"Good morning to you Mr President. My name is Craig Carter of the Space Control Centre."

"Mr Carter, do I know you?" asked the President suspiciously.

"No Sir, but Commander Simms is my superior. As I'm sure you are aware by now, an alien being has taken over control of this department."

The President fixed his steely grey eyes on Craig. "I'm aware of this. Some strange woman contacted me and has given me some weird ultimatums. She wants me to destroy all our weapons so she can just march in! What kind of an idiot would grant such a request?"

"Uh Sir, she doesn't understand protocol," he put in quickly. "But that's why she has asked me to speak with you. We have had ... er, dealings before today."

"Mr Carter, where is Commander Simms at the moment?"

"He is indisposed at present. He went home due to illness, Mr President."

"Are you supposed to be his representative then, Mr Carter?"

"I guess so," he said, after glancing at Andocia for confirmation.

"Mr Carter, you say you know this woman. Will she destroy

America if we don't agree to her demands?"

"In all honesty, Sir, I don't really know, but she's capable of great mayhem if she puts her mind to it. I don't know how far she's prepared to go, but she's definitely trouble."

"Mr Carter, do you have any suggestions as to how this should be handled?"

"Well if it were up to me, I wouldn't agree to anything, Mr President," said Craig, ignoring Andocia's icy stare, "but I have been forced to communicate with you and Andocia told me that she will kill people if you don't meet her demands. I know she wants me to convince you that surrender is the best course of action, and while I love my country and all it stands for, I can't do it, even if it means I may have to forfeit my life. Mr President, this woman is dangerous, that's a fact, but I can't tell you what to do. It must be your decision."

"Mr Carter, I appreciate your honesty and I thank you for your candid reply. Does Andocia wish to speak with me?"

In response, the woman shouldered Craig aside and barked into the vidscreen. "Mr Carter is brave but foolish and I'll deal with him later. Mr President, I assure you that many people will die if you don't give in to my demands, starting with this fool here. I urge you to consult with your advisers and get back to me as soon as possible. You have one week!"

Without waiting to hear his reply, Andocia switched off the screen, and turned to Craig, who stood his ground. "What are you trying to prove, Carter? The only good hero is a dead one – is that what you want?"

"Of course not, but what did you expect me to do? This is *my world* and you are the infiltrator. How can you expect me to just stand around doing nothing, while you come in and decide to take over the planet that I live on?"

"Carter, you seem to forget that I can do just about anything I like with you. I have all the time in the world to finish what I started in my universe," she replied menacingly.

"I can't stop you doing that, but I won't change my mind," said Craig stubbornly. "If you want me to speak to all the other leaders in the various countries, I'll do it, but my answer will remain the same."

"Carter, you astound me! I know you fear me, but you persist in being stubborn. You may as well face facts though; you and I can exchange heated words all day but I'll still triumph in the end, so get used to it."

Craig ignored her and looked out of the window, but he deliberately kept his mind blank so that she couldn't read his thoughts.

The day passed slowly for Craig and Constance who were forced to do Andocia's bidding, but finally they were told to go home. Craig dropped Constance off at her apartment and went in to share dinner with her, as before. When Miss Gregg checked her mobile device, she found a message had been left which read: "*Highway Inn, 22h00 sharp*".

Craig and Constance exchanged looks.

"Well that was probably Keith. Are you going to see him tonight?" asked Constance nervously.

"I have to! Andocia is pretty mad at me and I don't know how long she's going to put up with my nonsense. I have a plan in mind, but let me talk to Keith and see what he thinks. Sweetheart, can I borrow your helicar tonight? It's parked at the back and Andocia's goons are only watching my car in front. I deliberately picked you up this morning, because I wanted Andocia to think your car was giving trouble. I won't be long, just in case they decide to check up on us and that'll spoil everything."

"All right Craig, but I wanted to come with you!"

"I appreciate that, but it's too risky. If Andocia calls you for some reason and there's no answer, we'll be well and truly in the soup. If she does call and wants to check up on me, make up a plausible excuse."

Constance nodded and held him tightly, afraid she wouldn't see him again, and then he crept out of her back door, dressed now in dark clothing.

He arrived at the appointed spot and ordered a beer. The owner wore a dirty apron stained with various mixtures and had two day's growth of beard on his face. He was built like a mountain, and spoke gruffly, but Craig wasn't put off at all for the man was well-known to him. He was an undercover policeman who worked in this bar, because he knew first hand when crimes were about to be committed. One of his functions was also to protect the underground movement, which was at present planning to overthrow Andocia. On a prearranged signal, Craig muttered that his beer was warm and demanded a cold one, whereupon the bartender took it away and offered him another can.

Craig took this one to the Gents toilet and opened it. Inside the empty tin was a map. He took it out and studied it for a few minutes. Then threw the can into a nearby dustbin and tore up the map, which he flushed away. Instead of leaving by the front door, he made his way to the back which led into an alley and from there he walked quickly, glancing left and right to see if he was being followed, but nothing stirred. He counted doorways and after the fourth one, opened it and stepped inside, closing it behind him once again.

As he turned around, another man searched him expertly and removed his weapon, then he was given further instructions. Keith and several other security men whom Craig knew well, occupied the next room he was directed to. Keith shook hands with him and he was welcomed enthusiastically. "Craig, it's good to see you once again! Did you manage to confuse your tail?"

"He didn't see me leave because I came in Constance's car. Listen, Andocia is watching Constance and me very closely so this has to be a short visit. Do you have enough weapons to take Andocia on?"

"We have quite a few but more are always welcome. Why, what did you have in mind?"

"I need your security card and the new code you punched into the computer. Tomorrow I'll slip into the Control Centre's armoury and open the back window, so I need to disarm the alarm. I'll lock the door once again, but your people can get through the window and take whatever you need. I'm sure Commander Simms would agree if we could tell him. Also, I've written down the address of the place where Andocia has him imprisoned and I think it would be a good thing if your people can get him to safety. I don't want to know where he'll be taken, but he is far too valuable to be left in her clutches. She's bound to question me when he's freed and I can't guarantee I won't talk, because she has ways of finding things out, so I want to know as little as possible. Constance tells me Andocia is telepathic, so she can read minds. If any of your men are caught, they would be better off killing themselves. I've had first-hand experience of her methods and she can be very persuasive, so be careful. I'd like to help you further, but she's watching me too closely. I wish you and your friends lots of luck. Now I'd better be getting back to Constance, or else those beings might become suspicious."

Craig turned to leave but Keith stopped him. "Craig, you're putting your life on the line for us and we won't forget this, but we'll have to meet tomorrow night to finalize the details. At 19h00, leave Constance's place and drive your own car in plain sight of your tail. When you get to Tower Bridge, park in the overhang where there's some shadow. My people will arrange a diversion and one of them will get into your car and lead Andocia's goons on a wild goose chase, while I pick you up and transport you elsewhere. Later on, he'll deliberately lose them, but when they find your car again, you'll be on your way home, so that'll allay their suspicions."

"All right, until tomorrow then," promised Craig.

He returned secretly to Constance and then, after bringing her up to date, took his leave and headed home.

The next day was particularly hectic for Carter, because Andocia was still angry with him and hardly let him out of her sight. However, he managed to slip away and do what he had promised. The evil woman made Craig take her to the spacecrafts in order that she might examine the weaponry aboard them. He never saw Constance at all, for Andocia had given her some task to do in another building.

CHAPTER 12

That evening, Craig again took Constance home. At exactly 19h00 he left her flat and Andocia's followers tailed him as expected. On nearing Tower Bridge, a large truck suddenly cut across the next lane and squeezed into the space behind Carter's car, causing his tail to hoot furiously and swerve violently. The truck driver waved in apology when his vehicle suddenly stalled, and he battled to get it started again, but he had ingeniously managed to block all the driving lanes. The explorer touched down in the shadows and quickly removed his jacket, which he handed to a man waiting nearby. The man smiled and nodded and then climbed into his car while Craig hid in the shadows, his dark clothes blending in perfectly. He watched in satisfaction as the car that had followed him continued, unaware of the change of driver. Once both vehicles had disappeared from sight, another one with tinted windows pulled up and the passenger door opened. Craig jumped in and closed the door and they were airborne once again.

"Thanks Keith, it worked like clockwork!"

"A pleasure, I assure you. Did you manage to do what you promised?"

"Yep, but it was close. Andocia is getting very suspicious of me. She hardly let me out of her sight," he said as he handed over the security card and keys.

The two men went to another bar and took a booth near the back of the place. There Keith outlined his plan and assured Craig that Commander Simms would be freed the next day. For a while they sat discussing strategy and both offered input to the situation and emerged with a plan. For the first time in a while, Craig began to feel optimistic, especially when Keith took him to a tumbledown warehouse, which contained the finest transmitter next to the one at Mission Control. Carter whistled appreciatively. "Keith, you astound me! Where did this come from?"

"Oh, mostly from recycled old parts when the transmitters at the Space Control Centre were stripped and replaced. It's not too bad even if I say so myself. With this we've been keeping tabs on the rest of the universe. We can't reach those in the Golden Way yet but we'll work on it. Saturn was looking for you, but didn't want to contact you at the control room for obvious reasons. They seemed to think you were fortunate to still be breathing. Anyway, they say their secret weapon is nearly complete and it shouldn't take more than a few days to put into operation."

"Oh, that's wonderful!" exclaimed Craig excitedly, "but we only have three days left before Andocia starts attacking the countries, so let's hope they'll be ready by then."

They settled the last few points before Craig was taken to another place, where his helicar was waiting. Keith shook his hand vigorously. "Craig, it's been a pleasure working with you! I look forward to resuming my usual duties in the not too distant future. I won't contact you again, unless there's an emergency, in which case I'll let Constance know. We'll rescue Simms and then come after that witch woman!"

They said their goodbyes and Carter returned home, elated that something was at last being done to rid their planet of the evil influence.

The next day dawned cloudy and dull, but Craig was feeling cheerful. He was doing Andocia's chores once again, when he saw two of the woman's followers hurrying to her office. Guessing rightly that Commander Simms had probably been rescued, he went to find Constance. He felt now would be a good time for her to go into hiding as well, and he planned to follow her soon afterwards, but before he could get to her, he was confronted by two of Andocia's followers. Craig's heart sank, as instinctively he knew something had gone wrong. Their weapons were pointing at him and he feigned stupidity.

"What's going on? I was just going to make myself something to drink."

"Not right now, Carter. Andocia wants to see you."

The odds weren't in his favour, so he decided to go along with them in the meantime.

Andocia was livid with rage and glared at him with contempt. "I should've killed you long ago when I had the chance, but never mind, even I can make mistakes."

"I don't understand! What are you talking about?" he asked.

"Someone rescued your Commander, but they were overconfident and some of my men managed to take a prisoner. He was very anxious to give us all the relevant details about all those involved in this plot."

"What do you mean? Is … is he …?"

"No, he's not dead yet, but he will soon wish he was. Come on Carter, we're going visiting!"

He was motioned forward and followed Andocia, his stomach in a knot. They moved down into the basement where the cells were located and she paused at a window.

"Look inside there, Carter and tell me if you recognize that man."

Unwillingly he looked and gasped when he saw the unfortunate man. His hair was disheveled and his eyes were wide and staring. Blood trickled down from a wound in his shoulder and it looked as though his kneecaps had been shattered. He was fighting against red bands that attached his wrists to the arms of the chair and his arms were beginning to bleed where the restraints chafed him.

"Do you recognize him Carter?"

Craig nodded dumbly. "He's one of the space police attached to this station."

"Is his superior the fugitive known as Keith?"

Craig nodded again.

"Your Commander Simms may have been rescued Carter, but if you know anything about this, then you'd better tell me, otherwise the next man in that chair will be you. Just for interest's sake, Keith was wounded by one of my men as he fled from the scene and we're closing in on him and his miserable organization. Now I ask you again, did you have anything to do with this plan?"

"No, I didn't. Why would I jeopardize my life?" he lied, "but I knew my boss was going to be rescued. I don't know where he was going to be taken though, and I expressly asked not to be informed. I don't sell my friends out."

Andocia stared contemptuously at the squirming man in the chair. "He had the same grand idea, but he sang like a canary. He gave us the names of everyone involved in any kind of plot to overthrow my rule and guess what? Your name appears prominently on the list."

"You flatter me, Andocia," said Craig modestly, "I had nothing to do with this. Most of it was probably Keith's idea. Anyway, judging by the condition of that poor man you probably bullied him into confessing what you hoped was the truth. I believe he would have said anything to appease you."

"Very well, but I'm sure you know more than you are letting on at present. Craig, you're a handsome man and I'd hate to disfigure you in any way, so why not save yourself the trouble and just come clean. I promise not to reveal my source and when all these foolish people have been dealt with, I'll let you live."

Craig shook his head. Andocia merely smiled and instructed her men to watch him very closely. She went into the interview room and the frightened man looked up at her in pure terror. The woman exchanged a few words with him and then pointed one of her forefingers at him. The colour drained from Craig's face and he knew what was going to happen. With a strangled cry he hurled himself at the one-way glass partition but was helpless to stop the woman, and he could only watch as his friend slumped in the chair, while a hole burned in the centre of his forehead, like a third eye. Instinctively, Carter knew his time would soon be up as well and he turned on the men clustered around him. They were taken by surprise, and sprawled on the floor in a tangle of arms and legs. Craig wasted no time and leaped over the writhing mass and headed up the stairs to freedom. His only thought was to get away and hide underground with Keith and his supporters, while Andocia screamed profanities behind him.

He ran on and on, with them in hot pursuit and several people turned to stare, egging him onwards. Suddenly Andocia changed her tactics and headed for another building, and with a sinking heart, Craig knew she was going to get Constance. He too changed direction, trying to get ahead of them and when he had neared the building he screamed desperately.

"*Run, Constance, run!*"

Suddenly a door at the far end opened and he watched as she began to run in his direction, but several of them were close behind her. One dived and managed to overbalance her, but she stumbled onwards. Then, when she realized they were very close behind, she turned to meet them head on. Craig had to admire her when several took a tumble, having fallen victim to her karate training, but his attempt to warn her had cost him precious seconds. He decided to change tactics and rushed headlong into the battle in an attempt to help his girlfriend out. Both of them lashed out at the enemy soldiers and they fell senseless to the floor, like puppets whose strings had been cut. They kept on coming and the duo continued to mow them down. More of Andocia's soldiers joined the battle, but Craig and Constance fought onwards, refusing to believe they were outnumbered.

Suddenly Craig gasped in pain as he felt something hit him. His knees buckled and he fell to the ground, conscious of a dreadful pain in his head. Carter saw stars and tried to fight the mists of unconsciousness that were threatening to overcome him, but he lost the battle.

When next he awoke, his entire body ached and he struggled into a sitting position. His head throbbed and he gingerly touched a bruise that had begun to form on his forehead. For a while he didn't know where he was, but then realized he had been imprisoned in one of the cells, and there was no sign of Constance anywhere. To add to his headache, Andocia appeared and he groaned unhappily. "Ohhh you're the last person I want to see. What have you done with Constance?"

"She's in a cell similar to yours, in another block. I'm afraid both of you have outlived your usefulness. Tomorrow I'll officially take over your world and then you'll be executed, along with your precious girlfriend. However, you and I will have a cozy chat first."

Craig recalled how his friend had died and his skin crawled. Andocia's laughter rang in his ears long after she left him.

/ / /

It was after lunch that confusion reigned. Craig heard the sound of scuffling feet and wondered what had happened. There were sounds like firecrackers going off and then his face split into a grin. "Good old Keith – he came through for us. Well, he should keep Andocia pretty busy for now. I hope she beats a hasty retreat and we never have to hear from her again."

It wasn't long before one of Craig's friends found him and unlocked the door of his cell. Before he ran off once again, Craig grabbed his arm.

"Constance is also here somewhere. You have to rescue her as well!"

The man smiled. "It's already been done my friend, now let's get rid of this tyrant once and for all!" he said, as he threw a weapon to the explorer.

Craig was glad to oblige and they ran up the stairs side by side.

The battle was over within a few hours and most of Andocia's followers had been killed, but there was no sign of her. Craig and his companions ran to the hangar, but her ship had vanished, along with the barrier that had circled Earth. A loud cheer went up and the Americans decided to celebrate their victory. The planets in both universes were contacted and told that Earth had won the victory. Out in space, Petrovsky watched the cheerful scenes and smiled.

"Ah, so our alliance with the Americans has ended! Now I can go back to my favourite pastime, that of trying to capture the legendary Craig Carter."

/ / /

After a while, things began returning to normal again. Commander Simms had been restored to his position, safe and sound and together with Keith, they restructured the entire defence system. Despite all their efforts though, Andocia couldn't be found anywhere, so they assumed she had returned to her own universe once again.

Life continued as usual, with Craig and Constance both going out on separate missions, but there was always a nagging thought at the back of Craig's mind that the devilish woman was still somewhere about, waiting for the right opportunity. He knew she was aware that his intervention had turned the tide in Earth's favour. Now he had returned to Earth from another trying mission and was thinking of going home to sleep for a week. As usual, he went to Constance first. She put her arms about his neck and welcomed him with a kiss. "Oh wow, this is the best thing that can happen to me after a mission. You seem to make it all better."

She smiled and snuggled into his arms. "Oh Craig, tell me we'll always have good times like these!"

He tilted her chin up and kissed her on her nose. "We will, now and forever! I love you so much Constance and we've been through a lot lately. Things can only get better."

CHAPTER 13

Much later that same evening, Constance had gone into her kitchen to make them a snack. Craig sat in the lounge watching television, when suddenly a sweet voice sounded in his head.

"Listen to me, Craig Carter, there is trouble ahead for you!"

Startled, he concentrated on the voice and spoke in a whisper. "Who are you? Do I know you?"

"No, but I have to warn you that Andocia is at this very moment on her way to your home. No one has ever defeated her before and she is looking for revenge. Hurry, take Constance with you, for she comes in secret and will use your woman as a lever against you and force you to do her bidding. This time she'll finish what she started."

At that moment, Constance came into the lounge and her face was ashen. It took only a moment for both of them to realize they had heard the same voice simultaneously. Constance was confused by the voice in her head, but she spoke directly to the being in question.

"We can't just go into space and stay there forever! Both of us have lives here on Earth and we can't run away every time there's a crisis."

"I don't expect you to," came the gentle reply, *"but both of you must hurry to Saturn. Your friends there have to operate on Craig again, for Andocia can still influence him and she must be stopped. The Saturnians will know what to do, but the operation is a complex and delicate one, and he won't be able to operate his craft for a while. The recovery time will be a few days, but you mustn't stay in one place for long, not until the process is complete."*

Constance looked across at Craig who was nodding in agreement.

"Who are you?" he asked.

"A friend," replied the soft voice.

Instinctively, the couple knew they could trust the voice implicitly and stood up together. "Thank you, whoever you are," remarked Constance gratefully, but only silence greeted them.

At the Space Control Centre, they selected a spacecraft big enough to hold the two of them comfortably and before long, they were out in space. Craig contacted the Saturnians and explained the situation to them.

When they arrived on Saturn, they found everything was ready and Craig was prepped for immediate surgery. In the operating theatre, it wasn't his eyes they were operating on, but his brain. Even with their advanced methods, the procedure took a few hours. When the anaesthetic wore off, Craig was allowed a short time to recuperate. Karnd, who had taken Constance into another room, reassured her. "I'm sure you would like to know what we did to Craig. We cut into his brain and removed the memory of the first time he met Andocia. Remember he said her body just seemed to vanish and her eyes seemed to penetrate right to his brain, then later discovered he had gone blind?"

Constance nodded vigorously.

"Well anyway, he still remembers they met and the fact that she's very evil, but now if she does manage to capture him again, and I hope sincerely it doesn't happen, she can't make him blind again. Now I think you should go and visit your young man. He shouldn't suffer any after effects either, such as the attack he had in Russia."

"Thank you Karnd! We are both very grateful."

Constance went to see Craig and he smiled at her. The only evidence that anything had been done was a piece of sticking plaster on his temple.

"How do you feel now, Craig?" she asked solicitously.

"Much better – happier somehow."

"Good, it's as it should be," Karnd replied. "I just wish we could help you fight that evil woman, but you must try to avoid her at all costs," replied the scientist worriedly.

"Trust me, I'll do anything to avoid her," he replied fervently.

Lara joined them and smiled at her friends.

"Craig this woman is a menace! We are concerned about the way she tried to take control of your mind. I have never come across anyone so powerful before and I find it strange that she knew nothing about this universe. She is obviously telepathic as Constance said, but the way she influenced you concerns me deeply. I've heard of telepathic beings who could influence thought processes, but not to this extent. What made her target you in the first place?" the scientist asked curiously.

Carter shuddered as the memory of how she killed his friend came to mind.

"Andocia said she saw me land on Melton in the Golden Way and was curious about me. When she rescued me from Tyrus by using her mind alone, she told me she thought I was a criminal mastermind because everyone was after me. My so-called plan appealed to her, so she said and she was curious about me. However, when she read my mind, she realized I was in fact innocent of the crimes I had been accused of. She asked me to join her as her strategist and I refused. I guess she had never been refused by anyone before and it made her angry. Even the inhabitants of the Golden Way I met up with were afraid of her. It was then she decided to do everything she could to cause me harm.

"When the Russians rescued me from my cell, I decided to play along with them, because I needed to remain free and clear my name. I thought I was pretty convincing but Colonel Ivan Petrovsky obviously didn't believe me, because even though my friends were trying to capture me, I would never have defected to Russia. They tried to persuade me to give them sensitive information and tortured me when I refused. Anyway, until then I hadn't really realized just how much Andocia had influenced me and I had a flashback, which was the reason I was advised to came back here so that you could operate on me."

Lara's expression was grave. "You did the right thing and I have to tell you that whatever Andocia did to you went beyond anything we have ever seen before. Luckily we were able to help you!"

"I'm very grateful! If it hadn't been for your intervention, I don't know what I would have done."

Lara frowned. "That's something else I'm curious about. You said that someone spoke telepathically to you and told you that you should come here. Have you any idea who that person could possibly have been?"

Craig shook his head. "No, I have no idea but it was definitely a woman and she spoke to Constance and me at the same time. I must admit, I was curious but I knew instinctively she was to be trusted."

The Saturnians looked curiously at one another and Karnd spoke. "How was this possible? You admitted that neither Constance nor you had seen this woman, yet you trusted her implicitly. How could you have been so positive that she meant only to help you? What if she had been leading both of you into a trap?"

Carter shrugged his shoulders helplessly. "I can't explain it! I just knew she meant to help. There was some kind of *connection* I suppose. Anyway, she spoke the truth didn't she! You operated on me and took away something evil and I cannot thank you enough for what you did."

"I hope that this in some way makes up for the way we treated you when your colleague tried to frame you," Lara replied contritely. "You told us you were innocent and we should have believed you. After all the good you have done for us, we should have been more understanding and for that we apologize."

"I understand and anyway, all's well that ends well and Jorrick Baker got what he deserved. I certainly don't hold it against you and I can tell you honestly that it in no way harmed our friendship," Carter replied kindly.

"What happened to the real culprit anyway?" the scientist asked curiously.

"When he was caught, he was put in a maximum-security prison on Earth. I'm not sure what he was sentenced for but he was quite insane. He won't be released from prison for a very long time I can assure you."

The explorer put his arm around his girlfriend's waist and hugged her fondly. "I have Constance to thank for uncovering the plot to discredit me. If it hadn't been for her, I would still be on the run."

Constance smiled and they kissed tenderly.

The scientist smiled at her friend. "Well that is some consolation I'm sure, but it still cannot make up for the trauma you went through to prove your innocence. However, I'll never distrust you again, I swear! Our friendship will continue for the rest of our lives!"

Craig raised his glass and smiled. "To friendship!" he toasted.

Everyone raised their glasses. "To friendship!" they echoed.

They were silent for a time and then Lara stood up and indicated for Craig to follow her. She flew slowly so that he could keep up with her. The space explorer sensed she was still worried. "Craig if this woman was concerned enough to tell you about Andocia, she must be worried. You told me she suggested you should keep moving, but what if Andocia catches up with you somehow. What will happen then?"

"I don't want to think about that Lara, but I'll stay alert. Even with Andocia's incredible power, she cannot know where I am at present. Hopefully, we can avoid her. I would like to think Andocia will leave me alone now, but between you and me, I doubt it somehow. She strikes me as someone who will go to the ends of the galaxies to find me, but I still don't understand why! After all I didn't defeat her single-handedly when she tried to take over Earth. There were many willing helpers who did just as much damage to her self-esteem as I did. I just don't want Constance to worry about this."

Lara smiled gently. "Craig, that young woman is no fool! She knows you have made another deadly adversary. Anyway, enough of these melodramatic thoughts! My advice is that you take your unknown benefactor's advice and leave here as soon as possible. Hopefully when Andocia cannot find you she will just give up and return to her own universe!"

"I hope so! I had better get back to Constance so that we can leave as soon as possible. I would never forgive myself if Andocia did trace us here and took revenge on your planet for harbouring us."

They returned to the group for some refreshments quickly, and then Karnd examined Craig once more. "I'm pleased with the way the operation progressed. Just take care not to bump your head, because your brain is still very tender. Now you had better get going before Andocia gets a fix on your position."

The two space explorers lifted off Saturn and their friends waved to them. Constance was in control while Craig sat back and relaxed, as he was ordered to do.

"Okay, Craig, at least that's over and done with. I feel much better knowing she can't influence you again, but where should we go now? We have to find somewhere safe to hide, at least until your head heals."

"I think that we should visit Neptune and stay there, Constance. The King and Queen will see we're kept safe and I don't mind if they order armed guards to look after us."

Constance nodded happily. "Yes, I like that plan. I think at this point in time, safety in numbers would be a good idea, because quite frankly, if Andocia should appear now, I doubt we could hold her off."

The woman set course for Neptune and contacted the Neptunians. The King was delighted to offer them sanctuary.

When they touched down on Neptune, Constance sent the ship into space in time-lapse mode and they waited patiently for someone to bring them gills to wear. Both explorers were dressed in swimming costumes. They didn't have long to wait, before Lolita came to meet them. After embracing them happily, she handed them the gills and they all swam down to the underwater city.

The King and Queen were waiting to receive them and the couple bowed reverently. "Your Majesties, it's good to see you again!" said Craig as he kissed the Queen's hand. The King grinned and grabbed Constance in a bear hug.

"Ah my dear, it's such a pleasure to see you again! I'm glad you decided to come to us for protection and rest assured, as long as you are our guests, no harm will come to you."

"Thank you, Sire," said Craig gratefully. "We still aren't really sure what we're dealing with, but I don't relish the prospect of being in Andocia's company ever again!"

The King nodded and clapped his hands. Immediately a servant appeared and he issued instructions for the man to bring refreshments.

The next few days were spent exploring the underwater civilization with Lolita as their guide and Craig was once again fascinated by the wonders of the underwater kingdom. Not far from them hovered several of the King's personal guards and at night when Craig and Constance slept, trained personnel watched their room. During this time, the couple relaxed completely and rested well. Andocia never bothered them. Their time was spent in idyllic surroundings where the water was pleasant and the inhabitants were extremely courteous. Craig often sat with the King and reminisced about their relationship, while Constance kept busy exploring the underwater paradise with Lolita and her mother.

A few days later, Lolita came to find Craig. She took him into the privacy of her garden and sat down nearby. Her expression was contrite as she looked at her friend. "I've been meaning to apologize to you about what happened the last time we met. I was rude to you and so was my mother. On her behalf, I would like to say how sorry we truly are."

"I understand, really I do. You don't need to apologize for the way you both behaved. After all, I was a wanted criminal and all the evidence was pretty damning."

Lolita shook her head emphatically. "No Craig, I should have trusted you. Deep down I knew you were innocent, but still I let the doubts creep in. You have always been there for us and I let something so stupid get in the way of our friendship. All of us hurt your feelings and I wish I could take those words back."

Gently Craig took her hands in his. "Lolita, I'm not angry. I was hurt at the time of course but I couldn't blame you. Now at least I have been vindicated thanks to Constance having overheard Jorrick talking to the technician about their plans. That is ancient history now, so let's move on and pretend it never happened, okay."

"Are we friends again?" she enquired.

"We always were Lolita," he confirmed. "We just hit a rocky patch there for a while."

Lolita squeezed his arm affectionately. "I'm so glad things are back to normal again!" she sighed.

The princess spent some time with Craig and when it began to get dark, they returned to the palace.

A week later the couple decided to leave, for they had to return to work and Lolita waved goodbye to them as they lifted off and were soon out of sight. Then, taking the gills with her, she plunged into the water once again.

As the American craft moved away from Neptune, a trident ship moved stealthily behind them. Such was Andocia's technology that the couple was unaware of her presence, for nothing showed up on their screens and the computer gave no warning of the enemy approaching. Inside the American spacecraft, Craig was now piloting the craft, while Constance went to check on things in the back. The trident ship followed the smaller craft for a while, but Andocia made no move to intercept them.

Constance was sitting on one of the beds and reading up on the history of the Golden Way, while the computer related important points. She was looking for information about Andocia, but found very little to go on. It was almost as though the records had been destroyed deliberately. Despite the warmth of the cabin, she felt cold and she shuddered.

"I have such a bad feeling about Andocia, because she's still an unknown enemy. If only we knew what we were really up against, I would feel much better ..."

A soft thud interrupted her thoughts and she turned to see something coming at her from the other side of the room. Instinctively, Constance stood up to face this new threat and something closed about her throat, even before the being got to her. She found herself staring at a woman with green skin and dressed in a similar fashion to the men she had seen.

"What have you done to me?" she whispered painfully.

The woman smiled cruelly. "A simple trick really. We don't want your boyfriend interrupting us. Come Miss Gregg, time is short and Andocia requests the pleasure of your company."

Constance glared at this woman and moved in to attack, but the woman was fast. Instead of the explorer making contact with the stranger, the woman stepped nimbly aside and Constance missed, but she recovered quickly and whirled around to face the green woman once again. Her eyes widened in shock when she saw a strange weapon appear in the woman's hand, and before Constance could move, the trigger was pulled. A red blur emerged from the barrel and wrapped around Miss Gregg, effectively imprisoning her. Constance opened her mouth to scream, but only managed a soft croak. Even before she had blinked, the stranger had her in a grip as strong as iron. She struggled for her freedom but this woman was very strong. Andocia's follower spoke quietly. "I have her, mistress! You can teleport us now!"

The next minute they were in space. Constance barely had time to ponder the strange phenomena when she found herself on the trident ship, face to face with Andocia. The red cloud dissipated and she saw only females, many of whom were pointing their weapons at her, populated this ship. With her vocal chords paralyzed, Constance stared silently at her enemy, and stood her ground.

Unaware of the drama that had taken place on his ship, Craig continued checking all his instruments, while behind him the trident ship turned and silently disappeared from sight. Some time passed before he realized it was unusually quiet aboard and went to find Constance. When he reached the sleeping area, he stared in disbelief at the mess. A lamp had been overturned and smashed on the floor, and the bedclothes landed in a heap next to the bed. The computer was humming quietly and he hurried to it. There on screen was the history of the Golden Way. Craig pressed a button and spoke to the computer. "Computer, give visual display of this room half an hour ago!"

The hum changed to a whine and Craig watched in morbid fascination as he saw Constance struggling with a woman. The drama unfolded before his eyes and he could only watch angrily, his hands balled into fists so tight that they hurt. "Damn Andocia! So, she's been tracking us, has she? There must be some sort of stealth device on her ship which prevented us knowing about her."

Carter went back to his vidscreen and contacted his base so he could tell them the bad news. When he had been connected to Mission Control, he asked to speak to Commander Simms.

The moment his boss saw his crestfallen face, he tensed. "Craig, what's wrong? What has happened?" he asked worriedly.

"Sir, Andocia's ship must have been following me from Neptune. She must have a more sophisticated cloaking device than we do. I had no idea she was even nearby. Sir, she has kidnapped Constance."

"Damn that woman!" Simms exploded. Doesn't she know when to quit! Her plans to take over Earth were foiled and now she is obviously looking for revenge. That woman seems to have a fixation with you Craig. Why do you suppose that is?"

Craig shrugged his shoulders helplessly. "I have no idea, Sir. What am I supposed to do now? I don't know where she has taken Constance."

"My advice is to sit tight for a while Craig," remarked his boss. "If she wants you, she'll no doubt contact you sooner or later. She obviously wanted to get your attention."

"She certainly did that!" growled Craig angrily. "All right, I'll wait for her to contact me. I just hope she doesn't harm Constance in the meantime."

"I don't think so, Craig. If she wants you, then you will be hearing from her. She would have no reason to harm Constance if you are the ultimate target. Take care Craig and do the best you can to resolve the situation. Good luck, Son!"

"I'm going to need it!" he grumbled after severing the connection. He sat down and waited for the inevitable message from Andocia.

The computer screen lit up and spoke to him. *<Incoming transmission Craig. Do you wish to respond?>*

Craig sighed, "Yes, open a channel, computer."

The screen lightened and he stared at his enemy. "Hello Andocia."

"Ah Craig Carter, we meet again like I promised. By now you know that I have your woman, of course."

"Yes, I know," he said flatly. "What is it that you want?"

"I would like the pleasure of your company on my ship."

"What if I refuse?" he asked stubbornly.

Andocia shook her head in mock regret. "I wouldn't do that if I were you. I have no love for your kind and particularly not for you. Do you really want your girlfriend to die?"

"Your fight isn't with her Andocia. I'm the one you really want, so why go through this ridiculous procedure at all? Why didn't you just grab me and leave it at that?"

"Everything I do is done for a reason, Carter. My followers could have taken you, but I ordered it to be done this way. Would you like a word with your precious woman, just to prove she still lives?"

Craig nodded, "Yes, I would. If you have harmed her ..."

Andocia moved aside and Craig caught his breath when he saw his girlfriend bound to a chair.

"Craig, don't come to her please. She just wants to kill you slowly and painfully!" Constance pleaded.

"I'm so sorry my darling! I was sure we'd get away from her and now you're in danger."

"It comes with the job, you know that. I refuse to be your

Achilles' heel, so don't give in to her demands on my account!"
Constance begged.

"But Constance ..."

"No! I don't believe she'd kill me just to prove a point. She's
lying!"

Craig felt as though his insides were twisting out of shape and
his throat was dry. Andocia smiled maliciously and turned to
Constance, extending her forefinger once again, and then she
turned back to Craig. "Well, are you a gambling man, Mr
Carter? Do you dare gamble with your girlfriend's life? Am I
bluffing, or deadly serious?"

A shiver went up his spine as he remembered what Andocia
did to his friend on Earth.

"Damn you Andocia! All right, let's finish this once and for all.
I refuse to spend my life looking over my shoulder, wondering
when you'll finally get me, so you win! Just name the time and
place and I'll come. I want Constance freed in exchange for me.
She has done nothing to anger you!"

"Craig, no, don't do this, please!" begged Constance unhappily,
but he ignored her.

"That is a wise decision, Carter. There is an uninhabited planet
not far from your present position. It should take you about an
hour to reach it."

Craig looked at his computer screen and nodded. "Yes, I know
the one. Very well, I'll see you there."

His screen went dead and he set course for the planet.

CHAPTER 14

Craig hovered above the uninhabited planet and scanned the
surface. He saw the trident ship on the ground not far away, its
loading bay already open to receive him. He pointed the nose of
his ship downwards and flew into the lion's den, where a
reception committee waited. One of the women stared at him
appraisingly and removed his laser gun from its holster. The

explorer followed and soon came to a large room. Andocia sat in a chair facing him, but there was no sign of Constance. He saw many women who looked like Andocia, but there was no sign of any men he had tangled with on Earth.

"Where's Constance?" he demanded.

"Safe for the present, but whether she stays that way will depend entirely on you."

"I'm here, aren't I?" grumbled Craig.

She ignored him and pointed to a chair. One of the women lingered behind and Andocia waved her away. No one spoke until the door had closed behind her. Then Andocia addressed her captive. "Well Carter, I assume you know you're going to die soon."

He didn't answer and she continued. "You and I are going to get to know one another for the next few days, because I'm curious about your race. Once you have outlived your usefulness, then I'll see about your execution."

"Now that you have me, I want you to release Constance, that was the deal."

Andocia raised her eyebrows enquiringly. "It was? I don't recall agreeing to that. As long as I have your young lady with me, I'll have your co-operation. She's my insurance."

"But you promised!" exclaimed the explorer.

"No, I didn't."

Craig put his hands on the arms of the chair, determined to hurl himself at his tormentor, but she was ready and a strong red band wound itself around his body and the back of the chair, imprisoning his hands by his sides. Craig tried to free himself, but the bands were as strong as steel. Andocia got up from her chair and moved closer to her prisoner. Craig looked at his feet, afraid to make eye contact. His flesh crawled when she placed a hand under his chin and lifted his head up.

"Why waste time fighting me, Craig?" she aked gently. "Do the right thing and surrender your will to me."

"I won't! I daren't! I'd rather die!" he gasped.

Despite himself, he could feel he was succumbing to her will. Perspiration ran down his neck, when abruptly she turned away and he sucked in a lung-full of air.

Her gaze was murderous and confused. "How is this possible? It worked on you the last time, yet this time I couldn't blind you."

Craig refused to answer.

She recovered her composure quickly and smiled coldly. "Well I can't make you my doting slave by crushing your will, but you'll see I have many other suitable methods. What I want I usually get."

"What do you hope to achieve by killing me, Andocia? It makes no difference whether you do so or not, because my world is full of people prepared to fight for their planet. Even so, it changes nothing. Earth belongs to us again and your chance has gone. Why not just return to your universe and forget about this stupid idea of revenge you seem to be so focused on."

"You don't understand, Carter! You and your human friends have made me look an idiot in front of billions of beings and planets and I despise that. You have to be made an example of."

"So, if I die, it will make *you* feel better! Where's the logic in that? There were many people on Earth who contributed to our success, so kill me if you must, but don't expect me to plead for my life, nor in fact will Constance plead for hers."

Andocia stared admiringly at the bound man before her and he stared levelly back at her. Abruptly she left the room and the door closed soundlessly behind her.

An hour passed before she returned, but she seemed calmer when she spoke to him.

"All right Carter, let's not argue now. Will you co-operate with me if I ask you some questions?"

"I don't mind, just as long as we don't discuss matters of national security – but then you already took that information from me without my knowledge anyway."

The statement surprised Andocia, but there was admiration in her voice.

"So, you found out I'm telepathic! Well that's very interesting!"

"Actually, Constance discovered it and informed me. What do

you want to know?"

She questioned him at some length about his personal life and he answered the questions he didn't feel were too damning, but when she became personal, he clammed up.

"Andocia, I'd like to know more about you if I could. Constance was studying the history of the Golden Way before your friends captured her, but there's hardly any mention of you, except for vague references here and there."

"All you need to know about me is that I live in the Golden Way."

"Can you tell me about these women followers you have roaming about? Surely all the men couldn't have been killed on Earth?"

Andocia snorted in derision. "Bah, I underestimated the might of your planet, so I thought they would be suitable to do the job, but I should have known better than to place such a responsibility on the men-folk, for they are weak! If I had sent my female warriors, Earth wouldn't have got off so lightly! My mistake lay in not studying your planet at length, but the next time, I'll do more research."

"Who are you and where did you originate? The Meltonians told me your followers were destroyed years ago."

"You don't understand the concept of time, for what they meant to say was 'centuries' ago."

Craig's mouth gaped open in shock. "That's *impossible!* No one is that old."

"Ah but it's true. Actually, I am immortal. I've been around for longer than you could ever imagine. That means I can't be killed, no matter what."

There was silence while Craig digested this disturbing bit of news. "What about your followers? Surely they are not immortal as well?"

"These aren't my original followers, because they really did die. Unlike me they were mortal, just like you. These women are my elite group of warriors, and they are almost invincible. I choose only the best women to serve in my army! The men have their uses too, and I am just as strict when I employ them."

Carter stared at Andocia, taking in her green skin.

"But how come they are green, like you?"

"A chemical process I invented. All those who wish to serve me have to follow certain initiation rites, which eventually culminates in them becoming green."

Time wore on and Carter's muscles started to stiffen. Outside, the sun had begun to go down and he realized just how tired he was. He yawned and Andocia looked interestedly at him. "Are you bored with my company so quickly Mr Carter?"

He shook his head. "Look Andocia, you've had me tied to this chair for ages and I'm really tired. Tomorrow is another day, but I'd like to rest, preferably in the same cell as Constance."

"Very well you may retire for now, but not in the same cell as your precious girlfriend."

"At least let me see her! How do I know you haven't killed her already?"

"She's comfortable, I assure you, but that is entirely dependent on your good behaviour from now on. If you try to escape or cause some mischief, she'll die before your eyes, then it'll be your turn," threatened Andocia.

She snapped her fingers and the band fell away from Craig's body. He stood up stiffly and stretched his aching muscles. As if on cue, several women warriors came into the room and escorted him to the cells. They deliberately slowed down at one of them to judge his reaction and he looked inside. Constance was staring at the far wall, a faraway look in her eyes. They lingered only for a second and then he was pushed forward to another cell a little further away. Once the inner door had been locked, one woman laughed tauntingly. "Don't bother trying to call out to your friend, for once we close these outer doors, the room will become soundproof."

Carter ignored them and went to sit on the bed. Food was brought to him, but he nibbled listlessly at it. Later he fell asleep and when he awoke, was surprised to find it was morning once again.

Some of Andocia's followers came to collect him and he was marched back to the woman herself. His enemy smiled charmingly at him and immediately he became suspicious, especially when he was invited to dine with his hostess. He wanted to refuse, but the aroma drew him like a magnet and obediently he sat down and found, despite his reluctance, that he was very hungry. After breakfast, Andocia invited him to accompany her on a walk through the sparse vegetation of the uninhabited planet, to stretch his legs. No guards were in evidence and his suspicions grew. Finally, he could stand it no longer and spoke up. All right Andocia, what's going on? Yesterday I was treated like a criminal and suddenly today you trust me. What if I try to escape?"

The woman laughed. "No, you wouldn't dare, for we still have your precious girlfriend in our cells. You found her in good health last night I presume?"

Craig nodded. "All right, so you haven't harmed her, *yet.* What exactly do you want from me?"

His captor indicated to a rock under a tree and he sat down, while Andocia did likewise.

"You know, I was thinking about what you said yesterday and I've reached a decision. I was going over your exemplary record and it just seemed a shame to kill you, so I have a proposition to put to you. I resent that you thwarted me, but I have to admire your methods."

Craig looked suspiciously at the woman. "What are you trying to say?"

"Well, I thought I would give you another chance to redeem yourself. I could use someone with your capabilities on my side, so I've decided that if you join up with me, I can make you rich and famous. I'll treat you well, I promise and you'll lack for nothing."

"Aren't you forgetting something, Andocia? What'll become of Constance?"

"Well, I suppose I could let her go. It would be a fair price, if you agreed to my terms."

"What exactly are those terms?" he asked curiously.

"You'll have to live in the Golden Way of course, for that's where I operate from. All my followers will do your bidding if you ask them. In exchange of course, I'd need your undying loyalty, which means that everything you know must be passed on to me."

Carter raised an eyebrow and looked quizzically at her. "I thought you already had that information. Isn't that why you tried to take over Earth?"

"So, Constance has been busy! Yes, you were largely responsible for that. I must confess I cheated, but even now, I know your thoughts, for you don't know how to shield your mind from me."

"Give me time and I'll learn, that I promise you. Well if you know my innermost thoughts, then you must already be aware what my answer will be."

Andocia was puzzled and she frowned. "Carter, why would you refuse all this? Surely not for the sake of one miserable girl?"

"No, not just for her sake, but my own peace of mind as well. Andocia, what you know about Earth doesn't help you all that much. Ice courses through your veins, so you can't grasp what affection really means. Everything you want, you simply take, whether you have permission to or not. Well I'm not a possession."

"You prefer the alternative?" she threatened.

"No, I don't really want to die, but that makes more sense to me than betraying my world."

The devilish woman paced back and forth for a while and thoughtfully scratched her chin. "All right, let's be fair about this. I'll give you until lunchtime today to give me an answer. All I ask is that you think carefully about what we discussed here. If at that time your decision remains the same, then you die tomorrow morning."

She escorted him back inside and her warriors marched him back to his cell, but even as the doors closed behind him, he knew what had to be done.

At the appointed time, Craig was again invited to eat with his captor and he sat down opposite her. The meal was completed in silence, but when they went outside, Andocia was dumbstruck. "Carter, I'll never understand the human race! You have chosen death over all that I can offer, why?"

"Like I said, my loyalty lies with Earth and I just can't see myself serving you, not willingly at least. I've never come

against an enemy as strong as you before and it's most disconcerting, but what is fated will come about. I believe you when
you say that you could make me your slave, but it would be a
hollow victory and you know it. All I ask is that you free
Constance."

Andocia smiled and Craig felt like a fly that had just been
caught by a spider.

"Very well, you may have your wish then. In exchange for your
life, I'll free your girlfriend, but she's a very good fighter, so I'll
draft her into my army and she can serve me."

Helplessly, Craig stared at the evil woman before him. *"No!
That's not what I mean and you know it!"* he exclaimed angrily.

"Well that's my ruling on the matter. Unless you pledge
undying loyalty to me, that'll be her fate. If you agree to work
with me, then she may return to Earth unharmed."

Miserably, Craig shook his head. Andocia looked as though she
would kill him on the spot, but she recovered and snapped her
fingers. Immediately several of her followers came out and
seized Craig, who struggled furiously. "Andocia wait!" he pleaded.

She held up her hand and they stopped, awaiting orders.

"At least let me see Constance to say goodbye! I don't want her
to spend her time wondering what happened to me. I'd like to
tell her what's going to happen."

The evil woman considered for a second, then she gave the
order and he was taken to Constance's cell and locked in with
her.

His girlfriend jumped up and ran to him, embracing him
gladly and he clung to her. "Craig, what's going on? I knew you
surrendered to her yesterday, but no one wanted to tell me
anything. Are you all right? Have they harmed you at all?"

"No, I'm fine, but we're in quite a predicament now. I wish I
could tell you everything's going to be okay, but I can't lie to
you because it wouldn't be fair! Andocia propositioned me and
asked me to work for her, but I can't! She wants to take me
around like some little trained dog on a leash and I can't handle
that. It seems she doesn't take rejection well, so I'm going to be

executed tomorrow morning. I pleaded with her to let you go, but she says that she wants to use you in her army and make you into one of her female warriors."

"Over my dead body!" exclaimed Constance furiously. "I'll kill myself before I work for her."

Craig held his girlfriend at arm's length and stared into her eyes. He stroked her cheek lovingly. "Constance, listen to me, that isn't the answer!" he exclaimed earnestly, "I want you to do something for me please. I won't be around to stop her, but you must find a way, for my sake. If you love me, then do as she says willingly and without complaint, then when she trusts you, find a way to put her out of action. I'll die happier, knowing that the rest of mankind won't suffer because of what I did."

Constance stared at the man she loved and a tear emerged and ran down her cheek, followed by several more. "Craig, please don't feel guilty about what happened in the Golden Way! Granted, she saw you go through the portal into our universe, but you didn't even know about it. If you hadn't found the way by accident, someone else would inevitably have done so another time. You did nothing wrong, but there must be a way out of this horrible mess."

"I'm open to suggestions my love, but tomorrow isn't far away. I did think briefly about pretending to serve her, but she can read my mind and she would have known I was lying. It looks as though this is the end of the road for me. Just remember what I said," he begged, as the door opened and he was ordered back to his cell. He turned to face the woman he loved and silently mouthed the words, 'I love you!' then he was gone.

Craig paced nervously up and down his cell and watched as the time moved onwards, too quickly for his liking. Evening came but he wouldn't eat his food. That night he slept fitfully, waking up with a start every couple of hours.

Carter came awake suddenly, not sure what had woken him and looked around. His gaze fell on the cell door that now stood wide open and a voice he had heard once before, spoke to him. *"Craig Carter, make haste and leave this place! Fear not, for I have placed Andocia in a trance that will last several days. You will have enough time to return to your planet safely."*

Craig knew that he could trust this stranger and he did as he was told, but at the door, he hesitated. "Thank you for helping me, but where's Constance?"

"Don't worry, she is already safely aboard your ship and waiting for you. No one will stop you leaving, as I have taken care of everyone here."

Carter walked down the empty passages and glanced inside some of the rooms, where he saw that even the women warriors were asleep. Gratefully, he boarded his ship and found Constance already programming the craft for immediate departure. Once they had lifted off, the voice spoke again.

"Mr Carter, Miss Gregg, you are both very brave and I salute you. I'm sure that once your escape has been detected, Andocia will no longer be interested in you."

"Who are you?" asked Craig curiously.

"Just someone who wanted to help," replied the sweet voice modestly, and then it was gone.

"What do you make of that, Constance?"

"I don't know, but somehow I sense she's as good as Andocia is evil. I would've liked to have met her, but it just proves that good is far stronger than evil. She managed to put Andocia to sleep and none of us could even come close to that wicked woman because of the wretched barrier she erected around herself. Well I don't know about you my darling, but I can't wait to see Earth again!"

Craig grinned and agreed with her and soon they had touched down again in the Space Control Centre.

Back on the uninhabited planet, Andocia woke with a start and hurried to see if her prisoners were still about, but they were gone. She hurled a red bolt with all her force at a nearby tree, which burst into flame and consumed almost immediately.

"Damn it! *She* must have helped them to escape. Only one person can defeat me and it is her. So, she decided to help the foolish Earthlings!"

Andocia went back inside and shook several of her warriors who had just begun to wake up.

"Bah I'm wasting my time here! Let's return to the red planet now. I'm sick and tired of being in this foreign universe!"

"But mighty one, don't you want to finish what you started with the human man and woman?"

Angrily Andocia shook her head. "No, don't worry about them. By now they will have returned to their planet and I have urgent matters to conclude in the Golden Way."

The trident ship rose from the land on which it had stood for a few days and then disappeared in a red cloud.

Back on Earth, Craig and Constance were sitting in Carter's lounge when his mobile device rang. The screen showed a beaming Petrovsky. "So, we are enemies again, eh comrade! I prefer this situation, for life is dull when I can't pursue you."

Craig smiled, "Well you can always try, I suppose. Guess I'll be seeing you around then."

Petrovsky grinned enigmatically. "Count on it my American friend."

Constance sighed, "Well you can't complain about life being dull, can you Craig?"

"I guess not, but let's forget about Petrovsky, Andocia and all the others who despise us. I want to concentrate on us right now."

"No problem there!" she assented as she snuggled into his arms and their bodies met in a fiery embrace.

Later, while Constance slept, Craig sat up in bed and gazed fondly at his girlfriend. *"I love you so much, sweetheart, but I sense our troubles are just beginning! I know Andocia will never leave me alone, but I still don't understand why she is targeting me especially. Of all the evil beings I have ever tangled with, she is by far the most dangerous. Whoever our benefactor was, I hope we get to meet her sometime! We could certainly use someone like her on our side. She seems to know a lot about Andocia. I think she probably lives in the Golden Way as well! We've just scratched the surface of that universe and I'm positive there are many more planets to explore, and hopefully we can befriend these as well. It'll be wonderful if we find more planets that are perhaps as intelligent as the Saturnians. Imagine what we could learn from them!"*

Carter went to the window and looked outside. It was early in the morning and still too dark to get up. The explorer stared thoughtfully up at the heavens. *"The universe as we know it has grown substantially over the years. With new planets and stars being created regularly, space exploration will never become boring, at least not as far as I am concerned. I hope I'll always enjoy my job and that I'll live to a ripe old age."*

He rubbed his arms vigorously and sighed. *"As long as Andocia leaves me alone, it might be possible. I doubt we've heard the last of her though. Why is she so interested in me, I wonder? She tried her best to take over Earth but she was prevented from doing so by many wonderful people, not just me. I cannot understand her interest in me specifically."*

Craig returned to bed but sleep eluded him and he was glad when morning came.

CHAPTER 15

While he and Constance were enjoying breakfast, Constance's phone rang. She answered the insistent ringing and listened for a few moments, then stared unhappily at Craig.

"Honey it's the old age home where my grandmother lives. She took a bad turn and is asking for me."

Constance turned her attention back to her mobile device. "What happened? Is my gran okay?"

"We have given her a sedative to calm her down, Miss Gregg," the nurse replied. "She often sees imaginary things as you know, but whatever she thought she saw this time seemed somehow different than before. This time she was terrified! She is asking for you. Can you come immediately?"

"I'll come as soon as I can. Do you want me to contact my mother?"

"I phoned her before I contacted you. She is already on her way and will meet you here."

Constance disconnected and her face was pale. Craig took her hands gently in his. "Sweetheart do you want me to come with you?" he asked kindly.

Miss Gregg clung to her boyfriend for a moment, taking strength from his presence, and then she gently pulled away. "No, I'll be okay! She isn't ill, just unsettled and I need to go to her, but thank you!"

Craig wondered briefly how she could know what her grandmother's mental and physical state was, but he knew they were very close and didn't question her further. His girlfriend went upstairs to change and soon she left, promising to meet him later.

Miss Gregg arrived at the old age home and hurried to her mother. "Mom, what happened to gran? Have they told you anything more?"

Alexis Gregg shook her head. "No, I know just as much as you do. The doctor is with her right now and when he's finished his examination, he'll tell us what's wrong."

Mother and daughter waited for approximately fifteen minutes before the doctor emerged from the ward. He smiled at the two women and took them to his office. When they had all sat down, he began to explain. "Beth was very lucky today. The nursing staff was alerted to the fact that there was something amiss when Beth began to scream and shake uncontrollably. She fell out of bed at that point but fortunately no bones were broken. We did various scans and X-rays earlier but found nothing wrong. Apart from some bruising, she should be fine in no time at all. Beth was in a great state of agitation though and kept on muttering that someone was trying to kill her. This has never happened before and it is my opinion that she suffered a slight stroke which has somehow also affected her brain. As you know her mental condition has been deteriorating over the years and unfortunately, we can do nothing about this ageing process. Despite her condition, she is in very good health for a seventy-nine-year-old. She was asking for both of you. Reassure her that everything is all right and I'm sure that by tomorrow she will be fine again. Meanwhile we'll keep monitoring her and I'll personally update you if there's any change, bad or good. If you have any questions, I'll be happy to answer them for you." The doctor stood up and smiled at the two women. "I have to do my rounds now. We'll talk later, okay?"

"Thank you doctor," Alexis replied.

She took Constance by the hand and squeezed it reassuringly. "Beth will be just fine, I'm sure. Come on, let's go and see her."

Mother and daughter went into the room and stood on either side of Beth's bed. Her eyes were closed and Constance tentatively reached for her grandmother's hand. She held it gently and her grandmother's eyes opened immediately and she smiled at her daughter and granddaughter. "You came!" she said, and the relief on her face was evident.

"Gran, you gave us such a fright!" Constance complained. "What happened?"

Her grandmother's lips quivered and a tear squeezed out. "I'm so sorry I scared you," she mumbled. "It was so unexpected!"

"What was unexpected?" Alexis asked tentatively.

"The voice in my head!" she complained. "It was a voice that came from something evil and twisted. She told me not to talk to you, but you have to know what she said! I have to tell you!"

Constance held her grandmother's hand and it shook violently. Her mother interrupted. "Mom the doctor said you may have suffered a mild stroke. You've been given a sedative. It will calm you down soon and then you can rest. Whatever you imagined you saw was just a nightmare. It wasn't real!"

Elizabeth sat up suddenly and ignored her daughter. She clung to Constance in desperation. "Alexis has never understood, but you do! You must listen to me!" she wailed.

Mrs Gregg wrung her hands together, lost for words and Constance smiled at her. "Mom just leave me alone with Gran for a few minutes please."

Mrs Gregg nodded and left the room.

"Granny, you have to tell me what's worrying you so I can help!" Constance pleaded.

Beth's eyes seemed to lose focus for a moment and Constance could see the sedative the doctor had administered to her grandmother was now taking effect.

"What was that dear?" Beth asked vaguely.

"Why did you call Mom and me to the hospital? I can see you aren't well. Please tell me what happened! I have to know!"

Her grandmother's eyes opened wide for an instant as she fought the effects of the sedative. "Constance, I have to warn you! Your mother has never believed me, but I know you do. We have a connection, you and me! I saw her!"

"Who did you see?" Constance enquired.

"Her! She appeared in my head and I saw her as though she was standing right next to me. She told me to shut my mouth or she would do it for me. I had no idea she even existed until recently. Keep away from her, I beg you! There is great danger ahead. She knows all about you!"

"Who does?" Constance asked desperately.

"That woman is evil!" Beth's eyes bulged as though she was fighting for breath and she clawed at her throat. "I … I cannot say her name," she croaked. "Constance, open your mind and you will know the truth; you will know *everything!*"

Beth's eyes closed and the death grip on her granddaughter's arm relaxed. For a moment Miss Gregg panicked, then reason prevailed and she put her hand against the pulse on her grandmother's neck. The sedative had finally taken effect and she had fallen asleep. Gently Constance pulled the covers up and stroked her grandmother's wispy soft white hair.

Her mother was waiting outside and she looked ill at ease.

"What did Granny say?" she asked nervously.

Constance shrugged her shoulders. "I don't understand a word she uttered Mom! It was all gibberish to me! She said something about opening my mind so that I could learn the truth."

Constance was looking pensively ahead and therefore missed the expression on her mother's face. All the colour drained from her face and she clenched her fists so hard that her nails bit into the palms of her hands. She recovered quickly and put her arm around her daughter's shoulders. "Just ignore her honey. I think she has truly lost her mind now. I guess it was to be expected. Gran has had a good life, but she is old and frail now and often gets confused. Try not to take what she says seriously."

"I won't," Constance promised. "Will Gran be okay, do you

think?"

"She has the constitution of an ox, sweetie. By tomorrow when the sedatives have worn off, she will be back to her old self again. Let's go home now."

Arm in arm they left the hospital. Constance paused for a moment and looked up at her grandmother's window.

"I hope you are okay, Gran!" she thought nervously. "The doctor will do some more tests on you in the morning and then I'll know for sure."

Reluctantly she waved goodbye to her mother, climbed into her car and left.

Constance contacted Craig and told him briefly what had happened at the hospital.

He reassured her that her grandmother would most probably be fine and that she should listen to her mother. They arranged to meet later for dinner. Constance went home to her flat to prepare for their dinner date.

In the meantime, Alexis had also gone straight home, where she brewed some coffee and made some tea for herself. She sat down comfortably and re-arranged the cushions on the couch in the lounge. A car parked outside her townhouse, and she opened the door.

"Hello Craig! You are precisely on time!"

Craig smiled at Alexis and they hugged one another. He sat down on the couch and Constance's mother poured coffee for him.

"Well Craig, I did what you asked and told no one about our visit. We shouldn't be disturbed."

"Thank you. I appreciate it!"

"You were so secretive when you contacted me yesterday! What is this all about?"

"I apologize, but it was necessary. As you know, I love Constance dearly, but I have some questions that have been bothering me lately and I really need to know the answers."

"What is troubling you?"

"I have given this a lot of thought and I hope you won't be offended. I wanted to speak to you privately, without your husband present."

Craig looked at his coffee mug as though he was trying to get some inspiration from it, then he put it carefully down on the table nearby. "I'm sorry to interrupt like this, but I hope you will understand why I felt it was so important to speak to you. Please don't be offended by my questions, but it just makes me wonder why you and your husband always look so tense when Constance goes to visit your mother. Surely you would encourage it, because she is lucky to still have her grandmother to confide in. I know she is getting on in years, and seems eccentric, but Constance loves her so much. Beth does seem confused at times, but your daughter expects that. Why does this bother you so much?"

Alexis looked sternly at her guest. "Craig, I know how much you love Constance, but aren't you being a bit personal. What has this got to do with you?"

"I'm sorry if I appear to be rude, but I am just worried. Call it a hunch if you like. I was hoping you had the answers I'm looking for," Craig replied. "When Andocia came to conquer Earth and forced Constance and me to work for her, I watched how Andocia kept staring at your daughter, as though she was expecting something unusual to happen. We were both heavily guarded, but Constance had more guards surrounding her than I did. Up until that woman came to Earth and tried to rule, she had never even met Constance, but she seemed very interested in her. I know for a fact that Andocia is telepathic and telekinetic, but she isn't human. I suppose these are powers her people possessed."

Alexis began to fidget with her cup and couldn't look him in the eyes. Gently he touched her on her arm. "I'm sorry for upsetting you, but I need to know what to expect. Let's discuss your mom for example! I really like Beth, but she does say peculiar things. I notice that you are quick to brush this off and put it down to Alzheimer's disease, or something else age related, but I am a good judge of character and she strikes me as a very intelligent woman, even though she is elderly. When she talks to Constance, you always tell your daughter it is old age, but is it really? I know you love both of them very much, but they do seem to have some sort of connection you never talk about. I noticed you get very flustered when Constance tells you the things her gran says."

"Naturally I get flustered! I love Beth dearly, but sometimes she says very strange things and Constance doesn't really understand how her mind works."

"Maybe not, but you do, don't you?"

Alexis bit her lip and wiped away a tear. "You will never understand, even if I tell you everything! Please, just leave it alone!"

Craig went to Alexis and knelt down in front of her. He took both her hands in his and held them gently. "Alexis, I'm sorry if I'm upsetting you, but I have given this a lot of thought and I keep coming up with the same answer. You know, secrets have a habit of being exposed when you least expect them. Please share them with me. I swear that if I think they are going to hurt anyone, I'll forget this conversation ever happened."

Mrs Gregg stood up and wiped her hands on her apron. She took Craig's mug to the kitchen and refilled it, as well as hers. She sat down again and looked at her daughter's boyfriend. "I have kept this secret for years and all has been well, but you are a very perceptive young man, Craig. I can see that you will never be satisfied until you know the truth. I just hope you'll understand why it has remained a secret all these years. I have only shared this with Mark, because like you he is a clever man. He understands the situation, but has difficulty coming to terms with it. Because he is a soldier, he is more interested in ridding this world of violence, than dealing with other things."

"I understand."

Alexis put her hands in her lap and began her story. "I come from a long line of Greggs, and they have a secret which goes back many generations. I don't know when it began, I just know that it exists! It is only carried over to all the females in the family. Every second-generation daughter is born with 'gifts' and not everyone has the same ones. One common factor though is that all the women are telepathic and telekinetic. Like any other family, there are weak and strong women, so some receive more 'gifts' than others. Each gifted girl child has to discover these, which can happen at any time in their lives. Those who are born with these soon become very much smarter or stronger than their cousins. Everyone is different, so each female has to decide what path they will take in life.

"What this means, in effect, is that every second-generation female born into the talented family, will be gifted. My grandmother didn't have these gifts, but her daughter, my mother, certainly did. Elizabeth was very powerful! She had a knack of learning things very quickly and she was a very outgoing person. Everybody loved her, but when she got married, she moved to a small town where people were afraid of her. The gossip and lies about her threatened to break up her marriage, so she and my father moved away where they weren't known. They settled down and had me and my brother. Everyone thought they were a wonderful couple and no one else knew about her 'gifts' except us. We were sworn to secrecy and my mother tried to have a normal life, but she would often lose her temper and take it out on the trees around the area, breaking them in half, or causing them to burn to the ground. I guess we were awed by her powers, and we tried to live a normal existence, but it's hard to lie to someone who knows how to read your mind!

"When Shaun was eighteen, he was killed in a freak accident and my parents never got over it. My father loved Shaun and had decided to let him help run their small business, so when he died, so did my father's dream and he eventually had to sell the business.

"I had met Mark, a distant relative, by this time and we got married. When I gave birth to Constance, she began using her 'gifts' almost from the day she was born, and I panicked, remembering what had happened to my parents, so I took her to the doctor and explained about the family history. He gave me tablets and told me she would have to take them for the rest of her life. She has been taking them ever since."

"That means Constance is very special indeed! It's not my job to interfere with your family life, but I was just wondering, why didn't you give her the choice? Surely she had a right to know she was ... different?"

"I couldn't take the chance! The fact that she started using her 'gifts' when she was just a baby, bothered me. I knew she would grow up like Beth. My mother hated her own abilities because she said it interfered with her life. It was never ordinary! I didn't want Constance to grow up with the same problems."

"Those tablets the doctor gave her years ago are 'inhibiters' I presume?"

"Yes."

"Well they obviously work. What would happen if she decided to stop taking them?"

"She must never stop! Years ago, I told her they were vitamin tablets she had to take to protect her immune system. We told her that if she stopped, all her organs would cease to function. The moment she stops taking them, she will exhibit symptoms of her 'gifts'. Unless she learns how to control them, she could cause irreparable harm to herself or others."

"I understand why you made that decision and I suppose I can't really blame you, but I'm still curious! What do the tablets actually do? Do they minimize her brain functions in any way?"

"No, they only stop the actual powers. Everything else will continue to develop normally."

"Constance is very special anyway. She has a sixth sense which enables her to differentiate between right and wrong. Even if someone looks friendly and isn't, she knows about it." Craig replied.

"I don't think that has anything to do with her hidden 'gifts'. She exhibits amazing talent. Constance also has a good memory and is talented in many other ways. That's why she passed her exams with distinctions. The loss of her 'powers' has in no way made her a lesser person. Incidentally, the Gregg family aren't the only ones who have certain 'gifts'. Many families have talented members and I have met a few of them over the years. Unfortunately, even though we have come so far with inventions and things that make our society work better, telepaths are still looked on with suspicion."

Craig picked up the cups and took them to the kitchen sink. He smiled at Mrs Gregg and hugged her again. "Thank you for answering my questions. I feel much better, knowing what the situation is. In some ways I guess I would have done things differently if I had been in your place, but I respect your motives. I swear I will never tell Constance about this conversation. You have my word!"

Alexis Gregg smiled gratefully. "Thank you for making me tell you. I feel much better now, knowing that someone else is sharing this secret with me. Now you had better hurry home! It's late and you have a date with my daughter."

$$\textit{ノ ノ ノ}$$

Back at the hospital, Beth awoke suddenly. She looked around but the hospital was in darkness. She peered at the luminous dial of her watch and saw the time was 3.00 a.m. A dim light burned in the hallway outside. The old woman was filled with a sense of foreboding and glanced nervously around the room. Her eyes lingered on a corner and she gasped as a shadow detached itself from the wall. Instinctively she gripped the bedclothes and pulled them higher up to her throat. Her eyes were bright in the dim light as she glared at the figure that had suddenly appeared. "*You!*" she gasped. "*What are you doing here?*"

"I think you know the answer to that question Elizabeth," the shadow replied softly. "It's good to finally meet you, but then I feel as though we are old friends and, in a way, I suppose we are."

Beth glared witheringly at the figure. Her voice didn't tremble as she spoke to the shadowy figure. Had Constance seen her grandmother now, she would not have recognized her. All traces of the weak 'insane' woman had disappeared as she faced someone she had hoped never to meet in her lifetime. "You aren't a friend of mine, nor of the rest of my family. What do you want and why have you come here?"

The figure made a gesture of impatience. "Oh, come on Elizabeth, you don't have to pretend with me. I know exactly who and what you are. It must be so annoying having people believe you are insane. No one believes you when you hear voices, but I do. You see, I'm just like you. One would think that in these modern times, you would be believed, but sadly humanity still has so much to learn about telepaths. All your knowledge and power; such a shame you had to hide it from the world and those whom you love. Now they have stuck you here in this old age home to rot away and they will never know what your gifts are."

"They aren't gifts!" Beth snapped. "They are more like curses!"

The figure sniggered. "Oh, that really depends on how you use them. I for one would certainly differ in that opinion. I've not been encumbered with a family as you have and as such my gifts have grown over the years."

Beth clicked her tongue impatiently. "I don't care what you have done with your life! All I want is for you to stop meddling in mine. Leave my family alone!"

The figure smiled wryly. "I don't think so! I've been away too long and they have evolved over the years – well some of them anyway. Take you for instance! How did you hide your talents from your husband? Surely he must have suspected something."

"That's none of your business!" Beth snapped. "Just go back to wherever you came from."

The figure sighed theatrically. "Sorry, I can't do that right now! I have so much catching up to do as I have been gone such a long time! Now it is your precious granddaughter that interests me. How has your family managed to keep this knowledge from her?"

Beth glared malevolently at her uninvited visitor. "Leave her alone! She has done nothing to deserve your attention."

"Oh, but I beg to differ, my dear! She certainly has your strength and tenacity. I think she is a worthy opponent! I cannot believe you and your family have kept this knowledge a secret from Constance. Don't you think she had a right to know about these 'gifts' some members of her family have?"

Beth sighed heavily. "I have tried to explain this to her in a very subtle way, but Alexis has convinced her I've lost my mind. I cannot hold it against my daughter though, because some things are very hard to come to terms with. She just wants the best for Constance and I have to respect her wishes, even if I don't agree with her methods."

The figure moved into a patch of moonlight and her red hair swayed gently. Andocia smiled again at the old woman in the bed. "At the same time though, I also have to admit her boyfriend is another person who could prove a nuisance in the future. He is definitely another human being I will have to keep a close watch on. I met Craig Carter for the first time when all the planets were looking for him. He had been branded a criminal at that time of course. You see, he thinks I am interested in him because I thought he was a criminal mastermind, but that isn't so. Although it was my first impression, I realized my mistake when he explained he had been wrongfully accused of stealing dangerous bacteria. Imagine my surprise when I realized who his girlfriend was! I read his mind and that is what got me interested in him. He is a very clever man! I'm certainly interested in him because he's tenacious and very clever, but Constance is the one I am most interested in. Already that young man has foiled me in my takeover of Earth. No one told you about that of course because they didn't want to worry you, but I'm positive you knew about it."

"I know everything. Not much escapes me," Beth admitted. "However, I wasn't sure who was responsible for that fiasco – until now!"

Elizabeth's hands balled into fists and she glared at Andocia. "Why are you still bothering him? He defeated you, now go back to where you came from and leave us all alone."

"No Elizabeth, I can't do that, not now. I have many plans that will involve both your precious granddaughter and her meddlesome boyfriend. No one knows what I am truly capable of."

"I do," Beth replied quietly. "I'll warn them about you."

Andocia moved closer to the bed and gripped Beth's arm painfully. "You can do nothing! Do you honestly think anyone will listen to the ravings of a mad old woman? They will think it is your overactive imagination!" the evil woman sneered.

Beth showed surprising strength and twisted free from her grip. "I'll make them understand! I'll tell Constance everything about you. She has a right to know."

"Her mother doesn't think so!" Andocia countered. "If she did, she would have told Constance everything ages ago. I don't think she wants to go down that road, so her silence is guaranteed."

Beth sighed and rubbed her hands tiredly over her eyes. "I should have told Constance about you ages ago but I wasn't sure if you really existed, until now. I'm going to tell her the truth and then she can make whatever choice she wants to."

"Your daughter won't like that!" Andocia smirked.

"I don't care! Alexis had her reasons and while I don't approve of them, I do understand her motivation behind it. I'm going to tell Constance tomorrow when she comes to see me and you can't stop me!"

"Oh, yes I can!" Andocia replied menacingly. She raised her hand and a red bolt flew from her finger. Beth retaliated in a similar fashion but the bolt that came from her fingers was green. Unfortunately, it went wide and slammed into the wall, making a scorch mark on the paint which blistered immediately. Andocia's energy slammed into Beth's arm and burnt a hole in her flesh, making her gasp in pain and surprise. She placed her hand on the wound.

"Oh, well tried Elizabeth, but you are out of practice. You should have embraced your talents, not hidden them. I have enjoyed this little reunion, but sadly I have to leave now. You may be old but you are dangerous, so I'm afraid that you have to die. I *will* rule this miserable planet one day and no one is going to stop me, least of all you. I've enjoyed our chat. Goodbye Elizabeth."

Beth stared in hate at the woman and didn't flinch. There was no fear in her eyes, only resignation. She spoke telepathically to the redhead.

"I am out of practice as you say and if it is my time to die then so be it. If I was several years younger however, we wouldn't be having this conversation, because I would be more than a match for you. I only wish I had known about you when I was younger and stronger. I would have made sure you were destroyed. However, you will never

succeed in your quest to rule this planet. The people have come a long way since you last visited here. Do you think I am going to submit quietly to you? No! You are going to pay for your evil crimes one day. Someone more powerful than you will succeed in destroying you. I just wish I could be there to watch it."

The elderly woman ripped the tubes from her body and stood to face her enemy. She extended both arms and hurled twin bolts of energy at her tormentor. Both hit home and Andocia gasped in sudden pain as they burnt her. Beth looked deep down inside herself and willed the power she had suppressed over the years to surface once more. She had promised herself she would never use the destructive forces within her ever again, but tonight was an exception. For a while they traded blows and inevitably the noise drew the attention of the nursing staff and they banged on the locked door, demanding to be let in. For an instant Beth was distracted and Andocia struck her with all the force that she could muster. Beth was slammed backwards and she hit her head on the iron railing at the top of the bed. The old woman lost consciousness and Andocia reached for a scalpel.

"It's over Elizabeth!" she crooned softly. "I cannot let you warn your family. You fought bravely but I won!"

Andocia took the scalpel and cold bloodedly slit the old woman's wrists. She watched as Beth's blood seeped into the sheets. The door finally slammed inwards when someone kicked it very hard, but Andocia didn't stay around to watch what would happen next. She sat on the roof of the hospital and reached out with her consciousness to touch the mind of the woman she had just murdered, but received no response. Satisfied, she disappeared from view, leaving the hospital staff to sort out the carnage.

CHAPTER 16

The next day Craig was surprised to receive a call from Constance. She was crying and could hardly get the words out. Her boyfriend only caught snippets of the conversation.

"Constance, wait for me. I'll come and fetch you immediately!"

He arrived at her apartment and gathered her gently in his arms. She held tightly to him and sobbed uncontrollably. He let her cry for a while and then gently wiped her tears away.

"Honey, what's wrong?"

"Oh Craig, my grandmother is dead! I don't know what happened! She was fine when we left her last night!" Constance sobbed.

"Have you spoken to your parents about this?"

"Yes, but they won't tell me anything! All they said was she had died, but my parents keep whispering under their breath and when I walk in to the room, they stop talking immediately."

"Have they been to the old age home yet?" Craig asked gently.

"They went there earlier this morning. My mother won't stop crying and even the police have been around. When they came to the house though, my parents asked me to go to the shop to get something. Craig, they aren't telling me everything and I'm so confused! Why are they being so secretive?"

Her boyfriend kissed her gently on the top of her head. "Sweetheart I'm sure they'll explain everything to you in good time. I know you loved your grandmother very much and you are going to miss her terribly. It's going take a long time for you to get over this loss. Just remember, I'm here for you whenever you need me."

Constance buried her head in her boyfriend's shoulder and the tears flowed anew. Craig held her and let her give vent to her feelings.

/ / /

The funeral was held a few days later. Constance had taken the death of her grandmother very badly and the family doctor had given her a sedative to help her get through the day. She sat next to her family and Craig held her hand. After the service, Craig commiserated with Constance's family once again. He subtly prodded them for information, but they remained tight-lipped about Beth's death. Carter's suspicions were aroused when they avoided making eye contact with him and his years as a space explorer led him to the conclusion that they were hiding something, but what?

The next day he left Constance at her parent's house and went to see Commander Simms. His boss was surprised to see him. "What brings you here Craig? I have no missions for you."

"I know that Sir, but I was hoping you could help me. I know it is probably none of my business, but I'm very concerned. Constance has naturally taken the death of her grandmother very badly."

"Yes, she has," Simms agreed. "Very few people understood the old lady. She was … eccentric at best. Only Constance seemed to connect with her. Just be there for her and this bad time will pass soon enough. Time is the great healer."

"Yes Sir, I agree with you and I'll always be available for her, but that isn't the problem."

Commander Simms arched his eyebrows enquiringly. "What exactly is bothering you so much, Craig?"

Carter shifted uneasily in his chair. "Sir, I know this may sound stupid, but something is very wrong. Mr and Mrs Gregg won't even discuss Beth's death. All they have told Constance is that her grandmother was very old and it was her time to go. I've tried to probe discreetly, but I'm just coming up against a blank wall. Maybe it's just my suspicious nature, but something just isn't right. Why do Constance's parents seem so agitated when the subject comes up?"

Commander Simms scowled at his employee. "Why are you so suspicious? Don't take offence Craig, but this isn't really your business. Everyone deals with sorrow in their own way. The fact that Mark and Alexis don't seem all that keen on discussing the incident is no concern of yours. You should just be there for Constance when she needs you."

"I am and I'll always be there for her for as long as she needs me," he promised.

"Well then, why have you come here? I can't help you. I didn't know Elizabeth all that well."

"I know that Sir, but I was just wondering if you could perhaps talk to Mr Gregg. He is a friend of yours so maybe he'll tell you what happened. I just have a bad feeling about this. He said she died in her sleep, but he's lying. If it had been an ordinary death, why would the police have gone to see the Greggs?"

Commander Simms rubbed his chin thoughtfully. "All right Craig, I'll see what I can find out, but say nothing to anyone about this."

"I won't, I promise! Thank you, Sir, I really appreciate it."

A few days later, Commander Simms contacted Craig and he went to see his boss. He knocked on the door and was summoned inside and told to close the door. Simms looked very agitated and asked his employee to sit down. He in turn paced uneasily back and forth behind his desk.

"Sir, what's wrong?" he asked nervously.

Commander Simms shook his head. "You know Craig, I thought you were just being paranoid when you voiced your suspicions. You always did have an instinct for sniffing out things that weren't quite right, so I decided to do as you asked."

Carter leaned forward eagerly and his boss sat down in the chair. "Look what I am about to tell you must not leave this room, do you understand? I don't want you to mention anything to Constance, no matter what. Will you give me your solemn promise?"

"I swear I will never discuss this with her!"

"All right then; I spoke to Mark Gregg but he refused to tell me what happened, so I did something I'm not very proud of. I went to the policeman in charge of the case. He didn't want to tell me what had happened either, but I outrank him and he couldn't refuse a direct order. Are you sure you want to hear what he told me?"

"I'm sure Sir," Craig replied.

"All right then, here's the story. Craig, as you know by now, Beth was a little unbalanced. She used to tell the staff at the old age home some very strange stories and they pretended to believe her, but I have it on good authority she had probably lost her mind long ago. Only Constance could reach her and even she would find it difficult to believe everything her grandmother told her. As you know, the doctor who was attending to her felt she had suffered a slight stroke. He told Mark and Alexis that his tests had proven conclusive. I think Elizabeth knew somehow and became depressed. She committed suicide, Craig. There was no note or anything like that, but she had somehow got hold of a scalpel and slit her wrists. It wasn't pleasant and I believe the unfortunate nurse who found her is receiving counselling."

Craig gasped in disbelief. "Dear heaven, that's awful! No wonder the police were there."

"Yes, but there's more to the story, unfortunately. The ward was damaged and several monitors were broken. It appears Constance's grandmother went totally insane. They say she smashed some of the hospital equipment before committing suicide. I guess she just couldn't deal with the fact that she would be more helpless than ever before. She had always been a very independent woman and the stroke unhinged her."

Carter put his head in his hands and groaned. "Poor Beth; I only met her once or twice. As you say she tended to ramble on a bit, but I must confess, I liked her. Well, I won't tell anyone about this conversation. As you said, it's better that Constance remembers her as she was before the stroke. Thank you for clearing this up for me. I know I was meddling and you went out on a limb to satisfy my curiosity. I wish she had just died in her sleep, but anyway her suffering has ended now. I think I should get back to Constance and just be with her."

"That's a good idea Craig."

Craig left his employer's office and Commander Simms stared thoughtfully at his departing back. "This is a trying time for you and Constance, but once again your instincts have been proven correct. I wonder how you manage to do that?"

The door closed and Commander Simms shuffled some of his data disks around as he returned to his work.

Craig went to see Constance and was reassured to find she was no longer crying. Her eyes were swollen and red rimmed, but she seemed calmer. "How are you feeling?" he asked her kindly.

"I'm still very sad but I guess I'll learn to deal with it, Craig.

It's just going to be difficult you know, because I could talk to my gran about things I never even shared with my mother and father and I knew she understood and never judged me if I did the wrong thing."

Her boyfriend pulled her close and whispered in her ear. "I don't mind volunteering as her substitute my darling. I promise I'm an excellent confidant. You can tell me anything."

Constance's lip trembled slightly. "I may very well hold you to that promise Craig."

"See that you do," he replied, brushing his lips against hers.

He moved gently aside and took her hand. "I bet you haven't eaten anything today have you?"

"Well no, I didn't really feel hungry," she replied.

"Then Dr Carter suggests you put on a beautiful dress and we go out on the town. I think dinner at Club Mystique and a play afterwards is just what the doctor ordered."

Constance smiled cheerfully for the first time in days. "Actually, now that you mention it, my stomach is rumbling. You have a knack of dispensing good advice!"

Her boyfriend gave her a pat on her behind. "Go on then! Get ready while I make the reservations. Miguel will be pleased to see us again because I plan to spend an obscene amount of money which will probably deplete my precious savings," he replied flippantly. "Make sure you bring your appetite along. I'm going home to put on something more suitable and I'll see you in an hour, okay?"

Constance brightened up immediately and hurried to get ready.

An hour later he returned and the door was opened by a vision dressed in a magnificent red dress. Carter stared at the portrait of loveliness and for a moment he was speechless. "Oh wow! I must be the luckiest man alive right now!" he sighed as he handed her a bouquet of flowers.

Miss Gregg sniffed them and smiled. "Oh! These are beautiful Craig!"

He grinned wolfishly at her. "Well I would say they have some serious competition, my love. You look absolutely stunning!"

His girlfriend laughed pleasantly and placed them in a vase before they left on their date.

They arrived at their favourite club where a private table set away from the crowds awaited them. Miguel greeted them personally and kissed Constance's hand. "Ah Miss Gregg, you are truly a vision of loveliness! If you were not dating this handsome young man here, I would be tempted to leave my wife and two children and beg you to elope with me immediately!"

Constance laughed and patted his hand. "Well, perhaps another time then!"

A waiter came forward to serve them and Miguel shooed him away. "No Philippe, I will take care of these young people personally. It will be an honour."

Champagne was already chilling in an ice bucket and the owner opened it and poured the sparkling liquid into crystal glasses. Then he left them with the menus and went to greet some more of his regular customers.

Constance smiled. "You must have told him you plan to deplete your savings. We are receiving royal treatment."

Carter took her hand. "Well, tonight nothing else matters but the two of us. Just for a while at least let's forget our troubles and concentrate on enjoying ourselves."

The meal was excellent and so was the service. No sooner had they finished the starter, when the main dish was placed in front of them. Miguel was true to his word and made sure everything ran smoothly. The night passed blissfully and they relaxed and enjoyed every moment. The show they attended afterwards was very funny and Constance laughed uproariously at the antics of the actors. Craig glanced furtively in her direction and was pleased to see she was enjoying herself so much.

He drove her home to her apartment later that evening and stayed for coffee. Afterwards he got up to leave and she stopped him. "Craig, will you spend the night with me?" she asked. "I had a wonderful time tonight but I guess I need a friend."

"If you would like me to, then of course I will," he replied gently.

That night, after they had made love, Constance fell asleep with her head on her boyfriend's chest. He lay awake for a while, stroking her dark hair and kissed her gently on the top of her head. *"I'll do everything in my power to protect you my love. I won't let anyone harm you, not while I still live and breathe,"* he thought. Afterwards he fell asleep, cradling her in his arms.

CHAPTER 17

The next morning, he returned to his own apartment where he checked his mobile device. There were several messages and he listened to them while having something to drink. When he got to the last message though, he sat up suddenly and shook his head. He wasn't sure he had heard correctly so he played the message again. Someone he did not recognize spoke to him.

"Mr Carter, you don't know me, but I have an urgent message for you. There is a certain Russian gentleman who would like to talk to you. He says he has a matter of utmost urgency to discuss with you. Ivan is looking forward to seeing you again. I will contact you again at twelve today with details. Please delete this message as soon as you have listened to it."

Carter was intrigued, but suspicious. He decided however that it couldn't hurt to hear what the unknown man had to say.

Precisely at twelve, his mobile device rang. Craig picked it up and found himself looking at a stranger. The man was about his age he guessed, with blond hair, cut slightly long. His eyes were a watery green and he had large fleshy lips. When he smiled, Craig saw that his teeth were slightly crooked and discoloured.

"Yes, can I help you?" the explorer asked guardedly.

"Mr Carter?" the man enquired.

"That's me," he confirmed.

"Yes, you match the description I was given. I have a message for you. Ivan wishes to meet with you."

"Who is Ivan?" Craig asked suspiciously. "I don't know who you are and what you want. Unless you give me a good reason,

I'll terminate this conversation. I'm not in the habit of meeting strange people for no apparent reason."

The man looked cautiously around, almost as though he expected someone to appear behind him.

"Look, if you meet with me tonight, I'll explain everything. Ivan said you would be suspicious so he told me to give you a message. He said he enjoyed the last partnership with you, even though it was short-lived. He mentioned a redhead who caused some trouble. He also said he had some important information to give you. His full name is Ivan Petrovsky!"

Craig nodded his head. "I thought you were talking about him. I just wanted confirmation. Why does he want to see me?"

The man bit his lip nervously. "Look Mr Carter, I have already said too much! Meet me tonight at the Galaxy Bar, at seven. I understand your reluctance but feel free to bring a weapon with you if you wish. I'll explain everything then."

Craig thought about it and nodded his head. "All right, I'll meet with you, but if I don't like what I hear, I'll leave immediately."

"That's fine. You won't be sorry, I guarantee it."

The screen went dead and Craig stroked his chin thoughtfully.

"Why would Petrovsky want to see me, unless it's a trap? That man is still one of my most cunning adversaries. Well I know the bar in question and it is always full in the evenings. No one would try anything underhand there. I'm pretty intrigued, but at the same time I won't relax my guard. I'll take along a few friends, just in case."

That evening he arrived and sat down at the bar. He ordered a drink and surveyed the room carefully, but no one suspicious seemed to be lurking about. Craig was taking his time with his first drink as he wanted to have a clear head when the man arrived.

Fifteen minutes after he arrived, a man wearing a hooded anorak sat down next to him and ordered a beer. He didn't acknowledge the explorer's presence, however, and Carter didn't want to seem anxious so he ignored the stranger as well. By the time Craig had finished his first drink, the man next to him had half of his left. The young man was considering leaving when someone whispered softly. "Mr Carter, there is an empty booth in the corner. Do you see it?"

He glanced curiously at the man next to him, but the stranger didn't acknowledge him at all. "Yes I do," he replied.

"Order another drink and take it there. I'll join you shortly."

Carter was aware of a young woman leaning over him and she smiled in confirmation. He glanced questioningly at her and she looked at the far corner.

He did as the woman had instructed and ordered a non-alcoholic drink. When he received his order, he made his way over to the table where he sat down. Soon he was joined by the young woman who had spoken to him. She had straight dark hair that hung to her shoulders and almond coloured eyes. Her nose was small and pert and turned up slightly at the tip. Craig guessed she was probably in her late twenties, but she looked younger. Her figure was hidden by a bulky jersey but he could almost sense the untamed power inside her and he knew she could probably hold her own in a fight. This didn't surprise him at all.

"I was expecting someone else," he remarked suspiciously.

"I know and he's around somewhere. He'll join us later."

"Who are you?" he asked the woman curiously.

"Names are not important," she replied dismissively. "I know who you are and that's good enough for me. I'm here to explain the situation in general and then it's up to you to decide what must be done."

"Well I'm listening. This had better be good or I'll walk away."

The woman nodded. "Mr Carter, believe me, this will be worth your while."

Carter put his hands on the table and leaned forward. "Well you look like an intelligent woman, so tell me why I should be so interested, in one sentence."

She smiled and sipped delicately at her drink. "Ivan Petrovsky wishes to defect to America."

Craig's drink was halfway to his mouth when he stopped suddenly, and his jaw dropped open in surprise. "What did you say?" he hissed.

"You heard me," she replied.

Carter shook his head in disbelief. "There's no way he would ever do that! Is this some kind of a joke?"

The woman met his gaze evenly. "Do I look like I'm joking?" she asked crossly.

"Petrovsky! But why would he do this?"

"I'm only delivering the message as a favour to Ivan. He asked me to contact you and I did so."

She stood up to leave and he put his hand gently on her wrist. "Wait, please stay! I need more details."

Reluctantly, she sat down again. "What do you want to know?"

"I'm just curious as to why he chose me to drop this bombshell onto. I'm a space explorer, just like him, not an agent of the government. He should talk to them. There are channels to go through, protocol, and so forth. I know nothing of these procedures."

"Maybe not, but you have contacts in very high places, so Ivan says. He said I should tell you that unless you handle his defection personally, it won't happen."

Craig opened his mouth to say something, when someone sat down next to him in the booth. He turned to the person in question, who slowly lowered his hood and grinned at Craig.

"Ah, the mystery caller I see!" Craig remarked. "It's nice of you to join us."

The man ignored his remark and spoke instead to the woman opposite him.

"So, is he going to do it?"

Two pairs of eyes turned to look enquiringly at him.

"Well Mr Carter, will you help us?" the woman asked.

"How do I know this isn't an elaborate trap?" he asked suspiciously. "Colonel Petrovsky and I have a long history, none of it pleasant. Mostly he was trying to kidnap me and force me to betray my country. Why should I believe that he wants to defect now all of a sudden? I need some proof or there's no deal!"

The woman reached into her handbag and slid a compact disk over to him.

"Ivan said you might be reluctant, so he asked me to give this to you. Have a look at it and then make your decision. Neither of us will contact you again, but if you are interested, then come back here on Saturday and wait in this booth. Someone will be here to discuss the terms with you. If you don't come then we'll assume you aren't interested in continuing with this. It will then be your loss and that of America as a whole."

Craig was still suspicious but he took the disk and put it in his pocket. As they stood up, the woman looked at Craig and whispered. "You're a very cautious man Mr Carter. You can tell your minders that they can relax now! We haven't harmed you in the least." She extended her hand and Craig shook it.

"It was good to have met you, Mr Carter. You're everything that Ivan says you are."

The man also got up and the two of them moved away. Craig smiled when he realized they were both professionals, for they had known about the policemen and woman who had watched his back.

Carter made eye contact with an innocuous looking man sitting a few tables away and shook his head in answer to the questioning look he received. The two strangers were allowed to pass unmolested and he watched as they left the bar together. The man turned left while the woman turned right and they disappeared from view. Not long afterwards he too left the bar and returned home. By now it was very late so he put the compact disk into his safe and went to bed.

The next morning after breakfast he put the disc into his mobile device and activated the computer icon. The innocuous phone turned into a holographic computer and he inserted the tiny disk which was no bigger than a small bottle cap. He started the device and watched the screen in front of him. Ivan Petrovsky's face appeared at once and he smiled at his arch enemy.

"Hello Comrade Carter. It has been a while since we last saw one another. I'm hoping that this will change soon.

"Firstly, why would I want to defect? I'm sure you are very interested in knowing my reasons behind this. Well suffice it to say that I have become somewhat disillusioned with Russia. My superiors are dull and unimaginative and if you must know, the fact that America seems to be jumping ahead of us in the race to explore space, annoys me greatly. I'm tired of being on the losing end and I want to join your team, if America will have me. As you are no doubt aware, I can give you a great deal of information on many top-secret projects. Just as Russia would love to have you tell them all about your upcoming projects, I have valuable information that your country could use. I don't expect you to take my word for it, so I'll show you some of the things that I can do for you."

The screen changed and Petrovsky's face disappeared from view. However, his voice could clearly be heard.

"First of all, here is the latest spacecraft that Russia is building. Notice the way the nose cone has been streamlined, as well as the wings. This spacecraft isn't in production yet, but Russia will be building it within the next few months. I have access to the data disc which will help you to improve your crafts. These will be fighter ships though, but their estimated speed, when completed, will be at least twice as fast as your crafts. I'm confident that your country will be able to adapt these to meet their specifications. If you decide to help me then I'll make sure you have the blueprints for these ships. The on-board computers have also been modernized and this enables the commands given by the pilot to be attended to much faster. You will no doubt agree that is a good thing, especially if some emergency arose that required split second timing. The system is designed in such a way that it does a diagnostic check every twenty-four hours without being told to do so. It also fixes any problems without the knowledge of the pilot, provided of course that it's nothing serious. If it detects something amiss, it informs the astronaut of this and suggests alternative action to be taken. Your people will know immediately where the parts can be found and if required, the computer will contact the relevant parties who would be able to repair the problem. Only the finest experts are listed, thus you would avoid taking the ship to someone who isn't qualified to fix the problem.

"As a token of my good faith, I'll bring you a new weapon that we are presently manufacturing. It's based on your stun guns, but has a great many useful features built into it. Unfortunately, I've had to compile this disk in secret and I was unable to film these for you. I'm still in Russia at the moment and will stay here until you have kept your end of the bargain. My friends will liaise with you and when I'm happy with the arrangements, we can discuss how I can be brought to your country safely. I realize this could take some time, so I'll be in touch. Just follow the instructions you will be given next week and then we'll talk again. Do whatever it takes comrade and I hope to see you soon. I must impress on you the need for secrecy though. Speak only to a few people whom you trust. Russia has spies in unlikely places!"

The disk blanked out and Craig removed it from his computer. He turned it pensively over and over in his hands, wondering what the next step should be. He knew he had no experience in helping people to defect and he knew Petrovsky was also aware of that fact. He needed help, but who could he trust? Ivan had bluntly warned him that spies existed in their midst and the knowledge came as no surprise to Craig.

He stared thoughtfully out of a window and then made up his mind and phoned Commander Simms, politely requesting a meeting. His boss was curious, but Craig refused to divulge anything over the phone. They agreed to meet after hours when most of the day staff had left.

That evening he went to Mission Control and his boss was waiting for him. Craig closed the door and sat down opposite his boss.

"Craig, what's going on? Is something wrong?"

"I hope not. I received a strange call last week and when I followed up on it, I discovered that Petrovsky wants to defect to America, or so he says. Don't worry," he replied hastily when he saw Commander Simms' mouth gape open in shock. "I took a few friends with as insurance."

Simms shook his head. "I don't trust that Russian as far as I can throw him! Why would he want to defect now? He's regarded as an icon in the Russian camp, and his exploits are as legendary as yours! Why would he give all that prestige up?"

Craig spread his arms out helplessly. "I don't know, Sir! He said he's becoming disillusioned because America is leading the race in space exploration and he is tired of being on the losing end. He said he wants to join us."

"I don't believe him!" Simms replied. "He's up to something."

"Well, Sir, I don't trust him either and that's why I've come to see you. He says that unless I organize his defection, he won't come to America. Petrovsky doesn't trust anyone else."

Simms stroked his chin thoughtfully. "You know, if he really means what he says, the information that he could provide us with would be priceless."

"Yes Sir, it certainly would. I guess he knew that because he provided me with a compact disc that has some interesting information on it. He said it was a sign of his good faith. I brought it along for you to see."

The Commander took it from his employee and placed it in his computer. They sat in silence until the disc ended and Commander Simms looked over at Craig. "It looks genuine though, but he really doesn't give out that much information."

"No Sir," Craig agreed, "however he does promise to give us more details after he has defected. I suppose this is just to convince us of his intentions. What should I do?"

"I must admit I'm tempted to go ahead with this so-called defection, Craig, but I do have reservations about it. If Petrovsky is genuinely interested in defecting, we will gain a very competent man, but this needs a lot of thought."

"Should I just tell his messengers to forget about the defection then, Sir?" asked Craig.

"I think you should meet with his contacts as he advised. Try to find out more about this arrangement and then report back to me. However, I don't want you to go alone at any time. Petrovsky only deals with professionals and you could be out of your depth. No offence Craig; your skills in hand to hand combat are legendary, but you cannot outrun a laser beam no matter how talented you are. The Russian hates you intensely and this could all be an elaborate trap. See that some policemen accompany you whenever you are negotiating with them."

"I'll do that, Sir. I promise to be very cautious."

Commander Simms took the disc out of his machine and handed it to his employee. "You may as well take this disc with you Craig. It doesn't have anything really classified on it. Just make sure you report back to me after your next meeting. Once you have more information, we'll take it from there."

Craig left his boss's office and went back home. He put the disc away in a drawer and went to do some errands.

The weekend arrived and Carter went back to the bar where he had met his contacts. Some policemen secretly followed him in and sat down at various tables. He didn't acknowledge their presence at all.

The explorer ordered a drink and sipped it reflectively. He took his time over it, as before. Several people sat down next to him and he spoke to them, wondering if one of them was his contact, but no one seemed interested in him. Carter had moved on to his second drink and still no one had approached him. He looked around the dimly lit bar and observed the people, making up stories about them just to pass the time. One particular woman was moving amongst the customers and smiling seductively. She disappeared once during the course of the evening and returned later, resuming her search for interested men.

Craig smiled wryly and thought that some things never changed. No matter how much technology advanced, there was always a need for female company. The woman wasn't unattractive he had to admit. She had long black hair and smiling green eyes, but she was too old for him. Anyway, he loved Constance too much to cheat on her, even for one night of passion.

As though she had read his thoughts, the prostitute came to his table. She smiled invitingly at the handsome young man.

"Hi handsome, I'm looking for some company and I noticed you were all alone! If your date has stood you up then she's a fool! I wouldn't let a man like you out of my sight! If you want some company, I'll be happy to oblige."

Craig grinned at her. "No, thank you. I appreciate the offer, but

I was expecting someone. I guess whoever I was supposed to meet isn't coming now. It's getting late and I'm not waiting any longer."

Carter downed his drink and put the glass on the table. As he began to get up, the woman sat down next to him and handed him a slip of paper.

"What's this for?" he asked curiously.

"That's my room number, Mr Carter," she whispered. "If you want more information on our mutual friend, meet me there in fifteen minutes. I get nervous around the law and we need to have a private chat. I promise not to seduce you, unless you want me to!" she grinned mischievously. "If you aren't at my door within fifteen minutes, then I'll assume you are no longer interested in the package."

She gave his hand an affectionate squeeze and left.

Craig headed for the restroom. One of the policemen got up and followed him. The man didn't look at Craig until another man who had been answering a call of nature, left the room. He checked that all the stalls were empty before speaking. "What's going on Craig? What did that woman want?"

"She's my contact apparently. I have to meet her in her room within fifteen minutes or the deal is off."

"You can't do that! We have orders to keep you in sight at all times," the policeman protested.

"I have to go!" he remarked stubbornly. "Her room number is twenty-five. If I'm longer than an hour then come and get me. Until then I must ask you to leave this to me."

The policeman wasn't happy. "I don't like this!" he complained.

"We have no choice," Carter replied.

Further protests were cut off by the arrival of another man who wanted to use the facilities and Craig left without another word, leaving the policeman to stare helplessly after him.

Craig knocked on the door of the prostitute's room and she let him in and waved him to a couch. She kicked off her high heeled shoes and rubbed her feet. "I hate these wretched things!" she complained. "They pinch my feet and I cannot understand why men seem to find them so attractive."

The space explorer smiled at her. "I suppose that comes from working undercover," he quipped.

She glared at him and suddenly began to laugh. "Oh, you are very funny! I have heard about you, Mr Carter, but Ivan has never told me about your humorous side."

"Probably because being around him was never a joke Miss … er?"

It was her turn to smile. "No names, Mr Carter. I was asked to speak with you and that is what I am doing. Would you like a drink before we begin?"

"No, thank you. I have already had enough for tonight."

She smiled and moved sensuously to the bar where she poured herself a drink. The woman placed it on the table between them and sat down, crossing one leg over the other. She glanced coquettishly at the man opposite her. "It's a pity you don't require my services! I'm good at my job and you would be amazed what I can do."

Craig smiled at her. "I have no doubt as to your abilities, but I have a wonderful girlfriend and she's all I need. Thanks for the offer, but no thanks. Can we discuss the other matter, miss?"

She shrugged her shoulders dismissively. "You come right to the point, don't you! Sure, why not."

She took a sip of her drink and placed it carefully down on the table once more. "First of all, the fact that you are here obviously means you're interested in the package. I noticed you when you first came into the bar and I purposely left you alone for so long because I needed to know how important this matter was. You watched the disc obviously."

Craig nodded.

"Am I to assume then that you are ready to continue with the negotiations?" she enquired.

"Well, let's just say I am interested. I need to know just how serious Ivan is about defecting. I have had many close encounters with him, so I'm naturally suspicious. The disc was interesting, but it didn't really tell me much. What I need from him is a little more information that could be useful to us."

"Such as what?" the prostitute enquired.

"Well I know there are some informants in high places and I want the names of at least two of them as a sign of good faith. If you can persuade Petrovsky to part with this information, then I'll continue with the negotiations."

The woman frowned at him. "Mr Carter, you are asking for something that could be difficult to obtain. Ivan may not like that!"

Carter shrugged his shoulders indifferently. "Miss, if Petrovsky really means to defect, then he'll provide me with the information. I have to assume that if he is really serious about defecting, then we will learn these things anyway. Once he comes over to America, there will be no turning back. Until I have this information, I'll not discuss the matter further."

The prostitute sighed and brushed a piece of hair away from her eyes. Craig looked at this beautiful woman and couldn't resist asking her some questions. "How did a woman like you get involved with someone like Petrovsky?" he asked curiously.

She looked at him over the rim of her glass and their eyes met. "Mr Carter, things are never what they seem. I owe Ivan for helping me out of a difficult situation that I foolishly managed to get involved in. In exchange, he enlisted my help. It's none of your business, but I'm not really a prostitute. I do sleep with men as part of my job though, but only if this is required. Most of my clients are pre-selected. It's amazing what men tell me when I'm intimate with them."

Instinctively Craig believed her. He wondered if she was a government agent, but decided not to ask her, knowing she would probably deny it anyway.

Carter stood up and stretched. "Well Miss, whoever you are, I'm going to leave now. It's been a long day and I'm tired. Will you give the message to your friend for me?"

"Yes, Mr Carter, I'll tell him what you want. I'll be in touch."

She remained seated while he let himself out. Only when he had climbed into his car did he realize he hadn't given her his address. He debated whether he should go back, but decided against it. If Petrovsky was truly keen on defecting, he would find a way to relay the information, Craig was certain of that.

He started his car and drove away.

CHAPTER 18

One week later he opened his door and found a tiny data storage disc taped to it. There were no markings identifying where it had come from and he shook it experimentally, but nothing happened. He took the device inside and placed it on his dining room table where he noticed an indicator light flashing. He pressed the "start" icon and a message began to scroll down on a holographic background.

"Comrade, here is a present for you. I have enclosed another disc for you to look at. I understand your reluctance to believe me and I suppose if the situation had been reversed, I would expect the same commitment from you. On this disc are the names of two of our operatives currently active in your country. I understand they will have to be checked out and the data analyzed before you believe me. Your government has two weeks to investigate and then I want to finalize my trip. If you delay even one extra day, I will withdraw my offer.

"Now I too have some conditions that need to be met. When your people have verified I'm telling the truth, I want to deal solely with you. Have your security people do whatever is necessary to get me safely over to America and then I don't want to see another policeman shadowing you. If I see anything suspicious, our deal is off. I must state this emphatically! Hope to see you soon comrade!"

The space explorer took the disc and placed it in his mobile device, on computer mode. He watched as the faces of two people appeared on screen, together with their personal details. Carter watched in shock and disbelief at the screen for he knew both very well. One was Commander Simms' secretary and the other was someone in the space police force. He couldn't believe his eyes, yet he knew Ivan Petrovsky was telling the truth. Only then did he believe his arch enemy truly wanted to defect.

Carter felt numb and watched the blank screen, deep in thought. After a while he snapped out of his reverie and removed the disc from his machine. He hurried to Mission Control to inform his boss what he had learned.

When he arrived, he was met by Commander Simms' secretary and it took all his self-control to act as though nothing was wrong. Fortunately, his boss was in his office and Craig went in, closing the door behind him. He sat down heavily on the chair and rubbed his hands tiredly over his eyes.

"Craig, what's wrong?" his boss asked. "Has something gone wrong with the plans?"

Mutely his employee handed over the disc. "I think this is self-explanatory Sir. You should look at it yourself and then you'll understand."

Commander Simms looked enquiringly at his employee and then read the holographic letter. Laying it down on his desk, he placed the disc into his machine. The young man watched as the same emotions flitted over his boss's face. When he finished viewing the disc, he took it out of the machine with hands that shook slightly. "Craig, do you believe this? Isn't our mutual friend making this up to stall us?"

Carter shook his head. "I don't think so, Sir. He knows you'll investigate this thoroughly, and you should! Don't just take his word for it."

"Obviously I'll do that! My secretary!" he groaned. "Who would have believed it possible? She has top secret information on all of my employees, including you."

Craig sighed. "I suppose so and that does explain a lot, but I already knew that Petrovsky had my file. After all, Sir, we have his history as well. This is a competitive world that we live in and you can just bet he has a lot more spies around whom we have no knowledge of."

"You're quite correct, Craig. Well, I guess I can't just fire Betty without any reason."

"No, unfortunately not Sir, but you can give the relevant information to someone you know you can trust and let them deal with it. You have two weeks to uncover their treason, before I make contact with our friend's helpers. Afterwards I have to go solo."

"That's another matter that concerns me greatly Craig. You've had your share of narrow escapes but you aren't a professional spy. We both know just how determined that Russian is to capture you. Maybe this is just another scheme to get you."

Craig shook his head. "No Sir, that's not how he works. I'm in space often and Petrovsky knows he can get me there anytime, or at least he can try. Why would he risk exposure and give up two of his own people in exchange for our help? I also wasn't convinced in the beginning, but that has changed now. I have to do this, for the good of America!"

Simms sighed. "Very well then Craig, you must do what you can, and so must I. Sit tight and I'll take it from here. I'll be in touch soon, I promise."

Craig left the building with mixed feelings. He wondered what his boss was going to do about the two traitors, but it wasn't his problem any longer.

↓ ↓ ↓

The next two weeks passed slowly for Craig. Despite reassurances from his boss, he still agonized over the two traitors and wondered what had made them betray their country. After a week, Craig was asked to come into the office. When he arrived, he noticed Betty was no longer there.

He knocked on the door and went inside when summoned. Simms waved him to a chair and he sat down. Commander Simms looked tired and irritable. "Craig, I gave that disc to some friends of mine and they went over it with a fine tooth comb. The fingerprints lifted from the disc did indeed come from Ivan Petrovsky, so he genuinely handled it. Of course, yours were on there, as well as mine, but that was to be expected. We investigated Betty's background and discovered when she gave her allegiance to Russia. It seems Colonel Ivan Petrovsky was a very devious man and she had no choice. I'm not defending her mind you, because she could have told me about it, but she chose not to and instead she betrayed my trust. It appears she has a gambling problem and got into trouble with a casino owner who threatened to expose her when she couldn't find the money to pay her gambling debts, which were considerable as I understand. The casino owner was prepared to employ underhand methods to obtain the money. Somehow Ivan Petrovsky got to hear about it and stepped in to help. Her debt was cleared and when she promised she would pay him back, he told her not to worry. Instead he asked her to spy for him and obtain classified information. Betty didn't like the idea one bit, but she had no choice. She knew if she didn't comply with his conditions, her career would be over, so she did it. The staff believe she is on leave, but in fact she has been fired. The police have her at a secret location where they are interrogating her. Russia's man in the police force is also 'on leave', but there I have left the sordid details to his superiors and they will do with him whatever they feel is right. I want no part in that."

Commander Simms went to his liquor cabinet and poured himself a stiff drink. Craig didn't comment and when he was offered something, declined. His boss put the glass down on his table and pushed over another small data disc.

"This is what we have managed to put together so far. On that disc, you'll find the details of a light aircraft. The pilot's contact numbers are on it and it is up to you to organize the finer details. This man is a mercenary who works for the highest bidder and is prepared to pick up the 'package', but he doesn't know who the person is, nor does he care. I've paid him half his fee and the rest will be given to him on completion of the delivery. When you see Petrovsky's contact again, tell him or her of your plan and stress this must take place very soon. Once you have everything in place, you'll be given the address of a 'safe house' where you are to take him. I'm not happy you'll be doing this alone, but he kept his part of the bargain, so we must do the same with ours. All I can say is, 'good luck' Craig."

"Thank you, Sir," he replied sincerely. "I'll get him over here I promise."

Commander Simms shook his hand and the explorer left the building. He went home where he began to read the arrangements that had been made for the defection.

He spent the next few days planning Ivan Petrovsky's escape.

Exactly two weeks to the date, Craig returned to the bar and sat down in the corner booth. He ordered his drink and waited for someone to contact him. Even though the place was full he couldn't help feeling vulnerable, for this time he had come alone. There were no police shadowing him.

When he had finished his second drink, he noticed a familiar figure doing the rounds. The "prostitute" was greeting some men and he watched as she bent down to someone who whispered in her ear. Her dress was low cut and her excellent cleavage could clearly be seen. Craig's breath caught in his throat when he heard her giggle throatily and give the man an affectionate squeeze on his thigh. They spoke quietly for a few moments and then she came and sat down at Craig's table. She kissed him on the cheek and smiled at him. Almost immediately a waitress appeared and handed her a drink. She set another one down by Craig.

The stunning woman leaned over and whispered in his ear. Her breath sent shivers of delight down his spine. "All right Mr Carter, I assume the powers that be are happy with the information I gave you. Now have your drink and then you must come to my room. We have much to discuss."

She turned and smiled at the man she had obviously propositioned earlier and he waved back.

"What about him?" The explorer asked curiously.

She laughed softly. "I told him you are my brother and also my pimp. I mentioned to him that we have some business to transact and then I will return to him in about an hour, if he is still interested, and he will be, I guarantee it!"

Craig wondered idly what secrets the man had that Russia required and he felt sorry for the unsuspecting man.

He finished his drink and so did his companion. Then, arm in arm they returned to her room. Once she had locked the door and kicked off her high heeled shoes, she stretched her long legs out on the couch. Craig eyed them appraisingly and she watched him. "You know, Mr Carter, it's such a pity that our arrangement is just business. I would do you for free if you wanted me to."

The young man shook his head. "No thanks! I appreciate the offer and I must admit it is very tempting, but as I said before, I have a girlfriend."

"All right then, it's your loss," she replied as she took off her jacket and threw it over the back of another chair. She turned back to her visitor. "The fact you are here must mean you were satisfied with the information Ivan gave you."

"I was indeed," he assented.

"I noticed you left your minders behind this time, too. Excellent! So now let's get down to business."

Craig handed a small disc to her and she placed it in a reading device. They sat in silence while she read through the plan.

When she finished reading the documents, she nodded her head approvingly. "This is very good and should all go according to plan. I like your idea of having the aircraft land in this disused warehouse. It will make the transition so much easier for Ivan if he does this inside a building. I know the area where this warehouse is and it's remote enough not to arouse suspicion. How are you going to transport Ivan to a safe location though? I see no mention of this in your notes."

"I'll park my car down one of the alleys and take him personally. As you said, there must be no police involvement and I intend to honour that. Once the colonel has landed, I will be waiting for him."

The woman looked up quizzically. "You aren't accompanying the pilot to Russia then? Are you sure your pilot will do as you ask?"

"He will follow orders, I guarantee that."

The "prostitute" shook her head. "I'm sorry, Mr Carter, but unless you accompany the pilot to Russia, the deal is off. I can tell you now that Ivan will not accept anything less."

A knot formed in Craig's stomach and he felt uneasy. The woman saw his change of expression and stared piercingly at him. "Mr Carter, has Ivan not met all your demands? Why would he have allowed things to progress this far if he didn't mean what he said? I know how you feel about Russia, but you will be on Russian soil maybe ten minutes at the most. Surely that isn't too much to ask? Think about what you will get in return."

Craig had to concede they were getting a very good deal in exchange for a tiny bit of inconvenience. "All right Miss, you have a deal. Tell Ivan I'll accompany the pilot to Russia."

She smiled and got off the couch. "That's wonderful, Mr Carter. I'll contact you in a few days to make the final arrangements."

"So soon?" he asked disbelievingly. "Can he do this in such a short time?"

"Mr Carter, Ivan has been ready for months," she replied.

Their business had been concluded and the young explorer got up and extended his hand to the woman. She gripped it firmly and shook it.

"I'll be in touch!" she promised. "It has been a pleasure meeting you."

"Same here. I'll wait for your instructions."

Craig Carter returned home and the next day he contacted his boss. Commander Simms was very unhappy about the news that he should go to Russia, but reluctantly gave his permission.

Four days later Craig found himself on the light aircraft bound for Russia. The address he was to take Ivan when they returned was ingrained in his memory. The pilot spoke to him during the journey, but when Craig probed a little deeper and wanted to know why he did what he did, he replied offhandedly "It's a living."

When they arrived in Russia, Craig stared out of the window of the plane at the swirling whiteness below. The wind whipped the snow against the windscreen and the wipers barely managed to clear it away.

The airport soon came into view and Carter marvelled at the ingeniousness of the decision for it was a deserted airport which had once been occupied by elite Russian troops. The pilot landed without even a bump and opened the passenger door. Craig looked around but saw no one. He hesitated briefly at the door of the aircraft and then gingerly put his feet down on Russian soil. Here he knew he was at his most vulnerable and suppressed a shudder at the thought of what could happen if the tables were turned. His hand moved to his waist and he felt the comforting presence of his laser gun in its holster. He waited a few minutes longer, but no one appeared. He took a few steps towards the hangars and only then did a figure emerge from within the building. It stooped against the howling wind and came towards him. The explorer went to meet him. Both met in the middle of the deserted airstrip and Colonel Ivan Petrovsky pushed his fur-lined hood away from his head. His sparkling brown eyes looked into his enemy's ones and he grabbed his rescuer's hand and shook it firmly.

"Good to see you Comrade! You kept your promise!"

"Did you doubt me Petrovsky?" Carter asked.

The Russian shrugged. "I know how you feel about my country and I had serious doubts that you would come. I'm glad to see that they were unfounded."

Craig looked out into the distance and saw cars approaching at speed. He glared at Petrovsky. "Who are they?' he demanded angrily.

Petrovsky gave him a shove towards the plane. "It was obviously an unfortunate miscalculation on my part Comrade! It seems our secret deal wasn't so secret after all. I had noticed my superiors have been especially interested in my movements over the last week or so! I suggest we hurry before they get here. My government will not be happy to see me leave and they intend to use whatever means necessary to ensure that I stay."

Carter didn't need any further prompting and together they sprinted for the plane. They dived in and buckled their seatbelts just as some jeeps skidded to a halt on the deserted airfield. The pilot of the light aircraft had already started the engines and was taxiing away from the troops. He managed to get the plane airborne and gasped as some laser beams danced around his plane, but fortunately they missed and he was out of range before they could fire again. Despite the temperature, Craig found he was sweating and he mopped his forehead with a gloved hand.

"That was too close for comfort!" he gulped. "It was lucky your people are such lousy shots!"

Petrovsky looked back at the airfield, where the people now resembled dolls. He made no comment.

CHAPTER 19

After they touched down in the abandoned warehouse, both men got out. "Welcome to America, Comrade!" Craig smiled.

Petrovsky smiled, but the gesture didn't quite reach his eyes. "Thank you, Mr Carter, but you'll pardon me if I don't seem overly excited. Russia has been part of my life for many years and it will be hard to say goodbye."

"I understand," his rival replied. "I would feel the same way if the tables were turned."

Carter watched as Petrovsky looked around cautiously. "Now you are sure that there will be no unwelcome guests?" he asked. "We will proceed alone to your safe house?"

"As I promised," Craig replied.

"And there are no elite troops or snipers hiding inside or outside this building?"

Craig became impatient. "No, we are alone. No one will see this go down and we should reach our final destination without incident, I guarantee it. Why, are you having second thoughts?"

Petrovsky smiled lazily. "No, things are going according to plan."

Something in his voice alerted Carter, who stiffened. He became uneasy for some reason and took a step back. "I think we should get going. My car is parked outside and time is of the essence. I have this creepy feeling we are being watched."

Petrovsky smiled again. "Well I did see some homeless people outside when we arrived. They seem harmless enough though. Perhaps we should shoot them, just to make sure," he grinned.

"Oh, that's very funny! I saw them but most of them are so wasted on booze I doubt they even know we exist. It's not them I'm worried about."

Craig scanned the rafters and thought he saw a movement.

"I'm sure someone is up there. Come on, let's get out of here!"

Still Petrovsky made no move to leave. "Your imagination is running riot my friend. If you haven't brought anyone with, then there is nothing to worry about."

Carter scanned the upper areas and watched in disbelief as many people suddenly appeared. Everyone held long range rifles and they were pointed at the two men below. He looked nervously at his companion, who didn't seem perturbed at all and suddenly everything became clear.

"I know these aren't my people so they must be yours," he said angrily. "It's a trap!"

Petrovsky clapped his hands approvingly. "I knew you weren't stupid! You are correct, of course."

"You never intended to defect, did you? Craig growled.

They were interrupted by the pilot. "Hey, I only agreed to fly this man here! I want nothing to do with this. Whatever the two of you intend to do, I don't care. I want to leave."

Petrovsky turned to the man and smiled wickedly. "Oh sorry, I guess we failed to tell you that your services were no longer required. I hope you got paid well for this little adventure, because your family could use the money, seeing as they will have to pay for a funeral soon!"

Before Craig's astonished eyes, Petrovsky produced a hidden weapon and in cold blood shot the man through the heart. The pilot looked disbelievingly at his executor and fingered the blossoming stain on his chest, before crumpling to the ground in a heap. The space explorer spun around, determined to attack his nemesis, but Petrovsky pointed his gun at the man who had just "liberated" him.

"Uh uh, don't be foolish my friend! Hand over your weapon immediately, barrel first. I will hurt you and you know I mean what I say."

Carter looked up at all the guns pointed in his direction and handed over his laser gun as instructed. The Colonel slid it into his waistband. "Thank you, now the rest of your little toys if you please."

Craig blinked stupidly at him. "I don't know what you're talking about."

Petrovsky sighed and a laser beam just missed Craig's foot. "Has that jogged your memory?" he asked casually.

"Okay! Okay! Just wait a second!" Carter grumbled.

He reached slowly into a hidden pocket and took out a smaller laser gun. It looked like a toy but it was capable of firing several charges before the built-in battery went flat. This he also handed over very reluctantly. Petrovsky looked expectantly at him.

"What now?" Craig demanded.

"I think you have another little surprise hidden away somewhere. Give it to me now, or the next shot will pierce your knee and shatter it. You have ten seconds!"

The space explorer muttered under his breath and threw a knife at Petrovsky's feet. The blade became embedded up to the hilt, in a packing case.

"Thank you, Mr Carter. Now do you have any other surprises you'd like to tell me about?"

Craig glared at him. "Sorry, I left my rocket launcher and stun grenades in my other pants. I would have brought them along but I wasn't expecting any trouble. Silly me!" he replied sarcastically.

His humour was lost on the Colonel who looked contentedly at his prisoner.

"Why did you bother going to all this trouble?" Craig asked him. "You've had plenty of opportunity to come after me so why this elaborate scheme?"

Ivan Petrovsky laughed. "I had to give you some form of incentive so you would be caught off guard and I knew this plot to defect would please your country immensely. You see, I know how valuable you are to your government and you knew of course how valuable I was to mine. I dangled a carrot and you took the bait. The whole point of the plan was to make you handle the 'defection' alone, without support from your police force. Now you are all alone and I'm holding all the winning cards."

"It still doesn't make any sense to me! Why did you sacrifice two of your spies? We never knew about them."

"They were part of the bait that I'm talking about. You asked for a show of good faith and I handed them to you on a silver platter. You see they were going to be terminated anyway, so I just used them to make the deal more attractive. Commander Simms' secretary was a liability because she began to enjoy her job too much. She was beginning to feel guilty about her gambling problem and had decided to tell her boss what she had done. Her loyalty was shifting to your side and I couldn't allow that to happen. As for that idiot in the police force; he was useful but he started getting too greedy and demanded exorbitant sums of money in exchange for information. He had to be stopped and your government did that on my behalf. Did you know he shot himself when his colleagues went to arrest him?"

Carter remained silent and Petrovsky continued. "Well my noble friend, I suppose you would like to know what my plans are now that I have you?"

"Not really Petrovsky but I suppose you'll tell me anyway. What was the point of that display in Russia when your government pursued us?"

The Colonel smiled indulgently. "It was just a matter of simple theatrics, nothing more. I just thought the 'chase' would add authenticity to my so-called defection."

"It is obvious your government were in on the scheme from the beginning, then," he grumbled.

"They were," the Russian confessed.

"All right so what do you intend to do with me now?"

"I wasn't sure what to do with you when I finally had you in my clutches, but I have thought of a brilliant scheme. I could make you tell me secrets about your control centre by torturing you, but that is just time consuming and messy, so I discarded that idea."

Craig looked at the manpower at his enemy's disposal. His eyes roamed around the rafters, taking in the position of everyone around him.

"What brilliant scheme have you concocted then, my Russian friend?" he asked, stroking the man's ego.

"Oh, you'll love this, I guarantee it! I'm going to hold you hostage and make your boss pay for your safe release."

"Oh dear, has your government cut your pocket money?" he sneered. "Do you need a loan?"

Some of Petrovsky's friends snickered and he shot them a withering look.

In that instant, Craig sprang into action. He swiftly pulled a knife out of a holster under his arm and hurled it at Petrovsky. The man screamed in agony as the weapon pierced his arm. The movement was so sudden that it took everyone by surprise and Carter dived for the safety of some heavy crates. He heard Petrovsky swear loudly. "Get him you fools! Don't kill him, but incapacitate him any way you see fit. I'll make him pay for this!"

Gunfire hit the crates but Carter had already dashed for the next pile. Every step brought him closer to the entrance, but it was a desperate gamble and there were many shooters above him.

Craig stood up suddenly and watched in slow motion as someone aimed at him. There was no more cover left to hide behind and he watched in a daze as the man's finger tightened on the trigger. Suddenly from behind him, gunfire erupted and the sniper screamed, toppling off the rafters and slammed with a sickening thud on the concrete floor below.

The young man spun around and saw several homeless people brandishing weapons. They ran inside and began shooting at Petrovsky's friends. Someone threw a weapon to him and he waved in thanks, but he wasn't interested in any of the hired help. He was determined to capture Colonel Ivan Petrovsky and hand him over to the police.

Ignoring the beams that danced around him, he saw Petrovsky heading for the plane and fired a shot. It hit the aircraft and left a small hole, but it wasn't enough to damage the craft severely. Petrovsky fired a shot but it missed and whizzed past his opponent's ear. Carter kept coming, determined this time he would have the victory he so desperately desired.

All Petrovsky's friends were no longer interested in the two men fighting below. They were more concerned about saving their own lives as they shot at the people who began storming into the building.

Craig and Ivan fought like maniacs, each determined to cause the other great harm. The colonel's weapon was kicked out of his hand and he grunted in pain as his enemy's shoe connected none too gently with his already wounded arm. Despite the pain, Petrovsky managed to punch his enemy hard on the jaw, making him stagger back in surprise. He slipped on the fallen weapon and grabbed for it just as Ivan dived into the plane.

Carter tried to grab onto the door, but it closed painfully on his hand and he yelled in surprise and outrage when he saw his quarry was going to escape. The craft began to move and picked up speed, taxiing out of the hangar. Several policemen realized too late what was happening and they shot at the light aircraft, but it was too far out of range and they could only watch helplessly as the Russian colonel disappeared over the horizon.

Craig yelled in frustration at the loss of his worst enemy.

The fighting soon came to an end and those who still lived were led out of the hangar and placed in waiting police cars. Several of Petrovsky's friends would never move again and the young man was upset about the unnecessary loss of life. He berated himself for not having realized that no matter how sincere Colonel Ivan Petrovsky sounded, he was and always would be, a liar. He vowed never to trust the man again.

A "homeless" person came up to him, and he remembered seeing her scratching in the dustbins when he first arrived. She removed her dirty grey wig and smiled up at him with her incredible blue eyes. Craig hugged her gratefully. "Helen Spencer, it's so good to see you again! You saved my life!"

"All in the line of duty,' she smiled. "I guess you're pretty lucky to have a boss like Commander Simms. Despite your assurances that the Russian colonel was really telling the truth, he didn't believe it and organized a task force to go to the warehouse. He smelt a rat and it was him who saved your life, not me."

Craig put his arm companionably around the policewoman's waist. "Well I'm grateful to all of you for what you've done today. If you hadn't been here, it would have been a totally different story."

Helen nudged him playfully. "No, you are a survivor and I'm sure you would have managed somehow, but still I'm glad we could help."

"So am I," Craig replied as he reclaimed his weapons and stashed them away in their various places.

Helen Spencer watched and laughed. "Wow, you carry a veritable arsenal around with you!"

He looked at her and replied seriously. "Well you can't be too careful these days. Crime is rampant and I need to protect myself."

She shook her head and went to join her colleagues in rounding up the men and women who were being led out to the prison vans. Craig stayed nearby until the last of the prisoners were loaded into the waiting police vans that seemed to have materialized out of nowhere. They began to drive away and Carter approached Helen Spencer. "Thanks once again for your help, Helen! I think I had better go and see Commander Simms now. He'll want to know what happened."

"Go and do that Craig. I also need to leave now. I'll be in touch after we have questioned the prisoners."

"Thanks again Helen! I owe you a drink."

"Excellent, and when I have a free moment, I'll take you up on that offer!"

Helen waved to him and the convoy of police vehicles moved off.

Carter climbed into his vehicle and headed to Mission Control. When he arrived, he was told to go into his boss's office immediately.

The young man did so, but was embarrassed to face his boss, so looked down at his shoes. "Sir, I don't know how to apologize for the foolish way I behaved. I honestly believed Colonel Petrovsky was telling the truth when he said he wanted to defect. Instead it was just an elaborate plan to capture me. When will I ever learn?"

Surprisingly Commander Simms wasn't angry. He put a reassuring hand on his employee's shoulder. "Don't be too hard on yourself, Son. Petrovsky has a silver tongue and can be very convincing when he puts his mind to it. It's part of his charm!"

"I know, because he sure fooled me! Sir, I owe you my life! If you hadn't mobilized the police when you did, I don't think I would be here right now. Petrovsky wanted to hold me to ransom, or so he says, but there had to be another ulterior motive. I doubt whether I would have seen America ever again, had he succeeded."

"I agree with you. Well, anyway his plan failed dismally and all is well once again," Simms replied kindly.

"Well I can guarantee you, he'll never fool me again. I won't fall for his lies next time."

"I believe you! I'm glad you were unharmed, so go home and take it easy. I should have another mission for you within a few days. I'm just waiting for confirmation from the planets where you'll be going."

Craig left his boss and climbed into his helicar. He had an inexplicable urge to visit his girlfriend and hold her tightly. When he contacted her from his vehicle, she answered almost immediately and replied she would wait for him. He drove to her flat and she was waiting for him at the gate. They embraced tenderly and Craig kissed Constance passionately. They clung together like two lovers who had been apart for a year instead of just a few days.

Finally, he pulled away from her and stroked her cheek gently.

"Some days I don't know how I would ever manage without you," he sighed. "I seem to get into trouble on a regular basis. It must be some kind of record!"

"You certainly do have your share of the action, there's no denying that," she agreed. "However, I don't think it's anything unusual. Our jobs are dangerous most of the time anyway. I guess we just learn to deal with it."

"Well, there's nothing dangerous lurking in your flat I imagine!"

"Come inside and I'll make you something to drink. Are you hungry?"

As if in response to her question, Craig's stomach rumbled and he rubbed it. "I guess I am at that. I'll accept your offer!" Constance took his hand and led him inside.

After they had eaten, they sat in the lounge drinking their beverages. Craig's eyes fell on a picture of Constance's grandmother and the memory of how she had died returned to haunt him. He put the information out of his mind and reached for his girlfriend's hand. "How are you feeling lately Constance?"

She looked at the picture of her grandmother and smiled sadly. "I still miss her of course, but every day it becomes a little more bearable. I look forward to the day when it won't hurt as much anymore."

"I hear you," her boyfriend responded. "Yet always remember that as long as you keep her memory close to your heart, she'll always be with you and no one can ever change that."

Miss Gregg walked to the picture of her grandmother and stroked the lined face gently. "I know that," she replied softly. "You know, some nights I imagine she's close by, watching over me. It comforts me somehow."

"She loved you, as you loved her," he replied simply. "There's nothing wrong with the way that you feel. You were lucky to have known her."

"I know," she sighed. "She was my rock when I needed it the most. I know she had her idiosyncrasies, but I understood her. Even when everyone else thought she had lost her mind I knew it wasn't true. I guess her behaviour was a little odd, but she made life interesting – for me anyway."

"She certainly had a way about her," Craig mused. He thought about Beth's uncanny way of seeming to know what he was thinking. Despite the old lady's odd mannerisms, Craig had liked her and he too felt the void inside.

He pushed the depressing thought from his mind and gently held his girlfriend. He stroked her hair and their lips met in a gentle, probing kiss. Their drinks were forgotten as they came together in love and passion and soon all they could think about was the moment. Everything sad and depressing fled from their minds as the world ceased to exist.

CHAPTER 20

A few days later Craig boarded his spacecraft. He had a cargo hold full of various articles for some of the planets he would be visiting and was excited at the prospect of seeing his friends again. His first stop was Neptune where he would see Lolita and her family again.

He touched down on the dry, barren surface of Neptune and as usual Lolita was waiting for him. She launched herself at him and he hugged her wet body tightly. "Oh Lolita, it's so good to see you again!"

"Really?" she asked excitedly, her eyes shining with delight.

Carter laughed, and kissed the top of her head. "You know how fond I am of you, dear girl. You are like a sister to me and you know that."

The Neptunian princess smiled at him in a way that made his heart melt and he took her hand. "Come along and let's go to the palace."

They linked hands and jumped simultaneously into the water.

When they reached the palace, Craig was told to go inside. He met the King in the throne room and bowed reverently. "Your Majesty, it is an honour to stand in your presence."

The King smiled and embraced the explorer in a bear hug that took his breath away. "Craig, it has been too long! I have missed you!"

"It has been a while," the space explorer agreed. "Our planets are far from one another and time seems to catch up with us always."

The ruler of Neptune rang a bell which summoned one of his servants. "Get Mr Carter some refreshment," he ordered.

The man bowed and went to do his master's bidding.

The two friends spoke for a while and exchanged news about their planets. Supplies that had been ordered by Neptune were offloaded from Craig's spacecraft and taken to their respective recipients. Afterwards, the King took his friend on a tour of their latest spaceships. His designers had made a few improvements on their crafts and Craig's opinion was sought on these. He marvelled at the technology which was improving in leaps and bounds.

That evening he was invited to dine with the Royal family and was treated to a feast. During the meal, one of the serving stewards brought a large bowl of shimmering green liquid to the table. The liquid was poured into crystal glasses and handed to the guests who were seated around the large table.

The King raised his goblet and stood up. "A toast to our esteemed guest!" he exclaimed as he indicated to Craig, who squirmed in embarrassment.

"Your Majesty, this isn't necessary I assure you. I have done nothing to deserve this!"

"Nonsense young man, your feats are legendary and it is right that we honour them," he replied as he took a sip.

"To Craig Carter!" everyone murmured, and the young man smiled shyly.

The King downed his goblet in a few sips and reached for some more of the liquid, but Craig had only taken a sip before he put the drink down. It reminded him of greasy seaweed and made his stomach lurch. He pushed it away, but by this time the King had refilled his cup once again. Noticing that his guest had not had anything, the ruler addressed him. "I can't get enough of this stuff. Go on, drink!"

Carter smiled apologetically. "Sire, I mean no disrespect but this is just too rich for my taste. I will decline if you don't mind. What is it?"

The King reached for his guest's cup and drank the contents. "It would be a shame to waste this, young man, but I suppose we all have different tastes. It is a new plant we have discovered. One of my servants found it by accident and brewed it like one would do with the beverage called tea on your planet. It is left to boil for a long time and this causes it to ferment and give off the most wonderful fragrance. For the past month or so it has been my favourite drink. It invigorates me!"

Craig looked at the King and smiled, but he was more than a little perturbed by the King's appearance. His face looked flushed and his eyes were a little too bright. Craig exchanged a glance with the Queen who shrugged her shoulders.

By the time the meal was finished, the King had ingested a great deal of the green liquid. His wife took his hand gently.

"It's late now and His Majesty is tired. I think it is time for us to retire."

The remaining guests stood up respectfully and waited for their King and Queen to leave the building. Craig watched them go and his sharp eyes didn't miss the tremor in the King's hands and the slightly unsteady walk as he leaned against his wife. The explorer couldn't believe his eyes as he had never seen the King of Neptune in that condition. He was obviously drunk and a feeling of unease settled on Carter, but he waved it away. Soon after that the remainder of the guests left the dining room and returned to their homes.

The next morning Craig was woken by an urgent knock on his door. He went to open it and one of the servants bowed to him.

"Mr Carter, forgive the interruption but Her Majesty wishes to see you in the parlour urgently."

Craig hurried to change into his clothes and went to see the Queen. He was horrified by the sight of her. The space explorer had never seen the Queen without her customary make up and every hair always in place. The woman who faced him had red rings around her eyes and her hair was dishevelled.

When she laid eyes on him, she rushed into his arms and he held her, not sure what else to do. "Your Majesty, what's wrong?" he asked gently.

The Queen burst into tears once again and sobbed against his chest. "It's my husband," she wailed. "I went in this morning to wake him because he had overslept. He always wakes up before me, but today he didn't get up. Craig, it was horrible!"

"What happened?" he demanded.

The Queen continued to sob and the servant whispered in his ear. "Perhaps you should come and see for yourself."

Gently Craig extricated himself from the woman's arms and followed the servant to the king's bedchamber. The Queen shuffled behind like a robot, but she held onto Craig's hand as if she was afraid that he would disappear at any moment.

The threesome entered the bedroom and Craig closed the door against prying eyes. He made his way to the bed and stared down at the King. An involuntary gasp escaped his lips and he stared transfixed at the King. The ruler of Neptune lay in his bed and his eyes were closed. He seemed to be asleep, but something was very wrong, for he was a sickly shade of green. Anxiously Craig stretched out his hand and moved the sleeve of the King's nightgown up slightly. The Neptunian was green from the top of his head to the tips of his toes. His skin was icy cold. Carter felt for a pulse and sighed with relief when he found one. It was slow but steady, yet the King was obviously in a coma for he didn't respond to the gentle prodding of his friend. Craig spent a few moments trying to rouse the Ruler, to no avail. He turned to the servant and issued instructions.

"Bring the royal physician here immediately, but tell him nothing. Do this quietly and see that no one else is alerted. We don't want to alarm anyone."

The servant nodded and left the room, closing the door behind him. The Queen sat down on the bed and buried her head in her hands. "What am I going to do?" she wailed. "My husband had various meetings scheduled for today! What am I to tell the delegates who will be arriving?"

"When is the first meeting supposed to take place?"

"Not before 11 a.m. today," she replied, "but from that time onwards, he was due to be busy in meetings all day."

The Queen looked down at her prostrate husband and the tears began to fall anew.

Carter gently put his hand on her knee and she covered it with one of hers. "Listen to me Your Majesty," he replied earnestly. "I need you to be strong now and so does the King. You must be calm and think of what you are to say to those who have meetings scheduled. If you can deal with some of the issues, then do so. However, if you feel incapable of doing anything constructive, and no one would blame you if you did, then you must tell the guests that your husband has taken ill. Assure them that it is just a minor bug, and then have his secretary cancel all his appointments until we know what is wrong with him."

"I … I cannot face anyone today!" she sniffed. "I don't know what to do!"

The space explorer shook her gently but firmly. "Your Highness, please try to be calm! Once the doctor has been, you must go to your chambers and get dressed. Comb your hair and wash your face. Neptune needs you! You *can* do this!" he assured her.

She clung to him, drawing strength from his assurances. "Yes, you are right, of course! I must think of my people."

The doctor arrived and they were asked to move into another room while he conducted his examination. When he had finished, he called them in. "I've conducted some tests and it seems as though he has been poisoned by some organic substance. Has he been acting strange lately Your Majesty?"

The Queen thought about it. "I can't think of anything specific," she mused.

"Well has he added anything new to his diet for example?"

"He has been drinking plenty of that strange green liquid, Your Majesty," Craig replied. "Come to think of it, his skin colour is exactly like that of the drink you said he had begun to enjoy not long ago."

The Queen turned to her friend. "Oh, surely that cannot be the problem! He has been drinking that beverage for a few months already. Why would it only start affecting him now?"

Craig shrugged his shoulders helplessly. "I don't know, but your physician will need to look into this and report his findings. Your Majesty, time is moving on and you must go and get ready to meet with the delegates. I will liaise with the doctor and one of us will definitely report back to you. For now, you can do nothing for your husband, but reassure your people that nothing is amiss."

The Queen darted a worried look at the physician and he smiled reassuringly. "Craig is quite right Your Majesty. I'll get to the bottom of this and report back to you. Meanwhile don't allow anyone to enter this room, with the exception of myself. I have to do some tests. Before you leave though, I shall give you something to calm you down."

He produced a syringe and injected the Queen in her arm.

She left the room and her servant began to follow her, but Craig called him back. "Wait just a moment. I have some questions for you."

When the Queen was out of earshot, he questioned the servant. "Can you tell me where that green liquid originated from? I saw many people drinking it last night. It seems to be very popular."

"It is Mr Carter. Someone discovered it growing in an isolated area and tasted the leaves. You know how adventurous young people can be, I'm sure. Well one of the children decided to brew it like tea and found it most enjoyable. I think some of Lolita's friends most probably introduced it to her and she must have brought it to show her father. He obviously enjoyed it and the rest you know."

Craig's stomach clenched nervously but he kept his face impassive. "Thank you. You may return to your duties now, but you are under strict orders to keep this incident quiet. If word of this gets out, I will hold you personally responsible for the ensuing chaos."

The servant gawked at Craig but he nodded his head obsequiously. "I will say nothing, I swear."

Once he had left, Carter was worried and the royal physician glanced curiously at him. "Is something wrong, Mr Carter?"

"I think something is very wrong doctor! I only arrived here yesterday, but every time I looked at the King or stood in his presence, he was drinking this stuff. I don't mean the odd sip though; he drank it as though nothing else even existed. I think it has addictive properties and this led to him being poisoned. Go and run your tests, but quickly! I need to find out where this stuff originated from. I don't want the King to get worse. We can talk later. You know where to find me if you need me."

The two beings shook hands and went their separate ways.

Craig took another look at his friend before shutting the door behind him. He had no wish to instil panic in the kingdom, but he had to tell one more person about the King's condition.

He found Lolita sitting in her favourite spot in the garden. She got up immediately and beamed at her friend. "There you are! Isn't it a beautiful day!"

The smile died on her lips when she saw the expression on Craig's face. "Lolita, we need to talk. I have some bad news."

The young princess clasped her hands tightly in her lap. "What is it? What's wrong?"

"It's your father," he replied gently. "He isn't well! The Royal physician is with him and no one is allowed to go and see him."

"What has happened?" she cried.

Her friend brought her up to date on the situation and swore her to secrecy.

"What can I do to help him?" she asked miserably.

"You can do nothing right now. Just be supportive to your mother while the situation is being attended to. Lolita, do you know where those strange green plants were found? I promised the doctor I would get some samples to him so he can study them."

She nodded in the affirmative. "I know where it's growing. When would you like to get some samples?"

"How about right now?" he asked. "The doctor needs to get them as soon as possible."

Lolita stood up and began swimming away. He hurried to join her.

They swam for quite a while and Craig realized that they were heading towards the surface and he was puzzled.

"Why are we going to the surface?" he asked curiously.

"Well, that's where the plant is! It's just a small bush but it grows on the surface of Neptune. One of my friends discovered it and showed it to me."

Both of them climbed out of the water and Lolita began walking purposefully in one direction. Several plants were growing on the surface but even though Neptune consisted mainly of water, not many things grew above the water level.

Tests had shown that the soil was very acidic and killed most things before long.

Lolita turned a corner and stopped abruptly. Craig stopped behind her and gawked at the sight that met his eyes. As far as he could see, there was an enormous expanse of greenery. There was a moment's stunned silence which Craig eventually broke. "Some small bush!" he exclaimed in disbelief.

Lolita's eyes opened wide in surprise. "This can't be right! When I last came up here, the bush was about as tall and wide as me. There was nothing else!"

"When were you last here?"

"It must have been about three months ago."

Craig looked at the huge expanse of green and pursed his lips. Alarm bells were going off in his head and his heart thumped painfully in his chest. He kept his face impassive though and collected some samples of the plant for the doctor. These he placed in a container and closed the lid tightly.

"Come on, let's get back to the palace now."

They jumped into the water and returned to the palace. Lolita went to see her mother while Craig visited the doctor.

The royal physician took the samples from Carter and told him he would let him know once he had an answer. The young space explorer returned to the palace and sought out the Queen and her daughter. The Queen was immaculately dressed with every hair in place. She looked every bit the ruler she was, but despite her outside appearance, Craig saw the worry lines around her eyes and the stiffness of her posture. He knew Lolita had told her mother about their incredible find on the surface. Lolita, however, wasn't as strong as her mother. She wiped her red eyes with the back of her hand and Craig's heart softened at the sight of her distress. Unbidden, she ran into his arms and he held her tightly, stroking her long black hair tenderly. "Everything is going to be all right!" he assured her.

CHAPTER 21

The doctor sent for Craig and he excused himself from the women. He went to the doctor's surgery and the physician looked up from his microscope and smiled tiredly. "Mr Carter, I don't know what to say to you, but the news isn't very good. This plant is as you said, highly addictive and also poisonous. When taken in small quantities though, it is beneficial to the system, instilling a feeling of well-being, much like a drug. When someone abuses it as in the case of the King, it invades the nervous system and paralyses its victims. It lodges in the brain, causing a comatose condition. I'm not quite sure what will happen next, but the plant could attack the rest of his body and if I can't find a cure in time, he could die. The green colour is the first symptom of the illness."

"Well now you know what the problem is, can you cure it?"

The doctor sighed miserably. "In the early stages, yes most probably, but the King abused the plant to such an extent that I honestly cannot say what will happen. I've already started him on a course of medication in an attempt to slow down the rate of destruction, but this is a new threat and I don't know how to combat it."

"Will he die?" Craig asked bluntly.

"I sincerely hope not, but I cannot say for sure. I've been a doctor for more years than I care to think about, but this alien invader is strong. *I just don't know!"*

Craig's mind was racing as all the possibilities occurred to him. Whichever way he looked at it, Neptune was in serious trouble.

"I regret to tell you I have more bad news," the doctor sighed, "but on second thoughts, perhaps I should just show you."

He led the way into an isolated wing of the hospital and stopped at a bed. When he drew back the curtain surrounding it, Craig was horrified. A woman was lying on the bed. Her eyes were closed and she was the same colour green as the King.

Several beds stood in this ward and every one of them had curtains around them.

"All of them?" Craig gulped.

The doctor nodded. "So far, only these six have the same symptoms, but more could be infected. This woman here is in a worse condition than His Majesty. Her heartbeat is very faint. We have an epidemic on our hands."

Carter looked sternly at the doctor. "Don't jump to unnecessary conclusions doctor. Maybe these will be the only ones who get sick. Surely not many people knew about the plant."

"But what if they do?" the doctor countered.

"We'll worry about that later. I think you need to get some scientists to help you with this, but try not to get too many involved. The last thing we need happen is that panic sweeps through Neptune. I'm going to return to my ship and contact my boss. I daren't risk anyone overhearing what I have to say. I'll tell you what they advise. Meanwhile, just do the best you can doctor."

Craig went to his ship and climbed inside. He wasted no time in contacting Mission Control and speaking with Commander Simms. His superior was horrified and promised to call him back in half an hour once he had contacted some of the best scientists and doctors on Earth.

Craig meanwhile paced his ship restlessly, knowing that every minute which passed could be fatal. On the way to his ship, he had viciously torn a plant from the stony soil on the surface of Neptune. In a sudden fit of anger, he had crushed the leaves, and the juicy stem had leaked green liquid all over his hand, staining it. Apart from a slight tingling feeling in his hand, nothing had happened and he washed the liquid off. Some small deposits still remained in the creases of his hand though. He had fortunately taken another sample and put it in a bottle so that he could describe in detail what the plant looked like.

Fifteen minutes passed agonizingly slowly and he thought he would scream in frustration. Then he had an idea and contacted Saturn. It was one of the stops on his tour and he hoped that the delicate Saturnians would perhaps know something about the plant. They were the most knowledgeable beings in the universe.

He asked to speak to Lara and soon they were looking at one another. Lara smiled at her friend, but the smile died on her face when she saw how serious he looked. "Craig, what's wrong? You look very unhappy."

"Yes, I am. I'm fine but I fear for the Neptunians. Some alien plant species has begun growing on the surface of Neptune and it's spreading rapidly. It must be a very hardy plant because not much grows in the acidic soil above the sea of Neptune. This plant obviously thrives under these conditions. Some of the Neptunians have been drinking the juice from it and they have become sick. The King is also affected and is in a coma."

Lara was shocked to hear the news but she recovered quickly.

"Craig, do you have a sample of that plant with you perhaps?"

"Yes, I do! I picked one on the way to my ship, but what good is it when I'm on Neptune and you are on Saturn?"

"I might be able to identify it. Hold it up to the screen and I'll take a look."

Carter did as she had asked and Lara magnified the image one thousand times. The plant took on a whole new dimension with every single vein showing up like thick cords. There was silence for a while and then Lara spoke. "This plant is very rare and highly toxic. It is also very hardy and thrives in an acidic climate as you have no doubt seen. It isn't dangerous in small quantities, but if abused it certainly can cause complications. The King must have ingested an awful lot of the liquid to be in that condition."

"He has, but that isn't the worst of it! At least six others have been infected and more could be brought into the hospital. The Neptunian doctor reached the same conclusion as you, but he doesn't know how to reverse the damage. I wondered if you could tell me what to do so that I can relay this to him."

"It's a long and complicated process, but the good news is that it can be cured. The harmful side effects of the plant can be slowed considerably if the exact procedure is followed. No matter how strange the therapy sounds, and in some instances, it is contra indicative, but eventually the patients can be cured.

I'll send you the relevant documentation shortly. I just need to download it from our files."

The screen blanked out for a while and then data began streaming onto the screen. The explorer fed a data disc into the console and began to copy the information. A few minutes later the information stopped appearing and Lara's face came back into focus.

"All right Craig, I've downloaded everything I could find on the plant, as well as the medicines that the physician must use. It's a detailed description of everything he will need. If there are any problems then contact me again."

"Thank you, Lara!" he replied gratefully. "I'll give it to him immediately."

The Saturnian scientist's image faded from the screen and was replaced almost immediately with that of Commander Simms. He had the same information about the toxicity of the plant and gave whatever advice Earth's doctors had recommended. Carter copied all this as well and returned to the underwater world that was Neptune.

The royal physician took a break and went to study the documents in the privacy of his office. The young man returned to the palace and found the situation with the King unchanged. However, the doctor had recommended that the king be taken to the hospital for treatment and advised that transportation was on the way to fetch him. The Queen was trying to be very brave as she hurriedly packed some articles for her husband's stay in hospital. When he had been taken away, Craig explained what was going to be done and she felt reassured. He wanted to stay with them for longer, but had a schedule to keep and reluctantly informed them he would be leaving in the morning. Lolita clung to him and begged him to stay, but he had his orders.

The next morning, he was eating his breakfast when a servant approached him. The man was evidently very distraught and bowed to the human. "Mr Carter, my master has taken a turn for the worst. His heart stopped during the night, but fortunately the royal physician managed to start it again. He has asked to see you urgently."

Carter jumped up from the table and rushed to the hospital where he found the doctor waiting for him. He ushered him into his office.

"Mr Carter, as you have no doubt heard, His Majesty's condition has deteriorated. I started on the treatment exactly as the Saturnians said, but I think he was diagnosed too late. Our beloved ruler could die! Please contact the Saturnians and tell them about this latest development."

Craig wasted no time and went to the control room where he again spoke to Lara.

"This is most unfortunate," she sighed. "Perhaps the symptoms accelerate in the aged. He isn't as fit as he once was, I assume."

"Well, what must we do now?" he asked nervously.

Lara was silent for only a few moments before she spoke.

"Craig, could you bring him to Saturn immediately? I had better attend to this myself. It would be better if I could come to Neptune as our ships are faster, but we cannot swim. I could send a medical ship to pick him up, but our vessels are much smaller than both Earth and Neptune's crafts. If you go at warp speed you could be here in four days, five at the most. If His Majesty isn't on our planet by then, he will most certainly die."

Carter's brain whirled with all the possibilities but he nodded his head. "I'll make it to Saturn in time, I swear. Obviously, you'll need the good doctor to accompany us."

"Yes, he must come with you. Craig, don't delay! You were due to come to Saturn later on anyway. Just move that trip forward!"

Craig hurried to the doctor and found that the Queen and Lolita had also arrived. Hastily they went into the doctor's office to make plans.

"Mr Carter, I'll pack my bag just as soon as we finish here. I have given detailed instructions to my second in command and he will see that the others receive the correct treatment. However, we have a problem, because we cannot live without water for long periods of time. Your ship is fast, but it doesn't have the correct facilities for us. I would suggest you use one of our craft. I have taken the liberty of contacting His Majesty's private pilot and he's already standing by. I must take a small group of people with to ensure the safety of the King. He is not allowed to travel without at least two bodyguards and they too have been mobilized. We can leave within the next half an hour."

"As you wish," Craig agreed. "As long as we can meet the deadline, everything will be okay!"

"We will," the doctor replied confidently. "My King's life is in my hands and I will not fail him."

"*We* will not fail him," Lolita replied. "I'm going with you!"

"Lolita, I appreciate your feelings for your father but he's going to be fine," Craig argued. "The good doctor has his instructions and I have mine. You don't have to worry about him at all."

Lolita stuck her chin out defiantly. "He's my father and I want to be with him. You can't stop me. I want to help in any way that I can!"

Carter looked beseechingly at the Queen for some support, but she was twisting her hands anxiously.

"Your Majesty, please reason with her. This is a mercy mission and she should not be accompanying us. We need to coax every single bit of energy from your ship in order to meet the deadline that the Saturnians have set. Another passenger could slow us down."

The Queen glared at Craig and he was taken aback by the fierceness of her tone. "Craig, I understand what you are saying, but if I was able to accompany you, I would demand the same thing, but someone has to stay and rule while my husband is sick. Lolita can help nurse him if she wants. I insist that she go with you."

Carter sighed but nodded his head. "All right then Lolita, you have half an hour to get ready. Pack lightly and if you aren't waiting at the ship within that time, we leave without you, is that clear?"

She nodded and ran from the room.

↓ ↓ ↓

Twenty minutes later the ship rose from its launching pad and headed for Saturn. They stopped for a brief moment so the doctor could collect some samples of the alien plant before rising into the air and vanishing into the clouds. As per the Saturnian's advice, the doctor placed the plants in an opaque container and stored it in the refrigerator. This was done because the plant grew fast and its growth had to be inhibited. The Neptunian craft was making good time and when Craig checked with the pilot, he was happily informed that they would reach Saturn within four days. The young explorer was very relieved and went to check up on the King. He still lay in a comatose state but his condition had not changed drastically. Lolita was by her father's side, where she had been for most of the journey. Craig took pity on her and pulled up a chair. "Why don't you take a break Lolita? I'll sit with your father for a while."

She shook her head adamantly. "No thanks! I don't mind staying with him really."

Carter nodded and stroked her cheek gently. "He's going to be fine I promise! The Saturnians are wonderful people and very clever. He couldn't be in better hands."

She smiled at her friend and squeezed his hand. "Thank you for everything you have done for us over the years. I know my father would thank you if he could."

"There's no need for thanks among friends," he assured her. "I'll look in on you later, okay."

Carter left the sick bay and was about to go to his room, when one of the bodyguards called him. "Mr Carter, could you come to the observation deck immediately?"

Craig followed the man up the flight of stairs into the cockpit area. "What is it?" he asked uneasily. "Is something wrong?"

The pilot called him over. "I'm not sure sir, but a ship has been shadowing us for the last half an hour or so. Its design is unfamiliar to me, but you have travelled extensively so I wondered if you could perhaps identify it."

The human looked at the ship and immediately froze. "Yes, I know that ship! It's a trident ship! Why is it following us?"

"A trident ship, you say? What manner of being pilots such a craft?"

"I'm not really sure to be honest, but that's one of Andocia's crafts," Craig replied.

"*Andocia!*" the pilot gulped. "You mean that woman who tried to take over Earth some time ago."

"Yes," Craig replied. He put his hands over his ears in an effort to shut out the sound of her voice as she made contact with him.

"What do you think she wants with us?" the pilot stammered.

"She wants nothing as yet. I think that she's just curious about your people. However, just in case of trouble, do you have any weapons on board?"

The pilot swivelled in his chair and gaped at the human being. "We have some guns of course, but this is a passenger ship, not a war craft. There is no heavy artillery on board."

"How fast can this ship travel?" Craig enquired. "Can you go faster if you need to?"

The pilot shook his head. "I can go slightly faster but not enough to outrun that trident ship. How do you know she is just curious about us?" the pilot asked suspiciously. "We've had no communication from her. How do you even know that she's aboard that ship?"

Craig stared morosely through the observation window. "She's there, take my word for it. If I'm not mistaken, she'll be contacting you within the next few minutes."

The pilot stared at Craig and shook his head. "*Humans; Sometimes I find it so hard to understand them!*" the Neptunian pilot thought.

Sure enough, a few minutes later, the vidscreen beeped. When the pilot opened the channel, he saw a woman with red hair and green skin. She looked human, apart from the strange colouring. Her red eyes bored into his.

"Identify yourself!" the pilot exclaimed.

"I am Andocia," she replied haughtily. "I'm pretty sure your guest has already told you that."

The pilot gawked at Craig, who gave him an "I told you so" look.

'From the construction of your craft it seems obvious to me that you are from the planet Neptune," she continued. "Aren't you a little far from home?"

"The last time I checked, space was a free zone. I do not have to answer to you or anyone else for that matter," the pilot answered crossly.

Craig saw trouble brewing and he put a cautionary hand on the Neptunian's shoulder and whispered to him. "Don't push your luck with her. Believe me when I tell you she can cause you great harm. Answer her questions, but don't volunteer any additional information. That ship is equipped with weapons that could destroy us. Think about why we are on this mission and don't endanger the life of your King."

Suitably chastised, the Neptunian nodded and opened the channel once again.

"We are on a mercy mission and I request permission to pass." he replied to Andocia. "We do not want any trouble. This is just a passenger vehicle and we have no weapons on board."

"Where are you headed?" she asked curiously.

He darted a scared look at Craig, who nodded.

"We are on our way to Saturn," the being replied.

There were a few moments silence while Andocia pondered this. "Well then, if you are on a mercy mission and headed for Saturn, who is the patient?"

The pilot looked sick and Craig answered. "Does it really matter Andocia? The Neptunians need to get to Saturn urgently. They are not a threat to you. Just let us go about our business!"

"Well then, why are you with them? You look perfectly healthy to me."

"I too have business with the Saturnians," he replied.

Before Andocia could answer, the doctor burst in. "Mr Carter, what's the delay? The King's vital signs have begun to deteriorate! We must increase speed."

He saw Craig's anguished expression and stared at the screen in horror. His hand flew to his mouth. "Oh my, I didn't realize …" he gulped.

"The King of Neptune is on board?" Andocia replied incredulously. "I have never met a King before! Maybe I should come and introduce myself."

"It will serve no purpose! The King is unconscious anyway. You heard what the doctor said; we have to hurry. Let us pass unmolested!" Carter pleaded.

Craig's heart sank when he saw the expression on the evil woman's face. The pilot however was looking at another screen and he swallowed nervously. "Uh Mr Carter, we have a problem."

Craig looked at the monitor and saw guns emerge from the Trident ship.

"What must I do?" the Neptunian gulped.

"Whatever she says," the explorer replied unhappily.

"There is a planet not far from here," Andocia interrupted. "Follow me and land on it."

Her face vanished from the screen and Craig saw the indecision on the pilot's face. "If we turn around now, perhaps we can outrun her?" the Neptunian asked hopefully.

Before he could answer, several small ships circled them.

"She means what she says my friend. You had better follow her. Hopefully this won't take long. I had better go and tell Lolita what's happening."

Before he could leave, one of the bodyguards spoke up. "Our duty is to protect our King and we will fight this threat! Who does she think she is, ordering us around like this?!"

Craig turned to the angry guard. "I know you have your orders, but Andocia is not someone to be trifled with. This journey will have a very sad ending if you anger her. She could kill all of us with a few blasts from her guns. Stand down!"

The bodyguard reluctantly put his gun back in its holster.

Craig went to the sick bay where he found the doctor administering oxygen to the king. "How is he doing doctor?"

"He's hanging in there Mr Carter, but every minute counts! Andocia is jeopardizing this rescue mission."

"I know but we have no choice. Let's hope this will be a very brief visit. I'll explain the situation to her."

Lolita entered the room. She had left her father for a brief nap and had looked outside one of the windows. The princess had seen the trident ship and her eyes were wide with fear. "Craig, what's happening? Why are we following that ship?"

Her friend sat her down and gently took both her hands in his. "Listen to me Lolita we have had a minor setback. That's

Andocia in the trident ship and she is forcing your pilot to land this ship on an uninhabited planet not far from here. I'm sure we aren't in any immediate danger as long as we do as she says for now. I'll speak to her when we land and explain the situation. She has no quarrel with your planet and hopefully we will soon be on our way to Saturn once more."

Lolita looked miserably at her father. "Is he going to die?" she sniffed.

Carter put his hands on either side of her face and made her look at him. "Your father is a tough old man and he'll make it. I've seen your father overcome worse things than this. Just don't lose hope!"

She came into his arms and he stroked her hair tenderly. Lolita clung to him, taking strength from his presence. The space explorer looked over at the King and bit his lip nervously. "Hold on your Majesty, just hold on for a while longer," he mouthed silently.

CHAPTER 22

They followed the trident ship and landed nearby on the uninhabited planet. The Neptunians watched as the hatch opened and Andocia came out of her ship. Several of her female warriors followed and the small warships continued to circle the area. The evil woman was taking no chances.

Craig stepped out of the vehicle and greeted his enemy warily.

"Hello again, Craig," she replied conversationally. "You were the last person I thought I would run into. Space is a very big area, yet it is somehow still a small world."

"What do you want, Andocia?" he asked stiffly.

"Like I said, I wish to pay my respects to the King of Neptune."

"He is very ill and unless he gets to Saturn by tomorrow evening, he'll die. You can see him but he won't even know you exist. He's in a coma and has been for a number of days already. Every moment we remain here makes things that much worse for him and his people. This epidemic will kill the Neptunians and your obvious curiosity will hasten his death. If you want to see him then go ahead! No one will stop you, but make it fast! We have to leave soon."

The Neptunians began to come out of their ship. The King's bodyguards still wore their weapons and the determination on their faces left no doubt that they would defend their King to the end. Craig saw the situation could get out of hand and he alone knew the awesome power Andocia had. He looked warningly at the guards and shook his head. Reluctantly their hands moved away from their weapons.

Lolita emerged from the spacecraft and walked determinedly over to Craig. Andocia watched her with interest. "And who might this young lady be?" she asked Carter curiously.

"I am Princess Lolita of Neptune!" she replied haughtily. "My father's life is in danger because of you. So, if you wish to gawk at us then do so and satisfy your curiosity. Maybe then we can be on our way."

Andocia smiled at the young girl, and bowed from the waist. "I greet you Princess Lolita. It is an honour to meet such a brave young lady. Maybe my physician can help with your father's condition. Can she have a look at him?"

Lolita looked to Craig for his advice, unsure what she should do. "It can't hurt, I suppose," he offered. "Let her see him if she wishes."

Lolita nodded. "Very well, she may come and examine my father."

A woman approached, followed by Andocia. They went into the ship where one of the Neptunians led them to the sick bay. Craig and Lolita followed close behind.

The woman doctor greeted her counterpart and together they went to see the King. The woman doctor looked closely at him, noting his appalling green colour and quick breathing. She looked at the charts and the machinery that sustained the King. Taking a stethoscope from her pocket she looked to the King's physician. "May I?"

"Go ahead," he replied.

She examined him closely, listened to his heartbeat and looked into his unseeing grey eyes. Several minutes passed during which the woman gave the king a thorough examination. Finally, she straightened up and looked at the Neptunian physician.

"I know what this is. The name of the plant is 'Wellbenign' a very fast-growing plant that gives its victims a sense of well being and happiness. The more it is abused, the worse it affects its victims. I have seen this plant and the damage it can cause on occasion, but this is the worst case I have ever seen. Perhaps for a Neptunian it is more toxic."

She described the plant and the Neptunian physician nodded. "Can you help his Highness?" he asked desperately.

"No, you will have to go to the Saturnians to get him cured and time is of the essence as you so rightly have said, but I have a potion that can perhaps help slow down the symptoms. It can buy you some more time. I haven't tried it out on a Neptunian however, but in every other case it has been successful. Would you like me to administer some?"

The King's physician looked at Lolita. "Princess, may the lady give the medicine to your father?"

"If it can help my father, then yes she may. I'm desperate enough to try anything right now."

"I'll get some immediately," the doctor promised.

When she had gone, Andocia looked curiously at the Neptunian. "I must say I'm no expert, but he is certainly very green around the gills," she remarked laughingly.

Lolita glared at the woman, "That's not very funny!"

Andocia smiled, "Sorry, but I just couldn't resist."

Andocia's doctor returned with the syringe and Lolita bit her lip nervously as the woman injected her father. "There, it should take about fifteen minutes for the medicine to take effect. His heartbeat should become more regular."

Lolita stayed with her father but Andocia left the ship. Craig followed her out. "Andocia you heard what your doctor had to say. She confirmed what I told you earlier. Every moment we spend here on this planet is precious time that the King may not have. Let them go to Saturn where they can get the help they need! What could you hope to gain by keeping them here against their will?"

Andocia was silent for a while, then she sat on a large rock and patted the space next to her. He sat down beside her. "You know Carter, you make a very good case for the Neptunians. They are your friends, yes?"

"Yes." he replied.

"Princess Lolita is also a special friend, isn't she?"

"Yes, she is. I am very fond of her and the rest of her family. Her mother wanted to come with as well, but she had to rule Neptune in the King's absence."

"The King is very sick, I know. It certainly doesn't take a doctor to see the seriousness of the situation," Andocia remarked. "I suppose it would be humane of me to let them go."

Craig stared at Andocia. "Why do I sense a 'but' in there?"

"You know me well Carter, and yes, there is a 'but' involved."

She stood up and he followed her. "Will you let them go?" he asked pointedly.

"Yes, they can leave once my doctor has assured me that the King will make it to Saturn, but I want something in return."

"Why am I not surprised?" he sighed. "What is it that you want?"

"I want you in exchange for the freedom of that ship. No one will be harmed if you stay here with me. Imagine my surprise when I sensed you on the Neptunian ship. I have great plans and you are an integral part of them. Once your friends are safely away from here, I'll explain what I mean. Do you accept my terms?"

"And if I refuse?" he challenged.

Andocia glared at him. "You know what will happen if you refuse. I don't need to spell it out for you! The choice is simple! If you refuse, no one on that ship will survive and especially not the King and his daughter."

Craig began walking, "We should be getting back to the Neptunians now. It's time to see whether or not your doctor's potion has had any effect."

She fell into step beside him and they walked back to the ship in silence. They went into the sick bay where the King's physician smiled happily. "The potion seems to have helped His Majesty. He is breathing better now and I have taken him off the respirator."

"That's excellent news, doctor," Craig replied. "I think you had better get ready to continue the journey to Saturn then."

"We can continue on our journey now?" Lolita enquired hesitantly.

"*You* can Lolita," Carter replied. "I hope your father will soon be well again."

The princess looked into her friend's sad blue eyes and clasped her hands together nervously. "But you're coming with us, aren't you?"

"I would like to, but Andocia wants me to stay with her for a while."

"*I need you!*" she cried. "*How will I manage without you?*"

Craig put his hands on her shoulders and shook her gently. "Lolita, you are a princess and I was only along for the ride. Just give the Saturnians the packages I loaded onto your ship. You are a strong, capable young woman and you'll manage fine without me. Take care of your father. He's your main priority right now."

Lolita clung to him and he held her for a while. Then he kissed her gently on her forehead and brushed away a few of her tears. He removed her arms from around his waist.

"Doctor I have a message for you from my physician." Andocia remarked. "She says that your people must destroy that plant before it takes over the entire surface of your planet. Burn it to the ground and make sure that not even one root remains or it will eventually destroy all of Neptune."

Andocia said goodbye to the Neptunians and ordered Craig to follow.

"I'll be out in five minutes," he promised.

She nodded and left the ship.

"Craig, we can still get you out of here!" Lolita pleaded desperately. "She means to harm you!"

"I have to go with her Lolita. If I don't, she'll destroy all of you. That woman has no heart. I'll be okay! When you are a safe distance away, contact Commander Simms and he'll help you to destroy the plants on your planet. Leave quickly before she changes her mind!"

The doctor gently steered her away. "Do what he says, Princess. We must make haste to Saturn."

Craig left the ship and didn't look back. He heard Lolita's anxious sobbing until the hatch was sealed.

He went to Andocia and they watched as the Neptunian craft lifted off. Craig Carter waved until the ship was out of sight.

/ / /

Andocia began to walk back to her ship. "Come on then, time we were leaving as well."

Reluctantly Craig followed her aboard her ship. He had no idea what the woman wanted with him but one thing he was certain about and that was it wouldn't be pleasant. The hatch closed soundlessly behind him and he wondered if he would ever see Earth again.

He was directed to a room on another level and told to wait there until Andocia called him. A guard pulled up a chair and sat down near the door. Carter walked around the little room and saw that although it contained only the bare necessities, it was a comfortable space. The single bed looked comfortable and although the bathroom was very small, it contained everything he needed. The fact that Andocia stationed a guard outside his door told him he was a prisoner, but the fact came as no surprise.

Later he was escorted to Andocia. She was waiting for him in her stateroom and when he entered, she gestured to a seat. He sat down and kept his hands in his lap, alert for any nasty surprises, but he was in no mood to indulge in senseless chit-chat and he made that clear.

"I suppose you want to know why I insisted on your accompanying me," she remarked.

"That would be a good start," he replied.

"You are going to prove very useful to me, because I'm going to use you as bait. I want someone else and you are going to help me."

Craig frowned in confusion. "I don't understand what you mean."

"Of course not, but allow me to explain. I want your girl-friend, Constance Gregg."

"Constance? Why do you want her?"

"That little detail doesn't concern you right now. Let's just say that there are some loose ends to tie up."

"Are you saying that Constance is a loose end?"

Andocia smiled secretively, "She most definitely is."

"What has she done to you? I have annoyed you more than she ever did. Leave her out of this!"

"You certainly have a high opinion of yourself, don't you Mr Carter! Yes, originally when I first discovered you, I was in-trigued by your circumstances, but as you already know I found out that you were framed for a crime which you didn't commit. Then when I tried to take over Earth, you and she connived to dash that hope once and for all."

"Now look who's talking," Craig exclaimed angrily. "We both have our share of talents, but we didn't do it alone. A great many people helped us to defeat you and I'm grateful to them. There has to be more to this story than you're letting on."

"There is, but I have no desire to share more facts with you. Obviously, you don't know what I'm talking about, but that's fine with me. All will be revealed in time! I want to wait a few days though before you contact her, because I'm pretty sure the Neptunians have told your boss what has happened and thus he will have our previous location. Knowing Commander Simms, he will most probably send out a rescue craft or two to look for you, but we are going to be far away by the time he investigates."

"Where are you taking me?" Craig enquired.

"That is also none of your business. I have a number of safe places where you can be kept and we are heading to one of them now. When we arrive you can contact Miss Gregg. In the meantime, you'll have to be content as my guest. You may walk around this ship, with the exception of a few restricted areas. If you respect my orders, I'll only have you locked in your quarters at night, but there will always be someone watching you wherever you go during the day. We shall dine together at the same table, but be assured of one thing; no one can be persuaded to help you escape, for anyone caught in this act will die horribly and they know this. If you wish to remain in your comfortable room, take heed of what I'm saying. If you are caught trying to escape, you shall be moved to less pleasant quarters."

"I understand, but you are wasting your time and you know it! I'll never put Constance in jeopardy! Whatever you have planned for us, just forget about it. You used my respect and friendship with the King of Neptune against me and if it wasn't for him, I would never have agreed to this arrangement."

"Yes, you are certainly a sucker when it comes to those you love, aren't you Carter? I suppose your friends would consider that one of your most endearing qualities, but I see it as a weakness."

Carter kept silent and ignored his captor. Finally, she called to some of her guards. "I think Mr Carter is tired. Take him to his room and let him rest."

Craig went with them willingly enough but rest was the last thing he wanted. He lay face up and put his hands behind his head. Despite Andocia's threats against him, he was determined to escape before they reached their destination. He vowed he would rather die than expose his girlfriend to this woman ever again. Why he wondered, was Andocia suddenly so interested in Constance?

Dinner time came and he was escorted to Andocia's table. Carter hated Andocia more than any of his other enemies whom he had met so far in his lifetime and the fact that she was so powerful unsettled him immensely. What made matters worse was that she was telepathic and he knew she took great satisfaction in knowing this.

He picked at his food and hardly tasted it, while his captor chatted on about her plans for the future. He hardly listened to her, but took comfort from the fact that she didn't voice the desire to attack Earth again. When the meal was over, he complained that he had a headache and retired early to his room. There he spent a restless night thinking of ways to escape.

Despite his plans to get away from Andocia and the trident ship, he was unable to put any plans into motion, for his enemy never gave him the opportunity to try anything. Wherever he went, he was followed by several heavily armed guards.

A few days later they landed on a planet, but no one would tell him what the name of it was. He noticed with some degree of unease that the planet was in the Milky Way, for the sky was black. It was obviously one of the unexplored planets in his universe.

He was taken to a building and shown into a room. This one was bigger than the room he had occupied on the trident ship. However, it too was just a functional room which contained only the bare necessities. Once again, he was locked inside and he paced the floor restlessly. Craig hoped he would find a way to escape from the planet before he was ordered to contact Constance.

The next day he was allowed to walk around the planet, but he was forbidden to go very far and as usual was watched by some heavily armed guards. He glanced surreptitiously at the guards and was judging the distance between him and them. Carter began moving closer to the nearest guard in an attempt to grab her weapon.

She saw the movement and stepped backwards. As Craig tried to leap at her, a red beam kicked up the dirt at his feet and he knew he had lost the opportunity.

"You are a bad boy!" Andocia admonished her captive. "You really should take good advice."

The female guard came up to him, hate evident in her eyes. She raised her weapon suddenly and smashed it against his cheekbone. He stumbled away and grunted in pain as the skin on his cheek split open and the gash began to bleed. The evil woman grabbed him roughly and he was marched into a building. "All right Carter, the fun's over now. I want you to contact Constance and tell her what I want."

Craig shook his head. "I won't do it!"

Andocia smiled sweetly at her unwilling guest. "I know you are a stubborn man, so I have something to show you that may make you change your mind."

Carter looked at the screen as images began to appear on it. At first the picture was blurred, but gradually it became clearer and Craig gasped. He saw his parents sitting in their garden chatting to one another. His mother shook her head and wiped some tears from her eyes and his father comforted her. Alice Carter wrung her hands in misery and Brian Carter stood awkwardly by, not sure how to comfort his wife.

"Just in case you were wondering what that was all about, let me enlighten you," Andocia cooed. "That little scene took place soon after we lifted off from that deserted planet. Your Commander Simms told them about your circumstances, after your friend Lolita explained what had happened. Now do you see that tree nearby? Well keep looking!"

Craig had a bad feeling in the pit of his stomach and he looked where Andocia was pointing. A woman was crouching behind the tree, cradling a rifle and the barrel was pointed at his family.

Noticing his distress, Andocia chuckled evilly. "Your parents are alive, but as you can see, I have someone watching their house. Now you have two choices. Either you contact Constance and tell her of my proposition, or your parents die. Choose!"

"*Damn you Andocia!*" he exclaimed angrily. "*How low can you sink? My parents have done nothing to you!*"

"You are wasting my time! Make up your mind now," his enemy replied unfeelingly.

The space explorer sighed in defeat. Andocia knew him too well! "All right I'll speak to Constance, but I won't plead with her. The choice will be hers to make."

"Well, for your sake she had better make the right one."

⫽ ⫽ ⫽

Craig contacted Commander Simms and he appeared on the screen almost immediately. "Craig, thank the stars you are alive! We have been worried about you."

"I appreciate that, Sir. It's good to hear your voice again.

Andocia has been treating me well, but there's no place like home. I'm sorry if I appear rude, but would it be possible to speak to Constance? Is she around?"

"Not at the moment Craig. She is in space on a mission for me."

Craig's heart sang with relief but he kept a straight face. "Oh, that's too bad then! I guess I'll catch her next time."

"Have you any idea where you are Craig?" his boss enquired.

"No Sir, none at all. Andocia won't tell me."

"I suppose that was too much to hope for anyway. That woman is very clever. She knew I would send out a rescue craft for you."

Andocia moved into focus. "Commander Simms, where is Constance at present?" she enquired. "I want her exact location."

"Don't tell her, Sir!" Craig pleaded urgently. "Andocia means to harm her!"

The Commander looked uncertainly at his employee's face, not sure how to respond. There was a moment of awkward silence, which was broken by Andocia. She took a gun from one of her guards and put it against Craig's head.

"If you don't tell me where she is Commander, you can watch me kill your employee in front of your eyes."

Carter was about to tell his boss that Andocia wouldn't carry out her threat as she needed him alive. Her hand rested lightly on his shoulder and he grunted as pain shot down his arm and his captor glared warningly at him. It was just a second in time and Commander Simms probably didn't even notice the exchange, but he changed his mind instantly.

"All right I'll tell you!" Simms gasped. "Just don't kill him! Constance is probably passing Jupiter right about now."

"Excellent! Now give me the coded frequency you use to contact her. I'll have a word with her."

Craig wanted to cry out that he mustn't do it, but something seemed to be wrong with his voice. Commander Simms looked at him, and, getting no answer, he relented. Andocia wrote down the code and switched off the screen. She rubbed her hands together in anticipation. "Now I can contact your girlfriend and invite her over. The two of you will be reunited for a short time anyway. Once I have done what I intend to do, both of you will die and only then will I be able to move on with my life. I think I'll take it from here. You can return to your room now."

Craig wanted to scream at her, fight her, do anything rather than let her get away with it, but he knew he would be wasting his time and energy.

He was taken back to his room and locked in. Carter looked out of the barred window and sighed. *"Perhaps Constance will refuse to come,"* he thought hopefully. *"She knows what she's up against."*

CHAPTER 23

Some time later he was startled by the sound of his door being opened. He sat up suddenly and rubbed his eyes. He had obviously fallen asleep earlier. Some guards waved him out and he looked at the time on his watch. It was late afternoon.

He was taken to another room and on the way, he passed a small spacecraft parked near the hangars. It had Mission Control's logo on it. He was both exhilarated and disappointed when he saw this, because it could only mean that Constance had come as ordered. The guards marched him into a room where two figures sat facing one another in chairs. The tension in the air was palpable.

Carter ran to Constance and she came into his arms. He buried his face in her soft hair and whispered in her ear. "I'm so glad to see you, but why did you come? I hoped this wouldn't happen!"

She smiled at her boyfriend and kissed him gently on his lips. "I *had* to because you have always been there for me when I needed you, so I'm just returning the favour."

Further conversation was interrupted by Andocia, who indicated to the chairs opposite her. She invited the couple to sit down.

Craig stared belligerently at their hostess. "What happens now? Despite my pleas for Constance not to come, she decided to do so anyway."

Andocia smiled at Constance. "She is a clever young woman and she knew what would be best for all concerned. It may surprise you to know that she didn't even hesitate when I issued my ultimatum. You are a lucky man Carter, because she loves you enough to do the right thing."

"That's just your opinion," he replied disapprovingly. "I wish she hadn't done so."

Without asking if they would like anything to drink, Andocia ordered one of her guards to fetch some beverages. The group drank what was offered, but Craig was feeling very uneasy.

Carter put his drink down and spoke to Andocia. "All right, now that you have both of us here you may as well tell us what's going to happen. I believe we have a right to know."

"Well of course you do!" the woman replied expansively. "For the rest of today the two of you may spend some time catching up on each other's news. Tomorrow, however, it will be a different story. I'll spend most of my time chatting to your lovely girlfriend. You may walk around the planet if you wish, but any stupidity on your part will result in Miss Gregg here paying for your insolence. If she tries anything stupid, I'll kill you instead, so for your own sakes, behave yourselves."

The couple nodded in agreement.

"All right then, you may as well go now. I'll expect both of you at suppertime."

Craig and Constance went out, followed by several guards, but they ignored them. The couple held hands and walked over to a bench not very far away, where they sat down.

"All right Constance, I'm dying to know how come you got here so fast. Where were you when that she-devil contacted you?"

"I was just passing Jupiter after I dropped off some things for them. I was going to go to a few other planets, but then I was told about your circumstances. Commander Simms warned me that Andocia would be contacting me and when I had finished talking to him, she did so."

Craig took both his girlfriend's hands in his and sighed. "You know how much I've missed you my darling, but why did you come? Andocia told me she means to kill both of us after she's spoken to you. Did you know she used me as bait so she could get to you?"

"She did? But why does she want to see me? Should I be flattered?"

"I wouldn't be," he remarked sourly. "She said something about you being a loose end."

Constance stared curiously at her boyfriend. "What did she mean by that?"

"I have no idea, but I don't like it! We have to get away from here as soon as possible; tonight even, if we can."

Constance shook her head. "I doubt we'll get the chance. I don't think she will allow that to happen. Maybe we should just wait and see."

Craig got up and paced around the bench. "*Woman, we are in danger here, don't you understand!* Andocia hasn't invited us here for a cozy chat! She is going to kill us once she has whatever she needs from you. You seem pretty calm about our position!"

Constance took his hand and led him back to the bench. "Listen to me," she demanded urgently. "It won't help either of us if you panic! I know we are in grave danger, but we can deal with the situation if we do so calmly and collectively. We'll find a way to escape, just give it time. Maybe after Andocia and I have had our chat, or whatever she wants, she might be a little more relaxed. Then we can escape when she least expects it."

"That's if we aren't dead by then!" Carter grumbled.

Constance sighed and rubbed his arm soothingly. "You've been through worse times than this. Be calm and just focus on an escape plan. When I'm with Andocia she won't be worrying about you, so you can spend that time thinking of a way to escape, okay?"

"All right, I can do that. I suppose I'll need something to pass the time, otherwise I'll go crazy thinking about what that woman is doing to you!"

Miss Gregg kissed her boyfriend gently on his cheek. "Now that's the Craig I know and love."

"All right, now I'm curious. If it only took you a few hours to get here, this planet must be close by. I thought you would take days to arrive so, where are we?"

"We are on an uninhabited planet not far from Jupiter. As far as I know this planet doesn't have a name as yet, but our scientists have known about it for a long time now. Obviously, they had no idea Andocia has a hideout here."

"Yes, and I'm willing to bet that if we live through this and tell Commander Simms, he'll find she has moved on elsewhere and it will be uninhabited once again," Craig remarked.

"Probably, but it isn't important right now," his girlfriend replied.

"I agree with you." Craig held both his girlfriend's hands in his and sighed. "You know I love you, but I have to know, why did you put your life in jeopardy? You could have stayed away from Andocia if you really wanted to."

"I could have," she agreed, "but I thought about all the times that you placed yourself in danger to rescue me and I realized I could never repay you for all those times. That's why I'm here now. You, my darling, have a reputation of putting others you care about before your own safety and that is a wonderful trait to possess. Lolita was very upset when she had to leave you behind and it took a lot of persuasion to stop her from coming back to look for you. I imagine if her father wasn't so sick, she might very well have braved Andocia and her minions."

Craig smiled at that, but he knew Constance was probably right. "Do you perhaps know how the King of Neptune is doing?" he asked hopefully.

"No, I don't. I did hear he wasn't getting any worse though. I'm sure that the Saturnians have the situation under control."

"I'm sure they have," he agreed. "What's happening about the abnormal plant growth on Neptune?"

"I don't have any news on that, but Commander Simms knows about it and I'm sure he'll see to it."

Before Craig could answer, they were interrupted by some guards. "Come with us please. Andocia wishes to see you both."

Craig looked at his watch and realized with a start that it was dinnertime. The afternoon had flown by!

They joined their hostess for dinner and it was a splendid affair. While they ate though, Craig wondered if it was their last meal.

When dinner had been eaten, Andocia led Constance away. Craig stood up to follow, but some guards barred his way. "You'll see Constance tomorrow sometime. Now you must return to your room!"

The young man locked eyes with his girlfriend and she smiled reassuringly. "Goodnight my darling. Sleep well!" she said as she blew him a kiss.

He responded in the same way and went quietly with his guards back to his room.

That night he tossed and turned in his bed and was glad when morning came.

He was given breakfast in his room and realized that Andocia wasn't wasting time. He wondered what she was doing to Constance.

Much later on he was allowed to leave his room. He wandered around aimlessly for a while, but found he couldn't settle. Despite Craig's promise that he would try to think of a way for them to escape, he found he couldn't concentrate. His mind was filled with thoughts of what Constance was being subjected to by their captor. Carter knew where Andocia would have taken his girlfriend and without even thinking about it, started walking in the general direction. When he got closer however, his way was barred by some guards.

"I'm sorry Mr Carter, but this place is out of bounds! Andocia has given us strict instructions not to allow anyone past this point. If you refuse then we will use force."

Reluctantly he turned around and went back to his aimless wandering. Later he returned to his room and decided to spend time there instead. His meals were brought to him and wordlessly he ate what was given to him, but later he couldn't even recall what he had eaten. That night he went to bed but there was still no sign of Constance.

The next morning, he woke early and soon afterwards his breakfast was brought to him. He demanded to see Andocia but was told she was busy. Finally, in desperation he asked for Constance. The guards left and returned a while later with the woman he loved and he hugged her gratefully.

"Oh Constance, I'm so glad to see you!" he exclaimed happily. Are you okay?"

She smiled wanly at him. "I'm fine, just very tired. I slept for such a long time and I still feel as though I could sleep for a week."

"What did Andocia do to you? Was it bad?"

Constance shook her head. "I'm not really sure actually! I know she asked me a lot of strange questions, but I don't remember what I told her. All I can recall is that she seemed happy with the results, whatever they were."

"What sort of questions did she ask you?"

Constance yawned, and then frowned. "Uh, what were we talking about again?"

"We were discussing the questions Andocia asked you," he reminded her.

"Oh, those," she replied vaguely. "I really am feeling tired. Can we discuss this later?" she pleaded as she curled up on his bed. Before he could answer her, she was fast asleep. Craig covered her with the duvet and left her alone.

He went outside and closed the door behind him. Later he saw Andocia and went up to her. "What did you do to Constance?" he demanded.

"We had a very long talk about a great many things. Why do you ask?"

"I'm just curious. She seems fine though, but she's very tired. I left her to sleep it off in my room."

Andocia nodded distractedly. "Yes, I suppose she would be! Well rest is the best thing for her right now. What did she tell you?"

"Well, not very much actually. She was too tired to tell me anything."

Andocia seemed to be in a good mood and Craig was relieved.

He still had doubts though but didn't think it would be prudent to ask any questions about their future, or lack of it for that matter. "Am I to assume by your mood that you found out what you wanted from Constance?"

"It was a satisfactory discussion, yes. I am pleased with the results. Somewhat surprised though, but definitely pleased. It was an interesting day!"

Craig frowned, but didn't want to question her further. Andocia excused herself and said she would expect both of them for supper that evening, by which time she was confident Constance would have recovered from her bout of tiredness. The young man left her alone and sat down under a tree. He looked over at the hangars where Constance's ship had been moved on the day she arrived and began formulating a plan to escape. He knew that no matter what Andocia's mood was like today, she still hated them enough to kill them and he liked living. Craig watched the movement of his arch enemy's troops around the heavily guarded building and knew it wouldn't be easy. Every two hours the guards were replaced by others and as far as he could tell, there was no gap where he could slip unnoticed into the hangar. He decided the best time to make their move would be at night when there was more shadow around. If only they could get to the ship, they would be free! On his way back towards his room, Craig glanced surreptitiously behind the buildings and found there were some bushes that would be perfect to provide cover. He planned to escape that evening, but everything depended on how Constance felt.

When he returned to his room, his girlfriend was stirring. She sat up on the bed and yawned. Oh my, did I fall asleep again? I'm so sorry!"

"Don't be. Whatever you went through must have been very difficult for you. You probably needed that rest. Do you think you could tell me what happened when you were with Andocia?"

Constance used the bathroom and splashed water on her face. She combed her hair down with her hand and then sat next to her boyfriend once more. Miss Gregg frowned and shook her head. "I don't understand it but I can't remember very much at all. I just know there were some questions about my family in general. I can't even remember what answers I gave Andocia."

Constance buried her face in her hands. "Craig, what's happening to me? Why can't I remember anything?" she wailed.

He took her gently in his arms and she clung to him. "Don't worry too much about that my angel. I don't suppose it's really important. The main thing is you're still alive. I hate to sound pessimistic, but I doubt whether we will live very much longer. I don't see Andocia just letting us go."

"Craig, do you think if the situation had been reversed and I had been on Neptune instead of you, she might have made me contact you?"

Craig thought about it for a while and then he shook his head. "I don't know how that woman rationalizes things. Maybe she would have been content with you and gone after me at a later stage, but I just don't know. One thing I know for sure and that's the fact she hates both of us. We have to escape, tonight if possible. I don't want to spend another day in her company. That woman gives me the creeps!"

Constance yawned again and apologized. "I understand what you're saying, my darling and I have to admit you're quite right; we must get away from here as soon as possible, but I'm not up to tackling heavily armed guards tonight. My head feels as though it's been stuffed with cotton wool and I'm getting a headache. Maybe tomorrow I'll feel better."

Craig put his hand against his girlfriend's forehead. "Oh no, you aren't coming down with a fever, are you? Your forehead feels very hot."

"No, I'm just recovering from whatever Andocia did to me, I guess. I'm sure that by tomorrow I'll be feeling better. Can we escape tomorrow night instead?"

Carter's nerves were on edge. He wanted to escape so desperately, but he wouldn't leave without his girlfriend so he decided, against his better judgment, to wait until the next day.

Meanwhile Andocia was discussing the couple with one of her confidants.

"So, mistress, I assume that all went well with the woman. You seem to be in a good mood."

"I am, and yes things did go well. I subjected her to the most intense tests and told her things I would not normally reveal to anyone else. She was shocked and horrified by what I told her and it pleased me to see the horror and disbelief on her face."

"Did you tell her everything?"

"Yes, I did."

"Even the fact that you were responsible for the death of her grandmother?" the woman replied curiously.

"Yes, even that. Actually, that was the part I enjoyed the most! If she hadn't been strapped to the bed at that time, I think she would have tried to kill me."

The woman shook her head. "I don't know why you told her anyway. I mean, what purpose could it have served?"

"I had to do it. I had to *know!*" Andocia explained.

"And did you get the answer you wanted?"

Andocia smiled. "I did. Despite my findings, she is still a threat to me. Not in the way I had expected of course, but the woman has incredible skills."

"Pardon my asking mistress, but if you wanted her to know everything, why then did you wipe the session from her mind?"

"That too was part of the plan. You see, I don't want her knowing everything about me, but at the same time I wanted the satisfaction of seeing her face when she heard what I had to say. So now she remembers nothing of what happened, but I have learned a great deal."

Andocia's follower didn't agree with her mistress, but she decided to leave the matter well enough alone. She knew what Andocia could be like if provoked and the picture was disturbing.

"What will happen now, Andocia?" her follower enquired.

"Both Constance and that meddlesome boyfriend of hers will prove troublesome if we ever meet again. They must be terminated."

Andocia's follower smiled happily. "I must agree with you! I see them as a threat too. When do you plan to kill them?"

"I'll do so very soon in fact. Tomorrow I have to go to another uninhabited planet in this galaxy and when I return, I'll do it.

They have at most another forty-eight hours left to live. For tonight and tomorrow they will be treated well and afterwards, both of those meddlers will be out of my hair!"

Both women laughed evilly and left the room.

That evening the couple was summoned to supper and they went reluctantly. Despite Constance's assurances, she still seemed very tired and had trouble concentrating. They were allowed to sleep in the same quarters that night. After Constance had relaxed in a bath, she crawled into bed and was soon fast asleep again. As Craig watched his girlfriend sleep, he was troubled. What had Andocia done to her, he wondered. He surmised that either the session had been so traumatic that Constance's defence mechanism had been simply to forget everything, or somehow Andocia had wiped the incident from his girlfriend's mind. A shiver ran up and down his spine when he realized just how powerful their enemy was and it reinforced his urgency to put as much distance between them and Andocia as they could. He hoped fervently that Constance would recover by tomorrow; they had to escape, and soon!

The next day dawned bright and clear. Constance woke feeling much better and they tucked into a hearty breakfast in their room. She went outside with him and they basked in the sun, but once again Miss Gregg felt the urge to sleep and she excused herself. By this time, Craig was frantic with worry. He had heard Andocia was away, but Constance was no use to him in her present state. Why was she still so tired he wondered?

Carter couldn't stand it any longer and was determined to escape that evening, even if he had to carry his girlfriend all the way to the hangar. It was nearly lunchtime by now and he began heading back to the room to see if Constance had woken up yet.

Suddenly he heard a voice in his head. The voice was familiar, yet he couldn't place it immediately.

"Mr Carter, go over to those bushes in the distance. There is a small shed there."

He began walking immediately, noticing that the guards weren't paying any attention to him. Suddenly he remembered the voice. It belonged to the woman who had saved him and Constance from Andocia before. He quickened his pace.

Craig got to the shed and closed the door. No one had missed him. He looked around but the room was dark and gradually his eyes adjusted to the light. A shadow moved in the distance and someone emerged from behind a box. Carter gaped at the being as it came slowly towards him. It was dressed in white completely from head to toe. Only the hair was dark brown and it made a dark splash of colour against the stark whiteness of the garments. His eyes travelled down the length of the figure, which was unmistakably female, despite the looseness of the white garment. Slowly he looked up at her face and saw she had blue eyes. He rubbed his own eyes when he tried to make out the features of her face, but saw only a blur around the mouth.

The woman stopped a short distance away from him and seemed to be smiling. Craig looked into the blue eyes and saw serenity there, which immediately put him at ease.

"Hello, Mr Carter. I have finally managed to meet you in person."

Craig looked wonderingly at this woman. "I know who you are! You saved Constance and me from Andocia twice before. I never really thanked you for that!"

"It was a pleasure, I assure you. No thanks were necessary anyway."

"Well, you have our heartfelt thanks anyway. I'm sure Constance would echo that if she could, but she has gone to lie down. Ever since Andocia took her away from me for the day yesterday, she has been feeling very tired. We have to escape tonight, before Andocia comes back, otherwise she will eliminate us. That woman hates us so much and, I must admit the feeling is mutual. Yet, unless Constance recovers soon, I'll have trouble trying to escape from this wretched place."

"I understand how you feel, but how is it that you are both here? Were you travelling together?"

"No, I was on my way to Saturn with the King of Neptune, who was sick. Andocia waylaid their ship in space and made me go with her. She threatened to kill the Neptunians if I didn't obey, so I had no choice but to go with her. Once we were far away from the deserted planet where she made them land, she informed me she wanted me to contact Constance and tell her to come here. When I refused, she showed me what would happen to my parents if I didn't do as she asked. Once again, against my better judgment, Constance was called and she decided to come here, even though I didn't want her to. Andocia showed great interest in my girlfriend."

"Do you perhaps know why?" The woman in white asked curiously.

Craig shrugged his shoulders helplessly. "I didn't know what Andocia meant, but she called Constance a 'loose end', whatever that was."

Carter bent down and kicked a stone viciously and therefore missed the look of anger in the woman's eyes.

"*So, it begins!*" she thought angrily. "*Why is Andocia doing this now, all of a sudden?*"

Yet even as she thought those words, the woman knew the answer, but she couldn't tell the man standing nearby and especially not his girlfriend.

Gently she reached for his arm and her touch calmed the man down. "I'm really sorry about your misfortune, but I won't allow Andocia to harm you. I know what she is capable of and you can only guess. She is much more powerful than you could ever imagine. As long as she bothers you, I'll do my best to help in any way I can, but I cannot spend my life protecting you."

Craig looked shrewdly at the woman. "You sound as though you know Andocia very well. Do you also come from the Golden Way?"

The woman in white nodded. "Yes, I do and Andocia is well known to me. We have been enemies for longer than I care to mention."

Many questions formed on Craig's lips but she stopped him. "Look Mr Carter, right now your first priority is to escape from this planet. You were correct when you said that Andocia is going to kill you because she's quite capable of it. If she has no more use for someone, she usually gets rid of them. Andocia will return tomorrow sometime because I heard her soldiers talking. You must be gone before then."

"But Constance ..." he began.

The woman looked piercingly at the astronaut. "Mr Carter, do you trust me?"

"Yes," he replied without hesitation.

"Good, then listen carefully. "You must escape tonight! You have already thought of a plan, I'm sure. However, you must go alone because in Constance's present state, she will prove a hindrance. I'll get her away safely, I promise."

"But ..." he began awkwardly.

The woman in white put up her hand to still further comment. "You did say you trusted me, so do what I have told you. Where will you go once you leave this planet?"

"I must go to Saturn. I need to know how the King of Neptune is doing. We were heading there when Andocia crossed our path."

The woman nodded her head. "I understand. I'll meet up with you in a few days' time. Miss Gregg will be in good hands I promise you that. Now go quickly before someone comes to look for you. Say nothing to Constance about our conversation. I'll enlighten her later once she is safely aboard my ship." She reached into the folds of her robe and took out a laser gun. "Here, you'll need this. Good luck, Mr Carter!"

Craig hid the gun under his shirt and tucked it into his waistband. He walked to the door and then turned back. "Wait a minute! I don't even know your name!"

"My name is Tanus," she replied.

Carter smiled gratefully at her. "Thank you ... Tanus!"

He blinked and she was gone. The young space explorer went back to his room and found Constance still fast asleep on the bed. Gently he stroked her head and kissed her on the forehead. She murmured in her sleep and rolled over. Her boyfriend sat down on the couch in his room and began to plan his escape.

CHAPTER 24

That evening after supper had been brought to them, Craig changed into dark clothing. Constance had woken briefly to eat dinner and then lain down once again. When Craig shook her, she was snoring softly. He knelt down beside her and whispered in her ear. "I'll see you in a few days! Goodbye my darling!"

The space explorer aimed his laser gun at the door lock and it sprang open. He pushed the door closed again so that it looked undamaged. He peered cautiously up and down the corridor but it was deserted. Carter went into a storeroom a few doors down and closed the door behind him. A small window opened onto an alleyway that was in complete darkness and he lowered himself through it, closing it once more. Keeping to the shadows, the man hurried down the dark street. Several people were walking around and he pulled the hood of his tracksuit top and joined them. No one gave him a second glance.

Craig walked down the street until he reached the end, where he turned down another dark alleyway. This led to the hangars where Constance's ship was housed. There was a part of the street that was brightly lit and he had no choice but to enter it. His heart was racing but he walked at a leisurely pace and thankfully no one challenged him. Slipping behind a bush, he crawled to the hangars and climbed through a bathroom window.

As he was about to leave the room, the door opened and a man came in. Hurriedly he turned back to the taps and began washing his hands. The security guard smiled at him and he nodded. Andocia's follower turned to enter one of the stalls, when suddenly he turned back. "Excuse me ..." the man began, "What are you doing here?"

Craig smiled. "I'm just about to start my shift. I'll see you in a short while pal."

Recognition dawned and the man took a step back. He was just about to cry out when Craig hit him on the jaw. He went down immediately and hit his head on the door panel. Carter checked his pulse and saw he was still breathing, but would have a headache when he woke up. Hurriedly Craig undressed the man and put on his uniform. It was a little too tight, but it would have to do. Then he dragged the man inside one of the stalls and sat him on the toilet. He closed the door and walked nonchalantly out of the bathroom.

Craig went to the hangars and headed for Constance's ship. Several guards waved at him and he waved back. He pretended to check some of the ships, but no one seemed particularly interested in him. The space explorer climbed into Constance's ship and it began to rise in the air. Only then did the hangar come to life! Several people shouted and drew their weapons, but their laser beams couldn't penetrate the thick hull of the ship. He looked down on the planet with a mixture of sadness and exhilaration. He hoped fervently that Tanus would keep her word and save Constance.

At almost the same time as he had lifted off from the planet, another ship took to the air. Tanus had put Constance on a bed and they too were gone in a flash. As they were travelling in different directions, Carter failed to see the other ship lift off. He set a course for Saturn and was soon out of sight of the planet. When he was out of range of the planet he had escaped from, he contacted Saturn and told them he would arrive in a few days.

Two days later, a ship hailed Craig and when he opened a channel, Tanus greeted him.

"Mr Carter, I would like to extend an invitation to you to join us on my ship. Do you see the hatch opening?"

"I do, yes. Thank you, I accept. I'll see you shortly."

Craig flew into the cavernous hold and set down on a landing pad. He looked around the ship and saw several people coming to greet him.

"Mr Carter, our mistress wishes to welcome you. Please follow us and we'll take you to her."

Carter was fascinated by the design of this ship. It was large and everything fitted neatly together. The beings who had greeted him looked human, but he didn't want to jump to any conclusions.

They took him to an imposing room where he saw Tanus seated on a comfortable couch. Constance was sitting next to her and the moment she saw her boyfriend, a cry of joy escaped her lips and she flung herself into his arms. He kissed her tenderly. "I've missed you!" he sighed.

The woman in white invited him to sit down and he took the chair opposite her. "Thank you so much for rescuing Constance!"

"Doesn't she look wonderful?" Tanus beamed.

"She does!" he agreed. He turned to Constance and grinned happily. "I see you are finally awake!"

Constance smiled at the man she loved. "I have Tanus to thank for that! She found out what was causing the tiredness."

Craig looked expectantly at Tanus who began to explain. "I'm sorry to have to tell you this but Andocia was directly responsible for Constance's condition. She drugged your girlfriend's food so she would have no energy."

Craig was puzzled. "Why would she do that? It just doesn't make sense at all!"

"Actually, it makes perfect sense. She knew you wouldn't escape from the planet unless you could take Constance with you. It seems you have left a lasting impression on that woman. Andocia knew you would do everything in your power to thwart her so she exploited a weakness. When she tried to take over Earth, you were a thorn in her side and she hates to lose face with her staff."

Craig's eyebrows shot up in enquiry and Constance giggled. "I told Tanus about Andocia's takeover of Earth and how we sent her packing."

"Constance did and it was very refreshing to learn that," Tanus replied. "Your girlfriend and I have been discussing many things and I now know a great deal more about you than I ever did before."

Craig was puzzled and Tanus smiled gently. "Andocia may have 'discovered' you, but because of the way she went after you both with such ferocity, I started taking an interest in your career. It seems as though it has been quite an eventful one. Both of you have incredible talents in hunting down and capturing the evil beings in your universe but you, Mr Carter, seem to have an inordinate talent in that area."

Craig didn't quite know how to respond to the woman he had just recently met, but he knew that inasmuch as Andocia had become their enemy, this woman would be a good ally to have on their side.

Tanus stood up and excused herself. "I have some duties to attend to, so I'll leave the two of you alone for a while. I have asked my pilots to continue on a course to Saturn so that you don't lose any more valuable time. I'll see you both later."

She left them alone and as soon as the door had closed behind her, Constance's face lit up with joy. "Isn't she amazing? I have never met anyone quite like her before. I just met her a few days ago, yet it feels as though I have known her all my life!"

Her boyfriend nodded in agreement. "She does seem to have that effect on people! I feel the same way as you do. It's so strange!"

Constance lowered her voice as if she was afraid their benefactor would come in and hear her. "Craig, I know she is a kind person, but there must be something wrong with my eyes! I can see the top half of her face clearly, yet her mouth seems to be indistinct. It's almost as though she's wearing a veil."

Craig nodded in agreement. "There's nothing wrong with your eyes my love; I see exactly the same thing that you do. It seems the harder I stare at her, the more indistinct her features become."

"So, I'm not imagining it?" she replied.

"No."

"Why do you suppose that is?" Miss Gregg asked curiously.

Craig shrugged dismissively. "I don't really know! My best guess would be that perhaps she has some kind of disfigurement and she hides it. I'm certainly not going to ask her. I'm grateful to her for saving you and that's all that counts as far as I'm concerned."

"Do you know, she's also telepathic?" Constance enquired.

"I do, yes. Remember when Andocia was after revenge and she wanted to capture us after we thwarted her takeover of Earth? Well she spoke to both of us at the same time then, so that was a foregone conclusion. I don't know about you, but I trust her implicitly."

"I also do! We know so little about the Golden Way and its inhabitants. I wonder if we will be able to explore that galaxy one of these days and meet the beings who live there?"

"I hope so my darling! With the exception of Andocia of course, those whom I have already met seem to be very friendly."

"Well, time will tell, I suppose. Right now, though, I'm content to just be here on Tanus's ship and getting to know her better," Constance replied.

They spoke for a while before Tanus returned. She invited Craig to go on a tour of her ship and he agreed. As they walked, Tanus spoke to them. "So Mr Carter, Constance tells me you started your career as a spaceship mechanic."

"I did and that's why I'm looking forward to this tour. Tanus, please call me Craig. There's no need for formality amongst friends."

The woman in white laughed gently. "So be it! I like the idea of us being friends."

Tanus showed him around the ship and introduced Craig to her staff. Every one of them looked human and Carter was filled with curiosity, but he didn't broach the subject and Tanus didn't offer any explanations, so he decided to let the matter rest. Tanus would tell them when she felt the time was right.

After their tour, they returned to the room they had been in earlier. Over refreshments, Craig couldn't resist asking a few questions.

"Tanus, pardon my curiosity, but I just wanted to know why you're helping us. Please don't misunderstand me – I'm grateful to you for what you have already done, and I want you to know that I appreciate your promise to keep us safe, although we can't reasonably expect you to bail us out of trouble every time. Yet, you said it yourself, Andocia is a powerful enemy and like it or not, she hates us. I cannot understand why this should be so, but we'll have to learn to deal with it anyway. Hopefully, she won't bother Constance or me much in the future, but we are accessible out in space and that's our job, for better or worse. I thought Andocia would get over her pettiness, but I guess that isn't going to happen anytime soon. I suppose she gives you a hard time in the Golden Way as well."

Tanus looked contemplatively at her guest. "That's putting it mildly! Yes, we do have our spats as well, but it's nothing that I can't handle. You see, I know what she is capable of and you two can only guess. That's why I have some advice for you both. Never underestimate that woman. If you meet up with her in the future, run if you can. You aren't in her league as far as evil goes."

Constance shivered and hugged herself. "I get the creeps just thinking about her. Well I certainly hope she keeps away from us in the future. I have no wish to be around her ever again."

Craig looked at Tanus and their eyes met. He communicated his concern to Tanus and she nodded slowly. Turning to Constance she smiled. "My dear, you expressed an interest in watching my staff feed the exotic fish I have on board. It's nearly their dinnertime now. Would you like to go and watch?"

The woman stood up excitedly. "Yes, please. Do you want to come with me Craig?"

Her boyfriend shook his head. "No thanks, my darling, you go right ahead. I'll wait here for you."

When she had left the room, Craig voiced his concerns.

"Look Tanus, I appreciate what you said before but I must know something. I have the distinct feeling that something bad happened to Constance when Andocia took her away for the day. Do you know what she did to my girlfriend?"

For the first time since they had met, Tanus couldn't look at him. She spoke hesitantly. "Craig, you are very intelligent and not much escapes your attention. The answer to your question is yes, I do know what she did to Constance and it was unpleasant. However, she wiped the memory of that day from Constance's mind so it won't affect her in any way because those memories will never surface again. I must ask you to trust me when I tell you this. I could explain what Andocia did to her, but that wouldn't serve any relevant purpose. Besides which, there are things you don't need to know either. What's done is done and it should be left alone. Bringing these painful memories to the surface would be very bad for you and Constance."

Craig nodded slowly. "I guess I understand. I trust your judgment, but I have other concerns."

"You want to know if Andocia will ever leave you both alone in the future?"

"Yes, I do. I cannot think why she keeps bothering us. What makes us different from other humans?"

Tanus paced the room. "I wish I had the answers for you but I don't. Hopefully Andocia will get tired of you and your girl-friend. Whatever she wanted to know about both of you, Constance would have provided those facts, either willingly or unwillingly. I cannot say what she is going to do next. Just take each day as it comes, and just do your job to the best of your ability."

"I intend to do that anyway. Tanus, thank you for being honest. I really appreciate it. Mostly, thank you for rescuing Constance."

"It was the least that I could do."

The young man joined their benefactor at the observation window. "Saturn is just a day away. We should be leaving soon, unless you would like to meet the Saturnians."

The woman in white smiled at her friend. "I'm looking forward to meeting them sometime Craig, but, unfortunately, I have to be elsewhere soon. Perhaps we can do this another time?"

"I understand. I'll just go and get Constance. We must get ready to leave."

Craig went to look for his girlfriend and they packed whatever meagre belongings they had with them and loaded them into their ship. They returned to their hostess and spent a short while with her. She walked with them to the docking bay where their ship was stored and hugged both of them in turn.

"Goodbye dear friends! I hope your journey will be a success and you find the King of Neptune healthy once again."

The couple waved to their new friend and soon were out in space again and Tanus's Mother Ship disappeared from their telescreen.

CHAPTER 25

Craig contacted the Saturnians and told them he and Constance were on their way to Saturn. The inhabitants acknowledged this and replied they were looking forward to seeing them again.

One day later they landed on Saturn and hurried to the control centre where Karnd greeted them excitedly.

"Welcome my dear friends. Lara said I must bring you to her office the moment you land. We have been very concerned about you both."

"With good reason," Craig acknowledged. "Being with Andocia is hardly fun. I'm looking forward to seeing Lara again."

Their vehicle pulled up at the laboratories where Lara worked and even before it had come to a complete standstill, Craig jumped down onto the ground. Followed by Constance he made his way into the offices. Lara turned and with an exclamation of delight, hurried to her friends and embraced them happily. "Oh, it's so good to see you!" She scrutinized them carefully. "Are you both okay? Andocia didn't harm you?"

Constance smiled. "No, not physically, but I think had we stayed a while longer, she may have been tempted to cause us great harm."

Lara looked carefully at Constance and put her hand gently on the woman's arm. "You look tired my dear. I think you should get settled in your room and maybe have a short nap."

"I might just do that. Thanks Lara. Are you coming Craig?"

Her boyfriend shook his head. "No thanks; maybe later. I have something else to do first."

Constance nodded wisely. "Yes, of course you do! I'll see you later then."

When Miss Gregg had left, Craig got straight to the point. "Lara, how is the King of Neptune?"

She smiled at him. "Come and see for yourself."

The scientist took him to a building which housed an indoor pool. The King was seated on a step in the pool and had a drink in his hand. His face broke out in a huge grin when he saw who his visitor was. "Craig, it's good to see you!" he exclaimed happily.

"It's good to be here, Your Majesty. I had my doubts I can assure you."

Craig approached the pool and the King got up slowly and shook his hand. Craig noticed his grip wasn't as firm as usual and that the King of Neptune looked tired. Noting the concern on his friend's face, the ruler smiled wanly. "I'm feeling much better as you can see, but I still have a long way to go. I feel as weak as a baby Neptunian and I'm sure the slightest breeze would blow me over, but at least I'm recovering."

"It's good to see you anyway, Your Majesty. The last time you looked as though you were at death's door."

The King gripped his friend's hand. "It's thanks to you Craig! You saved my life that day! If you hadn't contacted the Saturnians, I don't think I would be here today. They say I must stay here for another week at least, just to make sure I don't have a relapse."

"You must do as the doctors say, Sire. It was touch and go the last time I saw you and I could never stand another scare like that one."

"I agree with you Craig and I will most certainly follow the doctors' orders. Have you seen Lolita yet?"

"No, not yet, Your Majesty. Constance and I have only just arrived. I'll go and talk to her in a while."

Carter spent some time with the King of Neptune and then went in search of Lolita.

He found her in the public swimming pool, moodily staring into space. At the sound of her name, she looked up and gasped when she realized who had called her. Instantly she jumped up and flung herself into Craig's arms and gave him a wet kiss on his cheek. He hugged her and then ruefully looked at the wet patch on his shirt.

"Well, I guess I won't need to shower tonight," he grinned.

"Oh dear, I'm sorry!" she gulped. "It's just that I thought I would never see you again!"

Craig stroked her long, wet hair. "You know me better than that Lolita! I would never have let you down. Besides, I had some help," he replied mysteriously.

"How is Constance? I heard she's here as well." Lolita enquired.

"She is indeed, but she was tired, so went to lie down for a while. Andocia wasn't very gentle with her, I suspect."

Lolita's eyes grew huge in dismay and Craig smiled reassuringly at her. "She is very strong and capable Lolita. What Andocia did to her was strictly psychological. Physically she's fine."

Lolita's voice trembled. She was afraid of Andocia and Craig knew he couldn't blame her. He didn't like the woman either.

"What did she do to Constance?"

Craig shrugged his shoulders helplessly. "I don't know! Tanus wouldn't tell me."

"Tanus?" she queried.

"She's our new friend, Lolita! She helped us to escape from Andocia's clutches. We are both in her debt and I don't know how we can ever repay her."

Lolita came to sit next to her friend. "What's she like, this Tanus person?"

"She's absolutely amazing! We didn't really get around to discussing much – in fact she was quite secretive. She answered some of my questions, but not all of them. Even so, I believe she is a good person to have on our side when things get rough out in space. It's the strangest thing Lolita, but I trust her implicitly! I have never felt like this about anyone in my life before, except for Constance and my parents, of course. We only met her a few days ago, yet I feel as though I've known her all my life. Does that sound strange to you?"

The Neptunian princess laughed musically. "No, I suppose it doesn't. You have such good instincts about right and wrong and that is what has saved your life on many occasions. If you like her, then she must be wonderful. I believe I like her as well, based on what you have just told me. Maybe one day I'll get to meet her."

"Maybe you will. I certainly hope so."

The conversation then moved on to the health of the ruler of Neptune.

"I see your father has made a good recovery. I went to see him when we arrived."

Lolita smiled radiantly. "Yes, he's definitely much better but still very weak. I cannot believe that not long ago he was at death's door. The Saturnians are amazing!"

"I told you so! Did you manage to speak to Commander Simms about the alien growth on your planet?"

"Yes, I did. He promised to send a clean up crew to destroy the plants. They should be arriving within the next few days, I believe. I spoke to my mother and she confirmed that your boss had been in contact with her."

"That's wonderful news. Have you heard any news about those on your planet who were also infected with this virus?"

"Yes, my mother told me about them as well. Apparently, Lara spoke to the doctors on Neptune and explained to them exactly what should be done. It seems the rest of my people are recovering nicely as well."

"I'm delighted to hear that," replied a relieved Craig.

Lolita looked gratefully at her friend and hugged him tightly. "I'll always be grateful to you for your friendship!" she smiled.

"Any time!" he grinned.

Constance arrived while they were embracing. "Hey, what are you doing to my boyfriend?" she replied playfully.

Lolita smiled at her friend. "I was just telling him how amazing he is," she replied laughingly.

"Well, he certainly is," she agreed, "but go easy on the compliments. He may develop a swollen head."

Craig released Lolita and took his girlfriend in his arms. They kissed passionately and he sighed. "Today is definitely one of the high points in my life. Here I am with two of the most beautiful women in the galaxy. Life can't get any better! The King of Neptune will soon be well again and a crisis has been overcome. Who would have thought that one little plant could cause so much trouble?"

"Yes, it's very strange," Lolita agreed. "You know Craig, I was wondering how it got to Neptune in the first place. Do you suppose someone did it deliberately?"

"The explanations are varied and many Lolita. It could have been dropped onto your planet by a passing spaceship, or perhaps it just blew there somehow. The fact is we could discuss this all day and no real explanation will come to light. I think it was just an unfortunate accident. Of course, Neptune was the perfect host for something as fast-growing as that, because of all the water on your planet. Once the clean up crew have been to Neptune and destroyed every single plant, your problems should be over."

"You don't believe it was deliberate then?" the princess enquired.

"I doubt it very much," he assured her.

The Neptunian smiled. "Well, that's a relief at least."

Lolita excused herself saying that she wanted to go and speak with her father. The couple watched her go and then hand in hand they walked a short distance away where they sat down on a bench.

Constance sighed and put her head on her boyfriend's shoulder. "This has been a traumatic couple of weeks for all of us. First, Lolita's father nearly died and then Andocia intervened, taking you with as her unwilling prisoner. Then she used you to get at me! At least now the King is recovering well and so another disaster has been averted. It would have been dreadful if he had died! Imagine the uproar, if that had happened."

"Well, thank the stars that he is on the road to recovery! You're right though, it's been a time I would like to forget, but I'll always remember this incident. Hopefully, we will never have to deal with Andocia ever again!"

Constance looked searchingly into her boyfriend's eyes. "Craig, do you really think we have seen the last of Andocia?"

"I hope so, but something tells me we haven't. I wish I could say we can get on with our lives in peace, but I doubt it somehow. I want to believe it, but no, I don't think so."

Constance bit her lip thoughtfully. "I have to agree with you. I also like the idea of the 'happily ever after' scenario, but I stopped believing in fairy tales a long time ago."

The couple sat in companionable silence for a few minutes, each thinking about their brush with Andocia. Hesitantly Constance placed her hand on her boyfriend's knee. "Craig, did Tanus say what Andocia did to me? I have no recollection at all of what she put me through. All I know is that I have been feeling drained of energy ever since I saw her. I know it was partly due to the drugs she put in my food to make me sleepy, but it's more complicated than that, isn't it?"

Carter turned to his girlfriend and wished he could put her mind at ease, but he knew she would expect an honest answer.

"My darling, I don't know what you went through with Andocia. All I know is that Tanus knew what had happened and that she was very angry, but she wouldn't tell me anything. I guess she thought it best if we didn't know. Perhaps we should just be satisfied with that explanation. While the King of Neptune is here on Saturn, you'll have a chance to recover from your ordeal, because I want to stay here until I'm sure the King has recovered completely. When Lara gives him a clean bill of health, then we can return to Earth."

Miss Gregg nodded, but she was still thoughtful. "Darling, I wonder if I could ask Lara to use a mind probe on me. Maybe then I'll know what Andocia did to me."

Craig shook his head emphatically. "I don't think that's wise, honey. If Tanus wouldn't tell us then maybe we should just leave it alone. What I do suggest though is that you speak to Lara and let her give you a physical check-up, just to make sure your tiredness isn't due to some other medical problem."

"I think that's a good idea, Craig. I'll go and see her now. I'll talk to you later, okay?"

"Sure."

Craig went to find Lolita and the King and they spoke for a

while. Evening came and they all dined together. After supper, Lara took Craig aside and they went to her office. "Is everything okay?" he asked her tentatively.

Lara's wings fluttered gently and she smiled reassuringly at her friend. "Constance is fine Craig. She seems a little run down though so I gave her a tonic to help her recover. She did seem a little concerned as to what happened when she was with Andocia because she has no memory of what was discussed. I did sense some trauma though. Do you know anything that I should be aware of?" she asked carefully.

"No, Lara, I have no idea what Andocia did to her, but I have a feeling it was something awful. That woman is very powerful and also telepathic. I believe she somehow invaded Constance's mind. She probably learnt everything about Constance and her family, but that can't be helped. I just don't understand why it would be so important to Andocia though. I know when I met that evil woman for the first time, she read my mind and learnt a great deal of sensitive information that she later used to try and take over Earth."

"I remember," Lara winced. "We didn't help matters either when we thought you had turned against your planet. She whisked you out from under our noses!"

"Well Jorrick Baker was caught and imprisoned so that's all in the past now."

"Yes, thankfully it is! Look Craig, I can perform a mind probe on Constance if you like. Maybe it will help."

"Lara, thank you for that suggestion, but I really don't think it's a good idea. I tried to get some information from Tanus, but she remained tight-lipped about it. Whatever happened between Andocia and Constance is best left alone. I don't think anything good will come out of it."

"All right then, I won't do it. Perhaps it would be best in the long run as you say, but aren't you just a little bit curious?"

"Yes – and no. I want to help Constance of course but at the same time I don't want her to remember what happened that day. If it had been necessary then I truly believe Tanus would have told us about it."

"You are probably right. Okay then, we can leave things the way they are. In a few days, Constance will be feeling just fine. When do you plan on returning to Earth?"

"I think we'll stay here until the King of Neptune is well enough to return home. Once I know he is out of danger I'll be able to relax."

"You don't think Andocia will come back to look for you, do you?" Lara asked, alarm creeping into her voice.

"No, I don't believe she will. We have satisfied her curiosity now, so we can breathe easily again. Besides, she wouldn't know where to look for us anyway."

Lara stood up and began flying slowly out of the room. At the door, she turned and looked back at her friend. "Craig, we have other matters to discuss. Will you be free tonight after dinner to chat to my colleagues?"

"Yes, I'll be available Lara. I'll see you later then."

She flew away and Carter returned to his girlfriend and the Neptunian royals.

The next few days while Constance and the others rested, Craig was having meetings with the Saturnians.

Each day Craig noted with satisfaction that his girlfriend and the others were doing well.

While Constance and the Neptunians were recovering, Craig climbed into Constance's spacecraft and contacted his boss on a secure channel reserved for those in command only.

Commander Simms answered immediately. "Hello Craig, I was wondering when you were going to check in with me. How are the talks between you and the Saturnians going?"

"Just fine, Sir. We have had a number of meetings and they are satisfied with the um … items that Mission Control gave them."

"Excellent! I'm very pleased to hear that. Do they want you to stay a while longer?"

"No Sir, they are confident they can proceed without me now. I can leave whenever the Neptunians return to their planet."

"Do you know when the King of Neptune will be well enough to leave Saturn?"

"He should be fine by the end of this week, Commander."

His boss nodded. "That is good news anyway. Was there anything else Craig?"

"Well Sir, we do have a problem. The King took ill so suddenly that I just left everything and accompanied them to Saturn. My ship is still on Neptune. What are your orders? I can't just leave it there!"

Commander Simms shook his head emphatically. "No, you cannot! The cargo you were delivering to the planets listed on your manifesto is too important! Only someone with an A level clearance can pilot that ship home. By the time you return to Earth, the deadline will have passed, even if you ride with Constance."

Craig was quiet for a few minutes while he thought of possible solutions to the dilemma, and then had an idea.

"Sir, can we use ROSE to pilot my ship home?"

Commander Simms grinned. "Yes, of course we can! There is no one more qualified to pilot your ship. See to it immediately. I will contact Neptune on your behalf and explain the situation. Meanwhile, I'll see if I can get more of those items that were left on your ship, and send them to the relevant planets, using Courier Drones. You can ride home with Constance. Your ship will probably arrive even before you do! Just tell me when ROSE has been activated and we can keep track of her and your ship."

"I'll do that, Sir."

Craig disconnected and returned to the others. Not long afterwards, he and Constance went for a walk and sat down on a bench nearby. He scrolled through the icons on his mobile device and selected one. The icon began to flash and he started typing instructions on the keyboard.

On Neptune, a light began flashing on the ship's dashboard and a message scrolled across the screen. One of the cupboard doors in the sleeping quarters opened and a metal case rolled out. A light on the case also started flashing, and it began to roll towards the cockpit area. It stopped at the pilot's chair and began to open by itself. A robotic figure unfolded itself from the case and stood upright. The android opened its vivid green eyes and looked around. It was feminine in shape and looked like a human woman. She climbed into the pilot's chair and immediately the harness encircled her body. The android stretched out her fingers and toes and they slotted into matching gaps on the ship's console. Both android and console communicated and the spaceship thrummed quietly. Once all the relevant lights lit up, the android spoke. "Attention Neptune Control, this is ROSE. I have control of spaceship number ACD2457CC and I must return to Earth immediately."

Neptune's control room gave permission and the ship rose flawlessly into space and disappeared quickly. When she had left Neptune's atmosphere, ROSE contacted Mission Control who began tracking her progress. She acknowledged their response and the ship accelerated and began speeding towards Earth.

On Saturn, Craig received confirmation that ROSE was taking his ship back to Earth. Constance smiled at her boyfriend. "It was fortunate Commander Simms had arranged for the ROSE unit to be put on your ship."

"Yes, it was. I had to deliver various top-secret items to some of the planets, and it is usual procedure to have one of these androids on board, just in case of an unforeseen emergency."

Constance nodded. "ROSE is also a top secret project that very few people know about. Only astronauts with A level security are aware she exists. ROSE, the Remote Operating Systems Entity."

"At least I can rest assured my ship is in good hands. It's almost suppertime. I guess we should return to our hosts and the Neptunian royals."